EDUCATING

Elizabeth

OTHER BOOKS AND AUDIOBOOKS
BY JENNIFER MOORE

REGENCY ROMANCE
Becoming Lady Lockwood
Lady Emma's Campaign
Miss Burton Unmasks a Prince
Simply Anna
Lady Helen Finds Her Song
A Place for Miss Snow
Miss Whitaker Opens Her Heart
Miss Leslie's Secret

THE WAR OF 1812
My Dearest Enemy
The Shipbuilder's Wife
Charlotte's Promise

ROMANCE ON THE ORIENT EXPRESS
Wrong Train to Paris

THE BLUE ORCHID SOCIETY
Emmeline
Solving Sophronia
Inventing Vivian
Healing Hazel
Educating Elizabeth

STAND-ALONE NOVELLAS
"The Perfect Christmas" in *Christmas Treasures*
"Let Nothing You Dismay" in *Christmas Grace*
"Love and Joy Come to You" in *A Christmas Courting*
"To Love a Spy" in *Where Dreams Meet*

EDUCATING
Elizabeth

A Victorian Romance

JENNIFER MOORE

Covenant Communications, Inc.

Cover image *Woman on Stairs* © Lee Avison / Trevillion Images

Cover design copyright © 2023 by Covenant Communications, Inc.

Published by Covenant Communications, Inc.
American Fork, Utah

Library of Congress Cataloging-in-Publication Data

Name: Jennifer Moore
Title: Educating elizabeth / Jennifer Moore
Description: American Fork, UT : Covenant Communications, Inc. [2023]
Identifiers: Library of Congress Control Number 2022950926 | ISBN 978-1-52442-400-8
LC record available at https://lccn.loc.gov/2022950926

Printed in Mexico
First Printing: September 2023

29 28 27 26 25 24 23   10 9 8 7 6 5 4 3 2 1

for Amanda Taylor,
novelist, runner, hostess,
lover of romance, and the life of the party

PRAISE FOR JENNIFER MOORE

The Blue Orchid Society Series

Solving Sophronia

"The detailed descriptions and gentle push and pull between the couple will please readers looking for chaste historical romance. A plucky heroine and engrossing mystery make this a treat."

—*Publishers Weekly*

"Strongly recommended, and watch out for more books in this series."

—Historical Novel Society

Healing Hazel

"History buffs and others will enjoy every aspect of this simply delightful tale!"

—*InD'Tale Magazine*, Crowned Heart review

"Jennifer More demonstrates a mastery of this art, staying authentic to the period in which [the novel] is set whilst using modern ideas of feminism to create a wonderful leading lady in the form of Hazel Thornton."

—Readers' Favorite five-star review

Educating Elizabeth

"I am a big fan of Jennifer Moore. I adore her writing style. She writes romances as you would dream about them, and I love her for that. That being said, I have high expectations whenever I read one of her new stories. *Educating Elizabeth* is a one-of-a-kind story in which the rake is not a rake but an absolute gem of a man. I love how Charles Chatsworth has this bravado and charisma, yet he is terrible at being flirty with Elizabeth when they first meet, which makes him adorable. He gets better and wins Elizabeth over, and the journey to the culmination is impeccable. The narrative style is fantastic, engaging you and allowing you to form alliances and choose the character you will root for until the end. I love Elizabeth's change of heart and her development as well. Little Alice is adorable, and the impact she has on the story is incredible. I highly recommend this story and Jennifer Moore to romance lovers!"

—Readers' Favorite five-star review

"This author has a special gift of describing her characters and their emotions. In fact, I cannot recommend this lovely and inspirational book highly enough. I am looking forward to more novels in the series."

—Sue Garland, Netgalley review

"These two characters find there is friendship and so much more in store. Clean and sweet read. Recommend this book!"

—Denise Boutin, Netgalley review

"The theme I have loved in this whole series is how supportive the women are of each other. It is beautiful to see."

—Maria Thomas, Netgalley review

ACKNOWLEDGMENTS

Thank you to everyone who made this book possible. To my family—Frank, James, Ben, Andrew, and Joey—thank you for keeping things going when I was working and other things fell behind. Andrew, thank you for your expertise and input on the birding sections of this story.

To my writing group—Josi Kilpack, Nancy Allen, and Becca Wilhite—thank you for all the brainstorming sessions, for being available when I needed to run a scene by you, and for all the pep talks when I felt like I couldn't find the right words.

Thank you, Liesl McMurray, for taking the time to explain the history of electricity and magnetism to me, and reexplaining when I didn't understand the first few times.

Thank you to my editor, Kami Hancock, for helping me fix plot points and character development. Thank you to Aimee Robbins for your copyedit and Skyler Garrett and Rebecca Tuft for your proofreads. And, Christina Marcano, thank you for this gorgeous cover.

And a very special thank-you to wonderful teachers my kids and I have had over the years. Words can't express how much of an impact you've had. Especially my very favorite teacher, Carol Spackman-Moss. Your kind words and praise of a shy fifteen-year-old's writing changed the course of my life.

PROLOGUE

April 19, 1873

THE DECOR AT THE MARCHIONESS of Molyneaux's annual ball was splendid, the music was extraordinary, the refreshments were delicious, and Elizabeth Miller hated all of it. "'Most anticipated ball of the Season,'" she muttered, repeating with cynicism the words her cousin, Dahlia Lancaster, had said innumerable times over the past weeks. "'Everyone of importance will be there.'" Elizabeth continued duplicating Dahlia's words beneath her breath as she took in the ceiling paneled with stained glass and the ornate globe chandeliers that cast a golden glow over the elite of London Society.

She picked up a glass from a refreshment table, sipping the cool lemonade as an excuse to avoid speaking to anyone. She was here for one reason alone: to show support for her cousin on what promised to be a memorable night. Lord Reuben was going to formally announce his engagement. And after a year of very public courting, it was a foregone conclusion that Dahlia was to be the future Marchioness of Molyneaux.

Elizabeth took another drink as her gaze moved over the guests clustered in groups around the edges of the ballroom. Dahlia stood with her band of close friends. The "Darling Debutants," they called themselves—young ladies from wealthy families, whose entire focus was upon their clothing, which parties they would or would not attend, and making certain they were seen on the arms of rich men. Although Elizabeth and Dahlia got on well enough when they were alone, the Darling Debs were another case entirely. Elizabeth would prefer a dunking in the stinking water of the Thames to an afternoon of small talk with the vapid young women.

"Doesn't she look lovely?" Henrietta Lancaster, Elizabeth's aunt, spoke from beside her.

Elizabeth realized she'd been staring at her cousin and looked away quickly, turning toward her aunt.

Based on the red in her cheeks and the slur in her speech, Aunt Henrietta's glass contained something much stronger than lemonade.

"Dahlia." Aunt Henrietta motioned with her glass toward her daughter, reminding Elizabeth that she'd asked a question. "She looks lovely, doesn't she?"

"She does," Elizabeth said, looking back at her cousin. It was true. Dahlia was more than lovely. She was so beautiful that she practically glowed. Elizabeth had seen from the time they were young children how her cousin held the attention of everyone in a room.

"It will be a perfect evening for her." Aunt Henrietta took another drink, watching her daughter with a pleased smile. "Imagine. My daughter, a marchioness."

Elizabeth nodded her agreement.

"And you look lovely as well." Aunt Henrietta spoke as if she'd just remembered whom she was talking to. She gestured at Elizabeth's gown and gave an approving nod. "This suits you, my dear."

Elizabeth looked down at her lavender dress. It had belonged to Dahlia, and while it was neither as new nor as expensive as many she saw around her, she would wager the cost of it could feed a factory full of workers for a month. She ran her fingers over the smooth taffeta. Wearing these clothes, attending this ball—it all felt like make-believe, as if she were an actor in a play or a child in a costume. And while she imagined most young ladies of twenty-two years would relish the opportunity to mingle with members of high Society, Elizabeth resented it. Not only did she detest the excess around her, but she was very aware of her position as a charity case. A poor orphan whose wealthy relations had taken her in.

She didn't belong here any more than she belonged in her uncle's household. And the lack of control over her own situation chafed like shoes that were too tight. *Shoes can be removed*, she reminded herself. One wasn't constantly at the mercy of one's shoes.

Remembering that she'd just been paid a compliment, Elizabeth opened her mouth to thank her aunt, but she was interrupted by the arrival of a long-necked man with a thin mustache. She knew immediately who he was: Lord Tynsdale, Earl of Dunford, and a major opponent to the proposed Poor Relief Laws. Elizabeth had personally written letters to his parliamentary office and even joined in a march of protest as the fate of London's poor was debated by men who had never been deprived of anything in their lives. She fought against her lip's urge to curl.

"Mrs. Lancaster, I am very pleased to see you tonight." Lord Tynsdale inclined his head graciously to the older woman. His gaze moved to Elizabeth. "You simply must introduce me to your friend."

"Oh, my lord, how delightful to see you." Aunt Henrietta curtsied rather more deeply than was necessary. "Elizabeth, dear, please meet Lord Tynsdale." Aunt Henrietta moved her glass between them as she spoke, the liquid sloshing dangerously close to the brim. "Miss Elizabeth Miller is my niece. She has come to stay with us from the north."

"How do you do?" Elizabeth inclined her head. She watched him closely, wondering if he'd recognize her.

"A pleasure, Miss Miller." Lord Tynsdale's brows rose. He turned back to Aunt Henrietta. "I did not know you had a niece, madam. How could you keep such a marvelous secret?" He shook his head as if reprimanding her, but Elizabeth could still see the calculations going through his mind. He was wondering who exactly she was. Who were her parents? What was her status? Her worth?

She clenched her teeth tightly behind her smile, but she did not drop her gaze. She would not allow herself to be intimidated by this—or any—man. If only she felt as confident as she told herself she did.

"She has been with us for only a few months," Aunt Henrietta said. "And, of course, we've been in the country for the winter."

The questions still swam in his eyes, and he studied Elizabeth behind his casually polite expression. "Miss Miller, if I may be so bold as to claim your hand for the waltz?"

"I would be very pleased to dance with you, sir." He hadn't recognized her after all. She tried not to smirk, letting the movement of her lips grow into a debutante-worthy smile as she took his arm, feeling like an agent of espionage, fraternizing with an unsuspecting enemy.

"How is it that Dahlia Lancaster has a cousin of whom I was entirely unaware?" Lord Tynsdale led Elizabeth to join the other couples on the dance floor, faced her, and placed a hand at her waist.

She tried not to flinch at his touch; she had always struggled with being this close to people—men especially—but she'd accepted this dance and willed her curiosity and annoyance to override her desire for people to keep their distance. She took his hand, placing her other on his shoulder. At his nod, the pair of them stepped together.

"You must tell me where you're from," he said. "Do I know your father, perhaps?"

"I don't suppose you do," Elizabeth replied. "He is, as my aunt said, from the north." She continued speaking before he could ask more. "It is through my mother that I am related to the Lancasters. She was a first cousin to Dahlia's father."

"Ah, I see."

Elizabeth could tell from the wrinkle in his brow that he had more questions and was thinking of a tactful way to ask them. "Miss Elizabeth Miller." He studied her face closely as they swept past the dais where the musicians played. "Your name is so familiar, but for the life of me, I cannot place it." He squinted. "We must have met before."

"I would have remembered, my lord."

"Elizabeth Miller," he muttered again.

She saw the exact moment when realization dawned. His eyes widened and immediately narrowed. "You." Without breaking the rhythm of the dance, Lord Tynsdale maneuvered the pair of them to the side of the ballroom.

His arm was tight on her waist. Elizabeth was wary of being touched at the best of times, but this . . . fear moved cold fingers over her skin.

"You wrote all those letters." His voice was a low snarl. "You are the one . . . how dare you come here!"

In retrospect, perhaps the wording of her letters could have been more courteous. Elizabeth pulled herself from his arms, standing with her fists on her hips and holding her hands tight to keep them from trembling. "Someone must speak up for the poor, my lord. When the government doesn't care for the most vulnerable of its—"

The shattering of a dropped glass interrupted Elizabeth's speech just as she was warming up to the topic. Her gaze was briefly drawn toward the sound, but she could see nothing but a commotion moving in that direction. Taking a breath, she turned back to continue, but Lord Tynsdale was stalking away from her, headed toward another man.

Elizabeth's stomach sank when she saw who it was: Lord Lockhart, a shorter man with a round belly and pale eyes. A news photographer had captured an image of Elizabeth marching outside of Parliament with a hand-painted sign that read, "Lord *Rock*Heart cares naught for London's poor." The photograph had been in every broadsheet, and the moniker had caught on, much to his embarrassment.

The men spoke together, and Lord Lockhart's face darkened as his gaze rested on Elizabeth. They started toward her. Would they force her to leave?

Elizabeth glanced around. The crowd had moved away, guests choosing to either dance or investigate the confusion on the other side of the room. She stood in a cleared space, her back to the wall, and they were bearing down on her.

She looked beyond the men to the other side of the room, where she could see her aunt's feathered headdress bobbing to the music. The men wouldn't dare confront her if she were with Aunt Henrietta. But Elizabeth couldn't very well cut through the dancers to reach her. Here, she was very much alone, and the idea of the two men cornering her sent her into a panic. She started away in the other direction, thinking to circumnavigate the room, and a moment later happened upon a door concealed behind a potted tree. A servants' door, she assumed. Or perhaps it was for the family's convenience in moving between the ballroom and other areas of the house. Elizabeth was through it before giving a thought to where it might lead.

Ahead of her was a corridor lit at regular intervals with yellow gas globes.

She hurried ahead, passing a room bustling with servers arranging refreshments on trays, and continued on, finding a closed door. She slipped inside, and a quick glance from the corner of her eye revealed a fire in the hearth and what appeared to be a gentleman's sitting room. The air smelled of cigars, the chairs were leather, and the wood-paneled walls held hunting trophies.

Elizabeth peeked through the crack of the door back into the corridor, listening for any indication that she'd been followed. She hadn't realized her heart was racing, and she breathed as deeply as her corset would allow, calming herself. She closed the door quietly, letting the handle latch with a soft click.

A throat cleared behind her.

Elizabeth gasped and spun around.

The man who had made the noise sat in a chair near the fire, completely hidden but for his fingers, his trousers, and his shoes, behind the open newspaper he was reading.

Her heart seized and she fought down a burst of panic at being alone with a strange man. She tried to reassure herself that there was no reason to fear but remained cautious all the same.

A corner of the newspaper folded down, exposing the extremely handsome face of Lord Chatsworth. Seeing her, he grinned, showing the famous white-toothed smile, cerulean blue eyes, and dimples that gave the ladies of London palpitations and had earned him the title of Charming Chatsworth.

"If it isn't Miss Elizabeth Miller." His smile grew even wider.

Elizabeth's fear abated and she gave him a flat look. "My lord." She folded her arms. She and Lord Chatsworth had met before, under less-than-ideal circumstances.

Lord Chatsworth sighed, his expression looking resigned. "Coming to see me in my altogether? I should have known." He lowered the paper, revealing that he was entirely bare from the waist up.

Elizabeth let out a shriek and covered her eyes. Heat flared over her face and neck. "What are you doing?" She peeked between her fingers and saw him toss the paper aside and lean back in the chair, resting an ankle on his knee. She closed her eyes again. "You are . . . naked."

"Only a little." Lord Chatsworth smirked. "I assumed that's why you were here." He reached for the glass of wine that sat on a table beside him. "Apparently you didn't get a good enough look last time."

"We were children," Elizabeth said. Somehow her already flushed cheeks flushed even more, a result of the embarrassment and anger that twisted like a cyclone inside her. "And I did not intend to come upon you thus." Hearing a noise in the corridor, she started and stepped away from the door. She had much more important concerns at the moment than Charming Chatsworth and his lack of clothing.

She looked for an escape route. On the far side of the room between two windows was a door that led, she assumed, into the garden. She walked quickly around the edge of the room, hand outstretched to block the view of Lord Chatsworth's chest and shoulders.

"Don't tell me you're leaving already." His voice held the same teasing tone she had loathed as a child. She walked faster.

The doorhandle rattled, and Elizabeth dropped to the floor behind the sofa, pulling her skirts out of sight. She froze, knees and palms on the floor.

"Good evening, Lord Tynsdale, Lord *Rock*Heart."

Lord Chatsworth's use of the man's nickname sent chills over Elizabeth's skin. Would he betray her? She lay her head down on the carpet, looking beneath the sofa toward the doorway. Two pairs of shoes entered the room.

"Chatsworth." Lord Tynsdale's voice held contempt. "What are you doing here?"

"And disrobed." The disgusted voice must belong to Lord Lockhart.

"Reading the *Times*." The glass was set down with a thunk. Papers shuffled. "I have the society pages here somewhere if you're interested."

"I'm looking for a young lady," Lord Lockhart said. "Did she come this way?"

"I am, unfortunately, quite alone," Lord Chatsworth said. "But if you remain with me long enough, one usually turns up. It becomes quite tedious, so many admirers clamoring for my attention." He sighed loudly. "But perhaps you don't have that problem and must resort to chasing young ladies through passageways instead."

"She's not here, Ro—Lockhart," Lord Tynsdale said. "Come along."

Elizabeth's racing heart began to calm. It seemed she would not be found out after all.

The two pairs of feet left and the door closed behind them. Elizabeth started to rise, but just then the door opened again and another pair of feet entered.

"The wine came out of your coat easily enough, my lord. But your waistcoat, neckcloth, and shirt will need more extensive laundering. I believe these should be near enough to your size in the meantime."

"Thank you," Lord Chatsworth said. Fabric made a swishing sound as he dressed.

The men spoke about the neckcloth and the pattern on the waistcoat.

Elizabeth was relieved, safe, but she remained where she was behind the sofa, watching their feet and thinking it would look silly if she should pop out now.

The man she assumed to be a valet left, and she hoped Lord Chatsworth would leave as well. With any luck, he'd forgotten about her in his eagerness to return to the party.

But luck was not on Elizabeth's side. Lord Chatsworth's shoes approached, and a moment later his head peeked over the back of the couch. "Tynsdale and Rockheart." He wrinkled his nose and made a clicking noise with his tongue. "No wonder you wished to hide."

Elizabeth did not think she could be in a more humiliating position, crawling around on all fours on the floor of the marquess's sitting room. She pushed herself up to kneel, but when she tried to stand, her feet got tangled in her skirts. She pulled on the yards of fabric, trying to push her shoes through the openings. Shifting to sit, she dug through the ruffles, heaving swaths of fabric aside and knowing she looked ridiculous. *This cursed dress.*

Lord Chatsworth came around the sofa and held out his hands to assist.

Mustering every bit of her bruised dignity, Elizabeth accepted, stumbling to her feet. "Thank you," she said, shaking out her skirts to straighten them and carefully not looking Lord Chatsworth in the eye. "For the assistance and"—she glanced toward the door—"for not giving me away." She gave a quick curtsy and started toward the garden door. "Good evening."

"You're leaving already?" Lord Chatsworth asked. "I'd hoped we might dance now that I'm dressed. Unless you prefer me disrobed. Give me a moment to change your mind." He unhooked a button on his waistcoat and grinned cheekily.

Elizabeth had had enough. She was flustered and embarrassed and furious that he would continue to tease her when she so obviously loathed it. "Lord

Chatsworth, you are a cad, and I will never dance with you as long as I live." She snatched up the glass of wine and tossed it at him, ruining his second shirt of the night, before rushing out the door and down the stone steps into the garden.

CHAPTER 1

March 1874

ELIZABETH STOOD IN THE CLASSROOM doorway, listening as a girl read to the class from a primer. "The hen has a neh—" The girl, one of the younger students, named Betsy Norris, hesitated, her small mouth wrestling with an unfamiliar pronunciation.

Mrs. Podmore, the teacher, lifted the child's finger, running it beneath the word as the child made the sound of each letter.

"N-E-S-T . . . nest!" The girl's eyes lit up and the teacher nodded.

"The hen has a nest." Betsy said the words—*read* the words with confidence and returned to her seat, a proud smile on her face.

Elizabeth left the doorway and came to the next, where Mr. Wilkie was writing an arithmetic equation on a large chalkboard. The girls copied the numbers on their slates. Sarah Baker's tongue poked out of her mouth as she wrote. Her bare feet dangled on the too-high chair.

Mr. Wilkie instructed the children to solve the equation and raise their hands when they arrived at an answer. Jane Lewis sucked on her chalk while she considered. Emma Walker screwed up her face, squinting in concentration until her eyes nearly disappeared. After a moment, she jolted, scribbling quickly, and shot her hand into the air.

Mr. Wilkie took Emma's slate, read her answer, and gave a nod affirming that she'd correctly solved the equation.

The girl beamed.

Elizabeth continued to her office on the upper floor. These moments were exactly what she'd had in mind when she'd petitioned months earlier to start the school for disadvantaged young girls. The process—applying to the city for premises, obtaining funds from patrons, securing craftsmen to repair the damaged workhouse and make it not only structurally sound but functionally appropriate as a schoolhouse—had been frustrating and at times arduous.

But the most difficult part of all had been convincing the residents of London's east end that education would benefit their daughters in the long run, making them eligible for employment as teachers, lady's maids, and shopkeepers. Families depended on income from each member old enough to thread a loom or stoke a fire, and in the end, Elizabeth had come to an arrangement with various factory foremen to allow the girls to maintain their employment while working only two days per week. The families sacrificed a few days of wages, but at least the girls retained their jobs.

Seeing her dream of a school come to fruition had become considerably easier thanks to Elizabeth's membership in the Blue Orchid Society. Her tight-knit group of friends had been together for nearly a year, and in that time, Sophronia and Vivian had married, one becoming a lady and the other a policeman's wife. Both were extremely happy. Another, Hazel, was engaged but was looking into options for married nurses before taking her vows. Along with Dahlia, the members of the Blue Orchid Society had raised funds for Elizabeth's schoolhouse through their families and connections. But the ladies had not been content to simply gather money. They had used their various talents and abilities to furnish the classrooms and gather donated supplies as well. This entire building was a testament to the sisterhood the women had formed those months earlier in the Marquess of Molyneaux's library when Elizabeth had fled from the unwanted company of Lord Chatsworth.

Each time she walked up the staircase that led from the classrooms to the upper level of the building, she was reminded of the night before the Spitalfields School for Girls had officially opened.

The five women had stayed until nearly dawn, arranging chairs and desks and filling the classroom cabinets with reading primers, pencils, paper, and chalk. Sophronia had printed spelling sheets on the presses in her newspaper office and donated piles of writing paper. Dahlia had purchased books for the classroom shelves and recommended the interior walls be painted in a light blue, claiming the color would be calming to the girls as well as very fashionably up-to-date. Vivian had personally appointed the chemistry laboratory, insisting on providing the very latest in scientific technology. And Hazel had converted a closet into an infirmary and volunteered to come after her hospital shifts to teach the girls about the importance of hygiene, nutrition, and emergency health care.

The Spitalfields School for Girls would never have become a reality if not for Elizabeth's association with these women. In that moment, sitting on the stairs with a glass of champagne, laughing with the four most important people in her life and looking over the fresh paint and new tiles of the entryway, Elizabeth's heart had been so full that she'd thought it could not possibly hold one more ounce of joy. She paused on the steps now, and the warmth filled her again. She stood there with a foot in both worlds: that of the ladies of high Society who had contributed to the school and that of the girls of the rookery who would benefit from their efforts.

When Elizabeth reached her office, she opened the casement window a few inches. A breeze was accompanied by the smell of east London factory smoke, which to many would be considered reason enough to keep one's windows closed. But the odor of burning coal and the resulting cloud that burned one's throat and turned the sky a shade of yellow-brown was as familiar to Elizabeth as the sound of raging furnaces and churning machinery. It was the smell of home.

The open window also provided access for a tabby cat Elizabeth had named Gaffer for his habit of sitting in the chair behind her desk and behaving as if everyone were his subordinate. In the West Midlands, where Elizabeth was from, *gaffer* was what one called the person in charge. If anyone were to come into the office when she was away, they could easily assume by his authoritative gaze that the cat, not Elizabeth, was the school's headmaster.

Tired of Gaffer's reproving look when he was ousted from his seat, Elizabeth had brought another chair to sit beside hers, putting a pillow on it to make it even more enticing to the cat, and the decoy had proven successful. Gaffer was entirely happy to supervise school operations from his position at her side.

Right on schedule, he slipped in through the open window, hopping down to the floor and stretching before taking his seat.

"Good morning, sir." Elizabeth scratched the cat's head and unwrapped a link of sausage from a napkin. He accepted his breakfast, and while he ate, Elizabeth settled into her chair and opened the envelope on the top of a pile of mail. "An invoice, I'd wager. What do you think?"

Gaffer didn't offer a guess as to what the letter might contain, but he didn't look surprised when she unfolded a notice from the plumbing company that had repaired a leaking pipe the week before.

Elizabeth set the bill to the side and picked up the next. As she inserted the brass letter opener beneath the flap, Ethel Boyle, her assistant, entered the room. She set an armful of books, files, and papers on the small table in the corner, unpinned her hat, and removed her coat with quick, deft movements. The woman was always in a hurry.

"Good morning, miss," she said, hanging her outerwear on the coatrack next to the door and patting her silver hair. "And good morning, Gaffer."

"How are you today, Mrs. Boyle?"

"Not well, not well at all." She slid a folder from the top of the stack, opened it, and then turning it around, set it on the desk in front of Elizabeth. Her foot tapped on the wooden floor.

Elizabeth and Gaffer leaned forward. "What is it I'm looking for?" she asked, studying the numbers, not exactly sure what she should be seeing. It appeared to be the school's financials, but Elizabeth was not familiar with the accounting, which was why she'd hired an assistant in the first place.

Mrs. Boyle stabbed her finger at one of the columns, sliding it to the numbers at the base. "The bottom line, miss. See here." She poked her finger at the paper. "We are deficient five thousand pounds."

"Five thousand pounds?" Elizabeth could only repeat the words back to her in a sputter. The figure was enormous. "But how is that possible? We budgeted our expenses so carefully."

"If you remember, two extra instructors were hired, the slate boards were double the price quoted by the manufacturer, and there has been maintenance on the building that we didn't foresee." She ticked the items off on her fingers.

Elizabeth glanced at the plumbing invoice and the pile of letters beneath it. "But five thousand pounds?"

"Since the school is a privately owned facility, there is also the land tax," Mrs. Boyle said. "And it is much higher than anticipated." She took the folder and put it on her own desk. "We need to find more money. If we can't produce five thousand pounds by June, the school will not reopen in September."

Elizabeth rubbed her eyes, imagining the symbol £5000 hanging like an anvil above the school. "This cannot have happened all at once. Why didn't you tell me sooner?"

"You told me you didn't want to worry about money," Mrs. Boyle said and quoted Elizabeth's words back to her. "'The children are the important thing,' remember?"

Elizabeth sagged back in her chair—or sagged as much as was possible in a corset. "I only meant . . ." She rubbed her eyes again. "I was certain the annual bestowments from our donors were sufficient that we did not need to fret about each penny. We have been given such an enormous amount of funding."

Gaffer jumped onto her lap and made himself comfortable, curling up and resting his chin on his tail.

Elizabeth's thoughts spun as she ran her fingers through his fur and panic edged into her mind. Close the school? Tell the girls they would have to return full-time to the factories and cut off their learning? She couldn't do it. She wouldn't.

"The most practical answer is to find another patron," Mrs. Boyle said. Now that she'd delivered the news, her shoulders slumped as well.

Elizabeth had already appealed to every person she even slightly knew in the city: her aunt's friends, acquaintances, the friends and family of the Blue Orchid Society members. So many had pledged annually as well as donated extra funding. How could she ask for more? The people who had believed in her so completely would think that she'd mismanaged their money.

"Lord Benedict?" Mrs. Boyle suggested.

"He has given so much already," Elizabeth said. Vivian's husband, Lord Covington—still called Lord Benedict by his friends—had used his influence in Parliament to secure the building rights and had funded the majority of the school's refurbishment as well as pledged an annual bestowment. She couldn't possibly ask him for more.

Her stomach was tight. She rubbed her forehead. All she'd wanted to do was teach. To make a difference in the lives of young girls who would otherwise never have the opportunity to break free from the cycle of poverty into which they had been born. Education was the key to a better life, and Elizabeth had seen firsthand the delight in a girl's face when she realized what she was capable of. She couldn't take this away from them. She would find the money somehow.

"Perhaps you might appeal to Lady Mather?" Mrs. Boyle suggested.

Elizabeth shook her head. Sophronia's grandmother had given a significant sum to the school and had gathered funds from her friends as well. Elizabeth smiled, remembering when the dowager countess had introduced her to Mrs. Griffin and Lady Chatsworth over tea.

Setting Gaffer on his chair, Elizabeth stood and paced in front of the window as she recalled the memory, and an idea began to form.

She had enjoyed herself immensely that afternoon with the older ladies, seeing in them the kind of person she hoped to be at their age. The three women were eccentric, diverting, and extremely intelligent, asking questions about the proposed school and listening with interest to Elizabeth's answers.

They had all supported the idea immediately and had given generously to the cause.

After her experiences with the pretentious Lord Chatsworth, Elizabeth had initially been hesitant to associate herself with one of his family members. But her worries were unfounded. Lady Chatsworth was nothing like her grandson. Elizabeth stilled, remembering what the woman had said when they'd parted. "This endeavor is a noble one. If you find yourself in need of further support, please do not hesitate to come to me."

At the time, she'd thought it simply a polite thing to say, but if Lady Chatsworth had been speaking sincerely . . .

Elizabeth made a decision. Returning to her desk, she opened a drawer, earning a complaining growl from Gaffer when he was jostled. Taking out a sheet of stationery, she composed a message beneath the school's letterhead requesting an interview with the noblewoman and gave it to Mrs. Boyle to post.

CHAPTER 2

A POKE ON THE ARM alerted Charles Seaton, Lord Chatsworth, that although his body was lounging on a wrought-iron chair in Mrs. Robinson's rare plant conservatory, his mind was elsewhere.

He glanced at his arm, then to the source of the poke, seeing that it had unsurprisingly come from the young woman beside him. Lady Priscilla Bremerton was frowning. He looked around the assemblage. The others in his company watched him as well, letting him know by their expectant expressions that he had been asked a question that he'd not answered.

"I beg your pardon." Charles turned more fully toward Lady Priscilla. He uncrossed his legs and set his feet flat on the flagstones, hoping he looked as if he were now completely engaged in the discussion. His thoughts attempted to stray back to his own . . . complications . . . at home, but he blinked his eyes, bringing his mind fully to the circumstance at hand. He smiled. "What were we talking about?"

Lady Priscilla gave an irritated sigh and pointed toward the refreshment table on the other side of a row of potted ferns. "Mr. Lewis and Miss Dayton." She widened her eyes dramatically, as if the reason for discussing the pair were obvious.

Charles looked toward the refreshment table again and saw that the couple in question were each holding a small plate and talking to their hostess beside a palm tree. Above them, stained glass set into the copper gothic-style arches of the ceiling turned the sunlight into beams of color that played over the white cloth of the refreshment table. He had always considered this glass-enclosed room to be exceptionally lovely, in spite of the constant humidity, and if he'd not been consumed with his worries, he would fully enjoy his surroundings.

As Charles watched the pair, Mr. Lewis took a bite of a pastry and wiped his thumb over the corner of his lip, and Miss Dayton handed him a napkin.

From her seat on Charles's other side, Miss Helen Rothschild snorted.

Miss Charlotte Gray, seated beside Miss Rothschild, gave her own sniff of displeasure. "They are so *conspicuous*."

"Exactly." Lady Priscilla pointed toward Miss Gray and nodded her agreement. "*Conspicuous* is precisely the word. And he is remarkably presumptuous to imagine himself her equal in any way."

Charles thought the couple's behavior hardly warranted such a reaction, but he kept his smile in place. He was content to let the ladies gossip if it would keep them occupied. There were few things more demanding than a bored debutante.

"Much like Benedict and that Kirby woman," Lord Ruben said. He was seated with his fiancée, Lady Lorene Stanhope, on a settee across from Charles, although the woman sat as far away from her intended as possible. How she managed to put so much space between them while remaining on the same piece of furniture was remarkable. And it couldn't have been comfortable.

"You don't approve of Benedict's marriage?" Lady Priscilla asked Ruben. The tone of her voice indicated that she knew the answer but was happy to hear him expound.

"It's not a matter of approval, my dear." Ruben took a deep drink and held up his empty glass to get the attention of a waiting servant, who rushed to refill it. "Benedict will be the Duke of Ellingham. His obligation to his family, his future, his house is clear, and yet he foolishly allowed himself to be ensnared by the artifice of a woman of low birth."

The young ladies nodded their agreement, and Miss Rothschild, in particular, looked irritated, as if Benedict's marriage had wounded her personally.

Charles looked to the other member of the party, Lord Meredith, for his reaction. Benedict had been a dear comrade since they were boys at school, and Charles was surprised to hear Ruben criticize their friend so openly.

Meredith, to his credit, scratched his side-whiskers and looked at his feet, his discomfort at Ruben's words evident. Meredith was a genuinely good man down to his bones, and Charles had never heard him speak ill about anyone. The four men (previously five, but Lord Everleigh was, unfortunately, serving time in a penal colony for his criminal acts) were known in the Society pages as the West End Casanovas, and truth be told, they thoroughly enjoyed the moniker and the celebrity status that came with it. Not that they needed it. They were all titled, wealthy, and if Charles did say so himself, handsome. A friendship spanning so many years and shared experiences had bonded the men tightly—all the more reason for Charles to take note of Ruben's disparagement.

As the self-appointed leader of their group, Ruben gave freely of his advice to the other members, but public criticism of a friend was unlike him.

"They do seem to be very much in love," Meredith offered in his typically good-natured fashion, defending Benedict without making accusations or causing further conflict.

Charles nodded. He trusted Meredith. Of anyone, he thought he might confide the details of his recent circumstance to Meredith.

"Love has nothing to do with it," Ruben said.

Lady Lorene was twisting a ring around her finger. She did not look up at her fiancé as he spoke, but her expression darkened.

"A marriage is a contract," Ruben continued. "A legal arrangement between two families that should elevate both parties socially and financially and provide their descendants with a legacy. It is an alliance of assets. Nothing more, nothing less."

Lady Lorene took a plate from the low table beside her and forked a bite of cake into her mouth.

Charles thought of this group of Casanovas and their counterparts, the Darling Debs, a year earlier. They were the same party, now with two permanently absent members. Missing were the aforementioned Lord Everleigh, along with a young woman who had, until the Marchioness of Molyneaux's Easter ball, been central to the young ladies' group of friends: Dahlia Lancaster. Last year she had sat on the settee beside Ruben, the pair of them hardly inches apart with eyes for only each other. Charles could remember clearly how taken she'd been with Mrs. Robinson's orchids, and Ruben's patience as the couple had walked arm in arm between the trees and displays of pots, stopping at each as their hostess described its contents.

The marquess's formal announcement of Ruben's engagement to Lady Lorene had shocked everyone—especially Dahlia. Her reaction had made it obvious that she'd had no idea of his intention toward another, and Ruben had watched her with cool eyes as she'd rushed from the ballroom, her standing in Society forever damaged by his cruelty. Charles had been disgusted with his friend for the way he'd treated the young lady. But, in the end, he understood. Ruben had done his duty. And one day, sooner than he'd like, Charles must do the same.

He glanced at the young ladies sitting in their company, his eyes lingering on each in turn. It would probably be one of them, he reasoned. It didn't particularly matter which. All were of excellent pedigree and familial reputation, though none stood out to him as someone with whom he wished to spend an inordinate amount of time, let alone share a home. He picked up his glass from the low table and took a drink.

He had no illusions that he would have love in his marriage. His grandmother spoke fondly of her late husband, but Charles thought it must have been an anomaly. He'd witnessed firsthand his parents' relationship. Their union had been the furthest thing from amiable. And those memories led his thoughts directly back to the concern at hand.

He sighed, running the side of his finger over the whiskers of his mustache. If only his grandmother's health spa retreat had not been this week. How could she leave him at such a time? He could not manage this without her.

"You seem distracted." Lady Priscilla poked his arm again.

If he kept allowing his mind to wander, Charles suspected he would end up with a bruise. "Once more, I apologize." He gave the young lady his most charming smile, raising a brow and winking. "I promise to make it up to you."

Lady Priscilla sat back, a smile on her face and pink on her cheeks.

Charles may have overdone it slightly with the wink. But he needed time to think, to figure out how to tackle the complication he found himself responsible for. And the small talk and gossip were not only distracting him from the more important matters; they grated on his nerves, making his already anxious thoughts even more consuming.

He spread his arms and forced a smile at the group. "I shall make it up to all of you—perhaps with a night of games and dancing? Or shall we have a costume soiree? A masquerade, what say you to that?"

His words had their intended effect. The ladies squealed and clapped, immediately suggesting costumes to one another. Even the gentlemen looked pleased by the idea, evaluating the different proposals of costumes and making recommendations of their own.

His plan had worked. Charles sat back and set his ankle on his knee, listening with half an ear to the excited discussion around him. If there was one thing he knew how to do, it was to give the appearance of a person completely at ease, even when his emotions were in a state of disquiet. It had been easy enough to don that persona, especially since Society assumed he would step into his father's shoes. Assuming the role of a carefree flirt, being "charming," as people called him, had its advantages. It kept anyone from getting too close, from seeing the true man behind the mask. His charm was a wall. Watching his mother's heart break again and again had taught him to keep his barrier strong. It was the only protection of which he could be certain. He would not allow himself to fall in love, not when pain would be the result.

He took out his pocket watch, glancing at the time and then snapping the watch closed as he scooted to the edge of his seat.

"Oh, you mustn't leave!" Lady Priscilla grabbed on to his arm before he could stand. She pushed out her lower lip in a practiced pout. "Everything will be so dull without you."

He took her hand from his arm, kissing the air above it before setting it back in her lap, and gave a bow. "It can't be avoided, I'm afraid." He bid farewell to the others and thanked Mrs. Robinson before stepping out of the glass building into the chill of the early-spring afternoon.

Charles indicated to his driver that he would be walking home through the park, preferring a few moments of quiet as he contemplated his situation and searched his mind for solutions. He walked up the familiar pathway, letting the quiet of nature ease his worries. He believed, just as his grandmother did, that immersing oneself in nature was the best cure for any ailment.

A trilling whistle came from a shrubbery beside the trail, and Charles paused, hoping to spot the bird who'd made the sound. It was early in the year for a yellow wagtail, but Charles was certain he'd identified the correct call. A rustle, then a moment later, the little creature came into view, hopping as it pecked the ground for seeds.

Charles smiled. The yellow wagtail was one of his favorite species. This bird wintered in Africa. The very idea of something so small instinctively migrating over such a distance was astonishing. He stood still, watching it peck the ground, looking for seeds. The bird wagged its tail before it hopped back into the cover of the underbrush.

As Charles left the park and walked along his street, he wondered idly how the creature could belong to two places. Did it consider one to be its true home and the other simply a place to visit for a season? Perhaps it felt at home in both locations. Or did it feel as if it didn't truly belong anywhere?

He glanced at the upper windows of Ivy House, his family's London home, as he stepped through the gate and approached its front steps, and his worry grew.

Nigel, the butler, opened the door, taking Charles's hat and gloves.

"How is . . . ?" Charles motioned toward the stairway with his chin.

"I believe today is a good day. There have been no tears—that I'm aware of."

Charles nodded.

"Do you still wish to take tea in the upstairs parlor, my lord?"

"Yes."

"It will be served in half an hour's time, if you are agreeable."

"Thank you, Nigel."

The butler took his leave, and Charles continued staring toward the stairs. He pushed his fingers through his hair, his worries refusing to settle. When he was a boy, he'd discovered a fledgling in the woods on his family's estate. The gardener had allowed him to keep the baby bird in one of the outbuildings. Charles had made a nest with leaves and grass and fed the creature crushed insects and even oatmeal. In spite of his attentions, the fledgling hadn't lasted through the night. Charles's own hubris was responsible for the little bird's death. He'd believed himself to be a competent caretaker. If he'd just left it where it belonged . . . the bird hadn't been for him to save, especially when he hadn't known what he was doing. And even now, twenty years later, he still didn't know what he was doing.

As a child, taking his father's title, becoming the Earl of Chatsworth, had seemed exciting. He would be in charge of the family, which meant everyone would have to do whatever he wished. But the reality was a far cry from his childhood imaginations. Now that his parents were both dead, the family responsibilities fell to Charles. Everything, good or bad, was brought to his attention, and he alone had to make decisions that felt far too important. Thank goodness his grandmother remained. She, at least, possessed a level head, which was more than he could say for the other members of his family.

A tray sat beneath a large mirror in the entry hall, and Charles absent-mindedly picked through the mail, noting that most of the letters were for his grandmother. But one caught his eye. The print on the stationery read *Spitalfields School for Girls*. It wasn't unusual for his grandmother to have associations with charity organizations. But in this case . . . He studied the stamp, puzzled, then closed his eyes, thinking. Something niggled at the back of his mind. He knew this name, but for the life of him, he couldn't . . .

Realization dawned with a flash, bringing with it a possible solution to his worries. "Aha!" His voice echoed through the entryway. He knew exactly who had sent this letter, and if he was correct, it was precisely the answer he had been searching for. Charles couldn't help a smirk as he thought of his previous meeting with Miss Miller in the Marquess of Molyneaux's sitting room. "Forgive me, Grandmother," he muttered, breaking the wax seal and unfolding the paper.

CHAPTER 3

THE DAY AFTER POSTING THE letter, Elizabeth's request was granted and an invitation extended for her to call at Ivy House that afternoon. "What do you think about that, Gaffer?" She held out the card for the cat, who gave it one glance and then licked his paw, brushing it over his face. "Lady Chatsworth remembers me after all."

After the students were dismissed for the day, Elizabeth set off across Town in a hired cab, fidgeting through the entire journey as she tried to imagine what she could say to a person who knew her exclusively through a third party. She couldn't help feeling as if this meeting was her only chance to secure the money the school needed. If she failed, could she possibly find another patron?

The cab neared Belgrave Square, and Elizabeth became more unsettled. Though she currently resided with her uncle only a short walk away, she did not feel completely at ease in the West end of London. And she'd never paid a call alone to a woman of Lady Chatsworth's standing. She should have planned the entire situation with more care, perhaps brought along a friend to help facilitate conversation. Sophronia would have been the best choice, but of course, as the head of her newspaper, she couldn't leave the office in the middle of the day with no notice.

Elizabeth paid the driver and stood for a moment on the paving stones before the grand house. One of the older residences on the square, Ivy House had a classic look with dark-red bricks and white windowsills and balconies. Pillars held a stone arch above the enormous wooden doors of the front entrance. And, true to house's name, tendrils of ivy climbed up its bricks, their green leaves stark against the red. Elizabeth had passed by Ivy House numerous times, but as she stood there alone, the house seemed to loom above her. In its shadow, she felt decidedly inferior. She shivered, crossing her arms against the chill.

She believed in the school, in the girls, but there were moments when the enormity of her endeavor made her wonder if she'd taken on more than she could manage. Her birth had put her far beneath Lady Chatsworth's notice. She'd lived in a boardinghouse in Staffordshire until she was thirteen, for heaven's sake. And the fear of being perceived as a poor manager of the funds she had already received made her stomach twist. Asking for money, even when it was for an important cause, was another reminder of her precarious place within a world that looked down upon women in her position. Not to mention the toll it took on her dignity. She straightened her skirts and brushed off her sleeves, knowing she was just delaying the inevitable. She'd run out of options. Better a few moments of discomfort than to lose the school. The girls needed her.

Reminding herself who she was advocating for, Elizabeth squared her shoulders, stepped through the gate, climbed the stone steps, and rang the bell.

The door was opened by a butler who, at hearing her name, gave a stiff nod and stood aside, indicating that she should enter. "You are expected, miss." He showed her into a parlor to wait.

The room was papered in colorful fabric with an intricate toile design. Ruffles of curtains held back by heavy tassels surrounded the large windows, and velvet Queen Anne–style furniture was arranged on a floral rug. Hanging over the hearth between a pair of gas-lamp sconces was a painting showing pheasants, a male and female, bursting from a thicket, flying in opposite directions. The birds were painted in intricate detail. Elizabeth moved closer, studying the pattern of the feathers. She'd seen her share of pheasants in the forest around the village where she'd lived as a child, and she appreciated the artist's portrayal. The scene was rather like a glimpse into her past.

Footsteps sounded behind her, and Elizabeth's heart caught. Now was the moment. She drew in a breath and turned to greet her host with a wide smile.

Seeing Lord Chatsworth standing in the doorway, however, she let out her breath in a slow puff and lowered her eyelids to half-mast. He was, as always, the last person she wished to see. "What are you doing here?" She folded her arms.

Instead of taking offense to her words and tone, he lifted his brows and one shoulder, gesturing to the ceiling with an open palm. "It is my house."

"I have come to see your grandmother," Elizabeth said. "So if you don't mind . . ." She stopped just short of dismissing him, but her intention was clear.

"Unfortunately, Grandmother is in Bath for another week." He stepped into the room and indicated a chair in front of the hearth. "Would you care to sit?"

Elizabeth ignored the offer. "She wrote to me just today, inviting me . . ." Her words trailed off as she tried to make sense of the situation. Had she misunderstood? She opened her handbag and took out Lady Chatsworth's card.

"I confess to some deception in that regard," Lord Chatsworth said.

She understood at once and fixed him with a glare. "*You* sent this? For what purpose?" He had tricked her. A tendril of discomfort slithered through her middle. She tossed the card onto a low table and folded her arms as her defenses mounted.

Lord Chatsworth rested his hand on the back of a chair. "I didn't believe you would come if you knew it was I who'd invited you."

"In that you are perfectly correct, my lord." His behavior now was different than she'd seen before. He seemed serious instead of his typically teasing demeanor. And his lack of arrogance made her nervous. What was he playing at? Elizabeth looked beyond him toward the doorway, not believing his innocent expression. If there was one thing she'd learned in her twenty-three years, it was that men were capable of any treachery to achieve their ends. "Please excuse me." She took a step toward the door but stopped when he held up a hand.

"Miss Miller, your letter presented a welcome answer to a . . . a dilemma. It seems we each have a need the other can satisfy, and I believe we might come to an arrangement that will be mutually beneficial."

Elizabeth's muscles tensed and trepidation turned to fear. She changed her course, walking around the table so fast she nearly knocked it over. Having the piece of furniture between them was small protection, but now the sofa blocked her path. She looked toward the doorway again, noticing that the butler and all other servants were conspicuously absent, and a feeling of dread descended like a wet cloud around her. She knew what type of proposition a philanderer like Charming Chatsworth would make. And as she possessed little physical strength compared to a man, she employed the most effective tool in her arsenal: her sharp tongue. "Lord Chatsworth, you are a scoundrel and a cad to assume that just because I am a woman working in the world, I am so far beneath your own position that I would be amenable to such a debasing proposition. You are sorely mistaken."

He looked surprised, then confused, blinking and staring at her with his mouth in an *o*. Apparently, women did not often reject his advances. "Miss Miller, I am not proposing anything . . . improper." The corner of his mouth twitched, which did little to reassure her. "I assume you requested an audience with my grandmother because you require funding for your charity school?"

Elizabeth gave a reluctant nod but did not allow her face to soften. He might take any sign of weakness for consent.

"I require a teacher," Lord Chatsworth said. "Someone with very specific . . . qualifications who will, out of necessity, remain discreet."

That explanation was not an explanation at all but the opposite, in fact. It was as if he were deliberately attempting to confuse her. She looked toward the door again.

"There is a girl," he said.

The timbre of his voice had changed. He was no longer speaking in a matter-of-fact tone. There was a vulnerability in his voice, as if he were trusting her with a secret.

Elizabeth was still suspicious. "What girl?"

"Her name is Alice."

"Who is she?"

"She is a member of my family." Something about the way he said it told her that he would answer no more questions about Alice or her origins. Was this a trick? At the moment, Lord Chatsworth was so different from the flippant, teasing man who so irritated her. He spoke with sincerity, and something inside her wanted to trust him. But she fought against the inclination, reminding herself how easily one could be duped. She and her mother had worked too hard and given up too much for her to fall into a trap.

"And Alice requires a tutor?" Elizabeth asked. "I'm certain, with your resources, you can find someone much more qualified than myself, my lord."

He nodded, his finger tapping where it rested on the back of the chair. "As I said earlier, I believe you possess precisely the skills required."

She waited for further explanation, but Lord Chatsworth didn't elaborate.

He offered her the seat again, and this time, curiosity compelled Elizabeth to take it.

He sat in the chair across from her. "How much money do you need?"

"Five thousand pounds." She winced. Saying the figure aloud felt audacious. It was such an enormous amount.

He nodded. "Very well. If you will uphold your side of the bargain, I will provide you with five thousand pounds."

"I still don't know what you would have me do," Elizabeth said, watching him carefully. "What *is* my side of the bargain, exactly?"

"Nigel," Lord Chatsworth called toward the doorway.

The butler stepped back into the room. "Yes, my lord?"

"Please invite Miss Alice to join us, and send for tea."

"Very well, my lord."

Elizabeth watched him go, her curiosity piqued. Who was this child that Lord Chatsworth protected so carefully? And what skills was he alluding to? Was this another of his jokes? Or something more sinister? She felt inclined to trust him at this moment, but remembering his history of teasing, of always throwing her off-balance and embarrassing her, she was cautious. One would be wise to guard herself around Charming Chatsworth. He was a rake. His motivation was his own pleasure, and he felt no compunction about tromping over people in his quest for diversion.

Elizabeth kept her gaze on the doorway, discouraging any further conversation from the man. She could feel him watching her and fought against the heat that spread over her skin at his attention. Was this a game? If so, she could not understand it. The rational part of her brain told her Lord Chatsworth was having a lark at her expense or tricking her into an agreement that would, in the end, put her at his mercy.

She scooted to the edge of her chair; the only thing preventing her from bolting was Lord Chatsworth's promised funds and the resulting futures for her students. Hearing footsteps outside the parlor, Elizabeth darted a glance at her companion, surprised to see that, rather than his typical smug smirk, Lord Chatsworth's brows were pinched together as he looked toward the doorway. He looked . . . concerned. Perhaps even worried.

Elizabeth didn't have time to think much more about it because, at that moment, a small girl stepped into the room. Her blonde curls were held in place with a wide bow. She wore a blue dress beneath a pinafore with ruffles that came just below her knees, showing legs too thin for their stockings and boots. Hands with chewed nails were clasped nervously in front of her, and her eyes were cast downward. The resemblance between the girl and Lord Chatsworth was astonishing. Was she perhaps a niece or a cousin?

Lord Chatsworth crossed the room to her. "Good afternoon, Alice." His voice was inexplicably gentle. "I would like to introduce you to my friend." At the word, he darted a glance at Elizabeth, but she didn't contradict him. She looked between the two of them, still trying to come to grips with the idea that the notorious rake, Lord Chatsworth, may actually possess a heart.

He touched the girl's shoulder gently, leading Alice farther into the room. "This is Miss Miller."

Alice performed a small curtsy, but she did not look up.

"We hoped you would join us for tea," he continued in his mild tone, then waited, as if to elicit a response.

But Alice was silent.

Elizabeth rose, coming closer until she stood right in front of the girl. "How do you do, Alice?"

"Bay too bah," the girl mumbled, still not raising her eyes.

Elizabeth's heart froze, then immediately started to pound as understanding dawned. Those three words made it clear why Lord Chatsworth had sought her out specifically.

She knelt in front of the child. "Ow ode'm thee?"

Alice lifted her gaze, and her blue eyes lit up. "Oy bin twelve."

She was so very small. Elizabeth would have thought her age closer to eight. "Dun thee want tae?"

Alice nodded, accepting the offer of tea, and a bright smile grew. "Oy'm clammed."

Elizabeth smiled as well. The girl's words brought with them a myriad of memories. The Midlands drawl was the sound of her childhood, and hearing it filled her with emotion. She remembered the hours of elocution lessons and speech training that rid her own diction of any hint of the regional speech. Elizabeth's mother had insisted it was necessary, however, and she'd spent every last penny on the endeavor. Elizabeth hadn't realized the wisdom of her mother's actions until she arrived in London and learned for herself how prejudiced people were toward what they considered to be a rustic way of speaking. If not for her mother's sacrifice . . . she blinked away her tears and sat on the sofa, patting the seat beside her in an invitation for Alice to join her.

The girl sat, scooting back on the cushion so her feet dangled above the floor.

Tea was served, and Lord Chatsworth and Nigel slid the table closer so Alice could reach the pastries from her seat.

"Now then, Alice," Elizabeth eased off her accent for Lord Chatsworth's sake. "Where are you from?"

"Staahbridge." Alice spoke around a bite of scone.

"And have you been in London long?"

"A few weeks," Lord Chatsworth said before Alice had a chance to respond. "She came to Ivy House at the beginning of February. Isn't that right, Alice?"

The girl nodded, agreeing with him as she took another bite, followed by a drink of tea to wash it down.

She was obviously a relative, just as Lord Chatsworth had said, Elizabeth noted. But, based on her table manners, it was clear Alice hadn't been raised among high Society. And His Lordship had conspicuously omitted a surname. "And what of your schooling?" she asked.

Alice looked back toward the parlor doorway. "Oy've lessons in the schoolroom."

"Tutors," Lord Chatsworth explained. "She studies French, history, arithmetic, geography . . ." He ticked the subjects off on his fingers. "And what else?"

"Readin'," Alice said. "Oy loik readin'."

"Oh, that's very good," Elizabeth said. "Reading is my favorite subject too." She sipped her tea and set the dainty teacup on the saucer. "Did you learn reading in Stourbridge as well?"

Alice nodded again. "Ar. But we day 'av many books at the orphans' 'owm."

"I see," Elizabeth said. She could sense Lord Chatsworth's tension, his worry that she would ask more. "I imagine Lord Chatsworth has a very extensive selection of books, doesn't he?"

Alice nodded, a wide smile pulling at her mouth. "'Ere's an entire room fer 'em. The loi-brae."

"And if Alice had her way, she'd spend all her time there," Lord Chatsworth said. He gave the girl a fond look. "She and I have been reading Sir Cornelius Poppleford's *Illustrated Handbook of African Insects* this week."

"Did thee know, 'eres a mantis as big as thy arm whot looks just loik a stick?" Alice asked. "And a moth the soiz of a sparrow?"

"I did not know about either of those creatures," Elizabeth said. "But I am very interested. I find learning about faraway places to be fascinating."

Alice continued to regale them with facts from Sir Cornelius Poppleford as they finished their tea.

An older woman in an apron and a cap came to the parlor door. She was pleasantly plump with kind eyes and graying hair.

"Ah, Mrs. Snowden." Lord Chatsworth motioned for the nanny to enter. "Alice is just finishing her tea now."

Alice set her teacup carefully on the table and stood.

Lord Chatsworth stood as well, giving Alice a warm smile. "I'm so pleased you could join us today."

At Mrs. Snowden's cue, the girl gave a curtsy. "Thank thee fer tae," she said, nodding to Lord Chatsworth and Elizabeth.

"It was lovely to meet you, Alice," Elizabeth replied.

Alice and the older woman departed.

Lord Chatsworth watched them go, then returned to his chair.

"She is a delightful girl," Elizabeth said.

"Utterly so," Lord Chatsworth agreed. "Her tutors report a bright mind and inquisitive nature. But I am concerned . . ." His words trailed off, and the wrinkles between his brows returned.

"You worry about her speech."

Lord Chatsworth nodded. "Alice will have every opportunity. She will be denied nothing money can buy. But even I cannot control how others perceive her."

Elizabeth looked back toward the doorway. No matter Alice's intelligence or her grand residence and expensive clothing, once she opened her mouth, she would be doomed in social and academic realms. "Eventually, her speech will become an impediment to her progress." She looked back at him. "If I understand the situation, Lord Chatsworth, you wish for me to provide speech training to Alice, and in return, you will contribute five thousand pounds to the Spitalfields School for Girls?"

"Correct."

Elizabeth studied his expression, certain she was missing something. "Five thousand pounds? You do realize you could find a much more experienced tutor for a fraction of that?"

"But I believe you are just the person to help her," Lord Chatsworth said. "Your backgrounds are very similar."

Elizabeth scowled, watching to see what he was implying, but his expression remained unchanged. Her background wasn't a secret, exactly. But it wasn't something she intended to announce to the gossip-loving *ton* anytime soon. Her mother had been dead for five years now, and with any luck, the rumors about her had died as well. Lord Chatsworth knew where Elizabeth hailed from, thanks to an encounter when they were young, but it was possible he knew no more than that. Elizabeth's face heated at the humiliating memory, and she looked down, frustrated that Lord Chatsworth could embarrass her without even saying anything.

She pushed away the thoughts, taking control of the conversation. "You mentioned the need for discretion in this matter, my lord. I do hope you can be relied on for the same."

"Of course."

"My origins are not known to many in London, and—"

"And I shall keep your confidence, as I expect you will keep mine. I have not made Alice's presence here common knowledge outside of this house. The circumstances of her birth and coming into my family are . . . delicate. And until I am ready for them to be known generally, I would like to keep my family's business private."

"I understand. But, with your permission, my lord, might I tell Dahlia? I can vouch for her discretion in the matter, and more to the immediate point, she can make my excuses to my aunt and uncle on days when I am tutoring Alice and will arrive home later than usual. I wouldn't wish for them to infer something improper, especially if they were to discover I was coming to Ivy House regularly." She winced, and her cheeks colored again.

"I'd not considered . . ." He brushed the side of his finger over his mustache. "That does present a problem." He thought for a moment longer and then nodded. "I believe Miss Lancaster to be trustworthy, and if her knowing your schedule will help maintain a consistency with Alice's tutoring, then by all means, tell her the truth. Perhaps my grandmother could assist in that regard as well when she returns from Bath."

Elizabeth was relieved. Not only would Dahlia help maintain her secrecy, but the idea of lying to her cousin made Elizabeth's stomach ill. She was glad such measures wouldn't be required. And if Lady Chatsworth could come up with a story to explain her regular visits to the house, that would be even better. Elizabeth stood and held out her hand. "If we are agreed, then, let us shake hands."

The corner of Lord Chatsworth's mouth twitched, putting her off balance again, but he rose and took her hand, giving a firm shake. "Very well, Miss Miller. We have a deal."

CHAPTER 4

AFTER THE DETAILS OF MISS MILLER'S employment were settled upon and she'd departed, Charles spent the remainder of the afternoon at his desk. Now that one of his more pressing concerns about Alice had been alleviated, he'd thought he'd be able to concentrate on the documents specified by his man of business. But he kept pondering his visit with Miss Miller.

Before Alice had joined them, the woman had sat with her arms folded and shoulders tight, leaning forward in her chair, as if she were ready to flee at the least provocation. In truth, it had been rather a blow to his ego. Young ladies typically found his company quite agreeable.

But when he was with this particular young lady, Charles became uncertain of how to behave. She didn't react with giggles and blushes to his flirting. His attentions seemed to only anger her. And when he'd come upon her earlier in the parlor, she'd seemed more than simply irritated. Her reaction had been defensive—frightened, even. That was an effect he'd never had on a woman before, and he couldn't understand what had brought it on.

Miss Miller was different from any woman he'd known. She'd always been different—ever since the day they'd met those fifteen years ago. He had been thirteen, and she must have been close to seven or eight. Charles and his schoolmates had been on summer holiday from school, visiting Meredith's estate in the Midlands. The Black Country had fascinated Charles. He had never seen anything like it. Though it was only a few hours away from his home near the sea in Sussex, he'd felt as if he'd come to an entirely foreign place. Enormous coal-burning factories and mines belched out smoke that covered the sky, and the sounds of the forges echoed on the wind. At times, the day was darker than the night. The world smelled burnt, and the people spoke what he'd at first taken to be a different language.

On their adventures exploring the countryside, the boys had found a pond in the woods near Foxborough Hall, and as he thought was entirely appropriate for young men on a hot day, they'd removed their jackets, shirts, and trousers, leaving them in only their smallclothes, and jumped in for a swim. He had found a thick patch of moss and covered his head with it, hollowing out holes for his eyes, and hidden behind a thicket, ready to scare his friends. But as he crept around to spring out at them, he'd come face-to-face with a young Miss Miller. They had both shrieked. Charles's mossy mask had fallen away, leaving behind dripping mud that covered his face, shoulders, and chest. He felt humiliated and skinny, standing there in his smallclothes, but the poor girl had been not only terrified at what she must have at first assumed to be a beast of some sort; she'd covered her eyes at his state of undress and run off.

When Charles had come upon her in town a few days later, he'd teased her mercilessly as a way of assuaging his own embarrassment over the incident, if he were to be entirely honest. He'd accused her of spying on them or plotting to steal their clothing.

Miss Miller had been furious at his taunts. He still remembered the red of her cheeks and the way she'd stamped her foot. Not entirely unlike when she'd come upon him in the marquess's sitting room last spring.

He'd wondered what she'd been doing that day in the woods. Had she been to the market? Running an errand from a factory? Visiting a parent at the mines? He'd burned with questions about a person whose life was so different from his. But asking in front of his friends seemed foolish, and he'd wanted to impress the other boys. So he'd teased her. And his words had embarrassed a young girl from a poor town.

Shame burned his neck. He owed her an apology, but in truth, he thought the delivery of it would only add fuel to her dislike of him. And why did it matter? Why was it of concern to him whether she liked him or not?

It should not matter to him in the least. Miss Miller was just a woman with whom he had a business arrangement. And seeing the absolute joy on Alice's face that afternoon as she'd spoken to someone who fully understood her had confirmed he'd made the right decision. And for that, and Alice's future success in the world, five thousand pounds was a small price to pay.

❧

A few hours later the Chatsworth family—with the exception of Grandmother, who was still attending a health spa retreat in Bath—gathered around the dining table as the dinner meal was served. Charles sat at the head of the table with his younger brother, Leonard, on his right side in his flamboyant fashion, wearing a paisley-embroidered waistcoat that was a few years out of vogue. Kathryn, their sister, sat on his left, in what was typically their grandmother's seat. She wore her blonde hair in a new style, which was becoming a regular sight, as she was daily trying out various arrangements before her debut next month. On Kathryn's other side was Alice.

The girl watched Kathryn with something akin to worship, imitating her movements. The sight warmed Charles's heart, and he hoped the pair would become close. There was only five years' difference between them. So far he and grandmother were the only two who had taken to Alice, but he believed that given time, Leonard and Kathryn would come to love her as well. How could they not? She was family.

Kathryn set down her spoon, motioning for a footman to clear away her soup. "You must tell me what Mariah Everson-Bowles wore to her debut ball," she said to her brothers. "I have heard mixed accounts. Andromeda Flynn tells me it was a periwinkle gown with sky-blue ruffles and a train."

Alice took a last spoonful of soup with a slurp, then set her spoon down as well.

Kathryn darted a look toward the girl, her lip curling at the sound Alice had made, but she continued on without turning. "But Caroline Sidwell is certain the gown was lavender with no train."

Footmen replaced the soup bowls with plates, and Alice snatched up her cutlery, sawing into her roast beef until she glanced at Kathryn and saw that the older girl was making delicate cuts in her potatoes and taking small bites. Alice halted her destruction of the meat and did the same.

"It would be social suicide if I were to wear something similar," Kathryn said.

"I couldn't say what anyone wore," Leonard said, swallowing and reaching for his glass. "Only women notice such things. Members of the more practical sex couldn't care less."

Kathryn frowned at Leonard. "Charles, surely you remember."

He dabbed the corner of his lips with his napkin and then returned it to his lap. "I'm afraid I don't."

"You two are no help at all." Kathryn's frown deepened, and she added a pout for good measure. "How shall I choose what to wear for my introduction to Society if I don't know whether or not it shall put people in mind of Mariah Everson-Bowles?"

"I cannot imagine a more appalling tragedy," Leonard said in a dry voice. He bit into a piece of bread.

Kathryn tossed her napkin onto the table, folding her arms and waving away her plate. "You cannot comprehend how difficult such a thing is for a woman. We have to worry about not only our gown and headdress but also what all of the other young ladies are wearing, not to mention what they have previously worn and how their presentations were received. It is much more complicated than you realize."

"It is just nerves, Kathryn," Charles said. "I'm sure every young lady has the same worries as her debut grows closer. You will be lovely, no matter which dress color you choose."

Kathryn folded her arms. "That is easy enough for you to say. I have been planning for my Season for over a year. The two of you will have to wonder only which dark coat to wear each night, while I must spend hours preparing for every event, just to arrive and realize I've worn a lavender gown when I should have worn periwinkle."

Leonard groaned and took a deep drink.

Charles decided it was time to steer the conversation in a different direction before Kathryn worked herself into a further agitated state. "Did you enjoy your lessons today, Alice?" he asked.

The girl glanced at the others, then nodded. Kathryn and Leonard had made no secret of their disdain for Alice's rustic dialect, and Charles didn't blame her for her reticence to speak in front of them.

She hesitated, then ventured, "Madame Chastain and oy talked in French."

"*Tres bien!*" Charles said, lifting his glass in a salute.

Alice grinned. "That's whot Madame Chastain said, too, when oy told 'er a book is *un lee-vrah.*"

Leonard smirked.

Kathryn looked down at the girl. "Dear, you really shouldn't speak with food in your teeth. It's unseemly."

The excited shine in Alice's eyes went out. She put her hands in front of her mouth, looking down at her plate, her face turning red.

Charles frowned at his sister. "Alice has been practicing etiquette with Mrs. Turvall as well, haven't you?"

Alice gave the slightest hint of a nod.

"Good for you, dear," Kathryn said in her sweetest voice. "And good for Mrs. Turvall for undertaking the effort. She will certainly be a wealthy woman with all the extra training required."

Leonard snorted, covering his mouth with his napkin in an ineffectual effort to hide his laugh.

Alice kept her face turned down, her hands still covering her mouth.

Anger heated Charles's skin. "Mrs. Turvall is very pleased with Alice's progress, as am I." He kept his tone steady. "Alice, I wonder if you might prefer taking dessert in the nursery tonight with Mrs. Snowden. You must be tired." He fixed the others with a hard look. "And I've some matters to discuss with Leonard and Kathryn."

Alice nodded without looking up, and Charles felt the weeks of progress they'd made slipping backward. How would the girl ever feel at home if these two continued to treat her as if she were an outsider? He missed his grandmother even more.

On cue, Nigel entered and pulled back Alice's chair. She rose and gave a small curtsy, mumbling something that Charles took as a farewell.

"Good night, my dear," he said.

The other two repeated the pleasantry, and Alice left.

Once Charles was sure the girl was out of earshot, he rose, set his hands on the table, and leaned forward. "Your treatment of Alice is entirely unacceptable." He looked from Kathryn to Leonard. "And it will not be tolerated."

"Oh, Charles." Kathryn waved her hand. "I was only giving her helpful advice. That girl eats like a monkey."

Leonard laughed. "A starving monkey."

Kathryn joined in the laughter.

"That is enough!" Charles's voice cracked like a whip, echoing in the high-ceilinged room. "I will make myself clear. This is my house. I am the head of this family, and I will demand respect for Alice, just as I would for either of you. She is your sister. And I expect her to be treated kindly."

"Half sister," Kathryn grumbled. "And we didn't even know she existed until a few weeks ago."

"If only Father could have left alone the tavern maids for once." Leonard's expression showed the depths of his disgust.

"None of that matters," Charles said. "Alice has no one else. And she is family."

"She doesn't belong here," Kathryn said. "She even told me she wished to return."

"Return to what?" Her words made Charles defensive. He'd had no indication that Alice wanted to leave. "Return to the orphan asylum? Or a workhouse?"

"Charles," Leonard said in a more thoughtful tone, "the way you've taken responsibility for this girl is admirable. I commend you for your worthy intentions. But you have to know she will never be accepted by Society. Her manners, the way she talks . . . she will be scorned by the *haut ton*. You do her no favors by keeping her here."

"I disagree." Charles felt a twist of guilt as his brother's words struck so close to his own worries. The image of a fledgling in its box came into his thoughts, and he pushed it back out. "In Stourbridge, Alice would inevitably have ended up as a worker in a glass factory. But with schooling, training in etiquette and speech, opportunities open for her. She can—"

"She can, perhaps, find work as a shopkeeper or a lady's maid, if she's lucky," Kathryn said.

"She can do whatever she wishes," Charles countered. "Opportunities for women are so much greater than they once were. With our support and the Chatsworth family name, Alice will be a respected member of Society. We will make sure of it." Seeing that his siblings were mustering further arguments, he didn't give them a chance to speak. "And if I hear either of you speak disparagingly to that girl again, then it will be the two of you taking etiquette lessons with Miss Turvall and eating dessert in the nursery." He slapped his hands down on the table, shocking them into silence before striding from the room.

CHAPTER 5

AFTER MEETING WITH LORD CHATSWORTH, Elizabeth had returned to Spitalfields and worked for hours with Mrs. Boyle on the school's finances. They'd scrutinized each expense, calculated the costs of supplies and the teachers' salaries, and in the end, they were left with a measure of relief. Lord Chatsworth's five thousand pounds would pay off the deficit caused by the extra taxes, repairs to the facility, and the other unexpected expenses. Once they were satisfied they'd not overlooked anything, Mrs. Boyle took her leave and Elizabeth was left alone.

The sky had grown dark, and the outside air was cool. Elizabeth bid Gaffer good evening as he slipped through the window, off to do whatever cats did in the night hours. She closed and latched the window and walked through the building, making certain the gas lamps were extinguished and the windows fastened. The classrooms had been straightened by their teachers, chalkboards erased, and wastebins emptied, but there remained some general tidying to be done. In the small library, Elizabeth spent a moment returning books to their shelves. She straightened the stacks of papers and boxes of pencils in the supply closet, then took a damp rag to the door handles and walls where little hands had left their marks. She swept the tiles of the entry hall, going over sticky spots with a mop, and only when her stomach began to complain did she realize how late the hour had grown. It was well past suppertime. Leaving the remainder of the cleaning for the morning, Elizabeth took her coat and hat and stepped out into the chilly evening, locking the school door behind her.

When she descended the stairs, she was surprised to find a cab was waiting for her. She recognized the horse and driver right away.

Clem waved from the driver's seat. "Miss Miller, there ye are!"

"Have you waited for me all this time?" she asked, looking up at the man. Clem typically drove her home after the school day was finished, but tonight she was hours later than her usual departure time. Was her daily cross-city journey of such value that he'd lose out on other fares for the job? She couldn't imagine that to be the case.

"Saw the light on inside and figured you was still 'ere," he said. "Not safe for a young lady to be wanderin' around on 'er own after dark."

Elizabeth hadn't even considered that. In spite of the school's location in an area with a reputation for crime, she'd never felt anything but safe. The rookery residents either knew she had nothing of value to steal, or they were appreciative of her efforts on their children's behalf. Perhaps her feeling of security could be attributed to both reasons. But it had made her careless. She glanced around, seeing shadows moving in the fog that hung low over the narrow streets and felt a welling of gratitude for the cabbie and his concern.

She stepped onto the mounting board, then paused before climbing into the seat. "Have you eaten supper, Clem?"

"Aye, miss. Th' wife always sends me with a bit o' somethin'."

"I am famished," she said. "If you would be so kind as to drive me to the best street vendor in the east end, I will happily purchase a meat pie for you as well."

Clem grinned, his few remaining teeth gleaming in the yellow light of a streetlamp. "I know jes' the place, miss."

An hour later Elizabeth bid Clem good evening and climbed the steps to the Lancasters' house on Eaton Place.

Jameson, the butler, met her at the door. He put a finger in front of his mouth, requesting silence.

By that simple gesture and the darkened house, Elizabeth knew exactly what sort of evening had occurred. Her uncle Eldon had likely been too ill to join the family for supper, leaving Aunt Henrietta to stare at his empty chair throughout the meal and drown her pain in whatever drink was being served until she excused herself before the dessert course, and the housekeeper, Mrs. Brimsby, would have assisted her to her bed. The supper routine was becoming more common, and Elizabeth regretted leaving Dahlia to endure it alone.

"Miss Dahlia is in the upstairs sitting room," Jameson said, as if hearing her unspoken thoughts. He spoke more warmly than one would imagine from his formal manner.

"Thank you. I shall join her presently." Elizabeth removed her hat and gloves. "How is my uncle this evening?"

"Much the same," he responded with a sober expression, taking her outerwear. Uncle Eldon's symptoms had waxed and waned for over a year. At times his strength would improve, giving the family hope that the disease was gone completely, just to return with a vengeance, leaving the man weak and fevered, his coughs echoing through the house. "He is awake now. Miss Dahlia read to him earlier."

"I wonder if I might bid him good night," she said.

"I'm certain he would like that." The elderly butler smiled and held out his hand, an invitation for Elizabeth to precede him. They climbed the stairs and followed the dim corridor, stopping outside the master of the house's bedchamber. On the other side of the corridor, Aunt Henrietta's door was closed, and no light shone beneath it. Elizabeth had been right about her retiring early.

Jameson gave a gentle knock on Uncle Eldon's door and pushed it open. He stepped inside. "Sir, Miss Elizabeth is here."

A nurse was straightening the bedsheets around the patient.

"Oh yes," Uncle Eldon said. "Bid her enter, of course."

The nurse curtsied and left, giving them privacy.

Jameson closed the door.

Elizabeth came forward, keeping a pleasant smile on her face in spite of the unpleasant sight of the sick man. He was thinner than she'd ever seen him, nearly swallowed by his pillows, his face sallow with dark smudges beneath his eyes. "How are you, Uncle?"

"Tired." He smiled, blinking slowly. He had probably already taken a dose of laudanum to help him sleep. "But happy to see you. How is the school?"

Elizabeth sat in the chair beside his bed and told him about Betsy Norris's reading frustration and then the delight on her expression when she'd at last managed to read the word *nest*.

"Figured it out, did she?" He chuckled. "Clever girl. And how old did you say she is?"

"Six."

"Excellent." Her warmhearted uncle beamed, delighted with the progress of a child he had never, and likely would never, meet.

"We hope to have a science demonstration soon," Elizabeth told him. "Professor Wallis and Lady Covington have offered to teach the girls about chemistry."

"Oh, won't the children love that? I—" Uncle Eldon's sentence was cut off by one cough and then another. He held up a hand, indicating that his coughing wouldn't last, but after a moment the coughs turned into a torrent, wracking his thin body until he bent forward, gasping for breath.

Elizabeth took a towel from the table beside his bed, holding it in front of his mouth as he coughed into it. She touched a hand to his back, wishing she knew how to comfort him. His fits were painful, and this one lasted particularly long.

When he at last sat back in the pillows, Elizabeth wiped his lips with the towel, unsurprised to see blood. She gave him a drink of water, glancing to the doorway, where Jameson watched, his worried face drawn in a frown.

"Thank you, my dear," Uncle Eldon said in a breathless voice. He took her hand. "Once I'm healthy and out of this bed, the Spitalfields School for Girls will be my first visit."

"Not the Queen's Head?" Elizabeth teased. Uncle Eldon had told her about the public house he and his university friends used to frequent, and she brought it up at every opportunity, loving the mischievous sparkle in her uncle's eye when she mentioned it.

"Perhaps we shall stop at the Queen's Head after." He winked. "And, of course, I must visit the dockyard. Dahlia has told me about the changes she's made, and I should like to see them firsthand." His eyes took on a wistful look. "Perhaps I will even take a voyage."

"When you are well, we shall all take a voyage," Elizabeth said with forced optimism. Both she and Uncle Eldon knew he would never be well enough to travel. "To anywhere you wish to go."

"Yes, we should—" His cough cut him off again, turning into another fit.

Elizabeth held the towel again, and this time, Jameson stepped into the room, followed by the nurse. The two remained at the doorway, but Jameson's meaning was clear. Uncle Eldon needed to rest. Elizabeth gave a nod of understanding, but just as she opened her mouth to bid him good night, Uncle Eldon took her hand.

"I'm so proud of you, Elizabeth." He held her gaze, his eyes wise despite the illness. "You are doing something of immense importance. Both you and Dahlia. I could not be more pleased with the young ladies you've become."

Elizabeth's throat went tight. She fought against the tears that threatened, not wishing her uncle to see her weep. "Thank you, Uncle. If not for you, neither of us would have the opportunities—"

He waved his hand to stop her words. "No thanks required. I simply provided the means and encouragement. You ladies are doing the work."

His words brought a rush of emotion. Elizabeth's eyelids itched, and she sniffed. Uncle Eldon's words sounded like a farewell. As if he were making certain things were said before it was too late to say them. Trying to control the tears pressing behind her eyes, she busied herself arranging the pillows behind him and pouring more water into his glass. "I'd better let you sleep."

The nurse came closer, bustling past Elizabeth to return to her patient.

Uncle Eldon sighed. "Yes, the doctor seems to think sleep is the thing. Sleep, vinegar massages, and cod-liver oil." He wrinkled his nose and grimaced.

Elizabeth laughed. "Good night, Uncle." She kissed him on the forehead and departed, exchanging a worried look with Jameson as she passed. Her uncle was weaker than he'd been even a week earlier, and his coughing . . . seeing him thus made Elizabeth's heart heavy.

In her entire life, she'd never known a man to believe so fully in the intelligence of girls. She'd typically encountered quite the opposite. But Uncle Eldon was different. He'd made Dahlia the heir to his steamship company, as well as been a significant contributor to Elizabeth's school. He encouraged them in their endeavors instead of telling them they were inadequate to accomplish them by virtue of their gender.

Elizabeth had worried that he would be angry when he saw her picture in the *Times*, but he'd actually laughed. "*Rock*heart. Good for you, my dear. Stick it to those Tories." But he hadn't shown the photograph to Aunt Henrietta, nor had either of them mentioned it to her, knowing she—and most of the people of her acquaintance—would disapprove of the impertinence and disrespect to a man of His Lordship's station.

Elizabeth walked past the staircase and continued on to the west wing of the house, stopping at the sitting room to see her cousin, but Dahlia wasn't inside. She must have gone to bed already.

As Elizabeth turned, a folded paper on a table beside the sofa caught her eye, and she picked it up. It was a brochure from Dr. Hugo Schneider's sanatorium in the Swiss Alps. Dr. Schneider had developed a treatment center for tuberculosis, believing fresh air and exercise to be a miracle cure for the lung disease. But Uncle Eldon had refused to leave behind his home and family, especially Aunt Henrietta. It appeared Dahlia had not given up hope.

Elizabeth continued on to her bedchamber, finding her lady's maid waiting for her. "Hello, Rosie."

"Good evening, miss," Rosie said. She laid out nightclothes on the bed as Elizabeth unpinned her hair and removed her shoes.

A knock sounded on the door, and Dahlia entered in a dressing gown. "You must have had an eventful day. You missed supper."

"More busy than eventful," Elizabeth said. She raised her brows, then darted her eyes toward the maid, wordlessly telling her cousin she had something to say, but it needed to wait until they were alone.

Dahlia sat on Elizabeth's bed, pulling up her bare feet and wrapping her arms around her knees. "Please don't tell me you ate street food again."

"A meat pie," Elizabeth said, allowing Rosie to unfasten the buttons on the back of her bodice.

"Oh dear," Dahlia said, grimacing. "You mustn't trust any sort of meat you purchase from a vendor's stall. You may have eaten a dog, for all you know."

"It was rather tough for dog meat." Elizabeth raised her arms for Rosie to lift off her gown. She made a show of smacking her lips in concentration. "Rat, I think." She nodded and pretended to lick the tips of her fingers. "Yes, definitely a rat pie with extra rat gravy and a sprinkling of cricket legs for flavor."

Rosie giggled.

Dahlia groaned and threw a pillow at her.

Elizabeth snatched it and threw it back. She took in a deep breath as her corset was loosened, then stepped out of her skirts and pulled her nightgown over her head.

Dahlia rose and motioned for Elizabeth to sit at the dressing table while she ran a brush through her cousin's hair and Rosie hung the clothes in the wardrobe.

Elizabeth closed her eyes, enjoying the feel of the bristles scratching her scalp and then tugging down through her locks. Once Dahlia was satisfied that the tangles were all gone, she wound Elizabeth's hair into a long braid, tying it off with a snatch of lace. As Elizabeth watched her in the mirror, she saw her cousin's eyes alight with curiosity. No wonder she was hurrying Rosie's work along.

"Do you require anything more from me tonight?" the lady's maid asked at last.

"No, thank you," Elizabeth said.

"Very well." Rosie gathered an armload of clothes for the laundry. "Good night, Miss Elizabeth, Miss Dahlia."

They bid her good night, and once she was gone, Elizabeth pulled her cousin to the bed, where the pair of them sat facing one another. "I went to Ivy House today," Elizabeth said.

"Oh." Dahlia looked disappointed. "Is that all? How is Lady Chatsworth?"

"I imagine she is doing well," Elizabeth replied. "But I didn't see her. My meeting was with Lord Chatsworth."

"Gracious." Dahlia's eyes widened. "The school must be in desperate circumstances for you to turn to him. If you need money, you should have come to me instead. I can't imagine Charming Chatsworth sullying his reputation by contributing to a charity school for girls."

Elizabeth shrugged. "In that you will be surprised. He contributed five thousand pounds."

Dahlia's mouth dropped open, and she shook her head. "Five thousand . . . I cannot believe it."

Elizabeth explained about the meeting with Lord Chatsworth and Alice, and when she was finished, Dahlia's surprised expression was tempered with confusion. "You're certain he said this girl, Alice, is a member of his family?"

"Yes. And she must be. She looks the very image of him. Perhaps she's a cousin or a niece. He gave no surname."

"Not a niece, certainly." Dahlia wove a pillow ruffle between her fingers as she thought. "Charles's brother is, of course, younger than he, and there is only one sister. Kathryn is seventeen, I think. And if Alice is a cousin, she is surely a distant relation. I don't know of any relatives of the Chatsworths in the Midlands. Lord Meredith's estate is there, but the Chatsworth seat is in Sussex."

"A distant cousin, then," Elizabeth mused. "I suppose it's possible. But if that's the case, why the secrecy?"

"I don't know," Dahlia admitted. "From the way you describe the conversation, Lord Chatsworth seems to be worried about a scandal, but how, I can't guess."

"Do you think . . . ?" Elizabeth took a pillow, holding it on her lap. "Might Alice be Lord Chatsworth's own daughter?"

"What?" Dahlia blinked, pulling back. "No, surely . . . you said she is twelve? I'd guess His Lordship is no older than twenty-eight."

Elizabeth did a quick calculation. He would have been sixteen when the girl was born. "Not impossible."

"No, but it is unlikely. You remember I was very close with Lord Chatsworth and his friends. A secret like this . . . I think I would have known."

"What if nobody knew? Not even Lord Chatsworth himself?" Elizabeth asked. "What if he found out only recently and that is why Alice was raised in Stourbridge until now?"

"And her mother never told anyone? Not even His Lordship?"

"Maybe she was sworn to secrecy."

"I don't know," Dahlia said. "I just don't believe it."

"I suppose it does no good to speculate." Elizabeth leaned back on the pillows. She considered whether to go down to the kitchen for something to settle her stomach. The meat pie was not sitting comfortably inside her. "The important thing is Alice, no matter her ancestry."

"Lord Chatsworth was wise to think of you," Dahlia said. "You are an excellent teacher."

"I think I will enjoy teaching her." Elizabeth yawned. "She is a lovely girl." Now that she'd shared her news and speculated about a potential scandal, she was growing tired.

"And you see yourself in her," Dahlia guessed.

"In some respects." Elizabeth pressed a pillow to her middle as her belly made a very impolite noise. "She seems much more well-behaved than I have ever been."

Dahlia laughed. "For that, dear cousin, you should be grateful."

CHAPTER 6

CHARLES TAPPED HIS FINGER ON the arm of his chair, glancing across his study to the doorway and then to the other side of the room where a clock sat on the mantel. Miss Miller would have arrived twenty minutes ago to begin her tutoring of Alice. They were most likely at this very moment in the schoolroom above him. And, try as he might, Charles could not keep focused on the task at hand.

His private secretary, Mr. Whitesides, pulled another stack of papers from his satchel. He glanced at them through his spectacles, straightened them, and then set them in front of Charles. "Petitions for expansion of the Poor Relief Laws."

"Of course." Charles pulled the stack closer, looking over the formal appeal and the pages of signatures attached. There were three such groupings, each of the petitions focusing on a different proposition for change to the existing laws. The vote was drawing nearer, and he couldn't help but wonder if he'd see Miss Miller among those gathered outside the Parliament building on voting day, waiting to hear the results.

Charles looked toward the doorway again, glanced at the ceiling and back down to the pages in his hands. None would contain anything he'd not already heard in the debates and news articles. And while to some the issues at hand seemed as simple as a change in social policy—allotting more funds to systems and programs to alleviate the afflictions of the poor—in reality, solving the problem of London's poverty crisis was more complicated. The money had to come from somewhere, and an increase of taxation would be a burden on an entirely different class of society, thereby adding to the problem instead of alleviating it. But on the other hand, something must be done. Should the government mandate increased minimum salaries for all workers? Such an act would raise the quality of life for some, but would the factory owners decrease their workforce as a result, expecting the remaining employees to work harder and longer to make up the deficit?

Sending impoverished persons to a workhouse or debtors' prison bordered on inhumane. But what was the alternative? Forgiving their debts outright? Obviously, that would injure the owed party. Leave them to starve? Another unacceptable answer.

Whether a person couldn't work or was physically unable to was a matter for a doctor to determine. Was the government to hire doctors solely for the purpose of deciding a person's work ability? And what was to be done for impoverished elderly widows? Slum housing? Hunger? Philanthropy had provided some temporary relief, but legislation was needed to address the issues at large. Changes had to be made, but deciding which problems to address and how was complex and had been the subject of years of intense debate. In the end, no one would be entirely happy with the decisions made.

Charles looked over one of the written petitions, and his gaze caught on a quote he recognized from the American president George Washington. *"Let your heart feel for the affliction, & distresses of every one, and let your hand give, in proportion to your purse."*

It seemed so simple. The wealthy class—of which he was one—must give more. He understood this, believed in it. His grandmother was an excellent example of supporting charity projects. She financed and even volunteered weekly at a soup kitchen. Unfortunately, not every person of means felt such a responsibility for those less fortunate than themselves. Asking the wealthy to contribute from their own purses when they were also the ones making the laws regarding who paid taxes and at what rate . . . it was nearly impossible.

Charles rubbed his eyes. He looked at the signatures—at places, the designations were only initials or marks of *x*—and he tried to imagine the people behind them. Some were those for whom the legislation was being written. The members of the population who would personally benefit or be hurt by the changing of the law. Those whose lives or deaths would be determined by votes. Others were no doubt crusaders, people such as Elizabeth Miller—advocates. Charles glanced toward the clock, the doorway, and the ceiling again.

He shuffled through the pages, then set them aside, feeling that if his thoughts were not entirely focused on the matter, it was a disservice to those he was supposed to be helping. "That is enough for today, I think, Whitesides."

"Very well." The secretary moved to clean up the papers.

"Leave them," Charles said. "I may read through them again later tonight."

Mr. Whitesides nodded. He took his satchel and inclined his head in a precise, nearly military manner, giving a bird's-eye view of the wisps of hair combed across his bald pate. "I will see you tomorrow, then, my lord."

Charles bid his secretary farewell, and then he climbed the stairs, making his way along the corridor, past the nursery. He slowed as he approached the schoolroom, placing his feet carefully on the carpet so as not to disturb the lesson.

"My goat is funny." Miss Miller's voice sounded clearly from the room. Charles thought she must be sitting near the door.

"Moy gawt ees foonay," Alice said, repeating the words with her heavy accent. Her tone held resentment, and Charles wondered how many times she'd been asked to repeat the sentence. He came close to the door and leaned back against the wall beside it.

"I know it's difficult," Miss Miller said in a kind voice. "But can you hear the difference? 'My goat' instead of 'Moy gawt.'"

"Ar, oy 'ear it," Alice said. "Mahee gooowt." She pushed out the vowel sounds, sighing loud enough for Charles to hear it. Her frustration was evident, even without him seeing her.

Miss Miller was quiet for a moment. "I have a trick," she said at last. "Or a game, if you'd like. Imagine you're in school or perhaps in church—somewhere you must behave—and your friend tells a joke or makes a funny face, or you remember something that makes you want to laugh. But, of course, you can't laugh. So you must hold it back, fight against it. Now, how does that look?"

The room was quiet for a moment as Alice presumably demonstrated how to fight against her laughter.

"Touch the sides of your mouth as you do it," Miss Miller said. "Can you feel the muscles in your cheeks and chin tighten?"

"Ar, oy feel it."

Charles touched the sides of his own mouth, testing his own anti-laughter muscles.

"Yes, that's right," Miss Miller said. "Now, remember how that feels as you repeat the sentence again. Keep those muscles tight and speak from the front of your mouth instead of the back. 'My goat is funny.'"

"Miee, gooot iis funnee."

"Oh, that was excellent," Miss Miller said. "Much better. Would you like to try again?"

Alice was quiet, and Charles dared a peek into the room. The teacher and pupil sat at a table across from one another, and the girl's head was bowed.

After a moment, Alice spoke. "Whot's wrong with 'ow oy talk?"

"That's a good question, Alice." Miss Miller's voice was gentle. "And the answer is not a simple one." She let out a long breath through her nose. "First of all, you must know, there is absolutely nothing wrong with your speech. Your words are the voice of your . . . of *our* people. They are the sounds of the miners deep in the seams, of the horizon filled with furnaces, of a sky that's black by day and red by night. The way we speak is the language of those who know the ways to appease fairies, of community, of industry. That part of you, your heritage—it is precious, and you must never allow anyone to let you feel as if you are lacking because of it." She breathed out again, speaking slowly, as if choosing her words. "However . . . our way of speaking is not recognized by everyone for its beauty."

"They think oy'm simple." Alice's voice was soft and filled with a shame that made Charles's heart hurt. He closed his eyes, remembering the cutting remarks his siblings had made with the belief that their insults were too clever for the young girl to take their meaning. But Alice understood.

"I know you aren't simple," Miss Miller said. "And Lord Chatsworth knows you aren't. Sir Cornelius Poppleford's *Illustrated Handbook of African Insects* is not for the feeble-minded." She was quiet for a moment, and Alice sniffed.

Charles glanced again through the doorway and saw Miss Miller offer Alice a handkerchief.

"Oy miss it," Alice said. "The Black Coon-trae."

"What do you miss? Your friends?"

"Ar, them too. But mostly oy miss the woods. The animals. Visitin' the market."

"You miss the countryside," Miss Miller said. "I miss it too. The tidy shrubs and manicured trees in Hyde Park don't quite have the wild feel we're used to, do they?"

"No. An' Kathryn says oy'm a babby if oy don't wear shoes in the garden. She don't think oy can be a propa lady."

Charles frowned. If only his sister knew how much her opinion meant to Alice.

"But I know you can be a proper lady," Miss Miller said. "And I will help you do it. But it will be difficult, I'm afraid." She shifted in her chair, making it creak. "Before my mother sent me off to school, she hired an elocution instructor to teach me the Queen's proper English. I hated every moment of it. It was difficult, changing my speech. And the way I was meant to talk sounded so pretentious. The sounds were strange in my mouth. But my mother would not allow me to quit. So do you want to know what I did?" Miss Miller lowered her voice, as if she were revealing a secret.

"Whot did thee do?" Alice asked.

Charles leaned closer to the open door.

"I made a game of it," Miss Miller said. "Sometimes I would imagine I was a spy from a far-off land, infiltrating the enemy. Or I would be a fugitive or a princess in hiding, and one wrong word would reveal me."

"Or a poy-rate!" Alice offered.

"Yes," Miss Miller said. "A pirate would certainly need to alter her speech to mingle among high Society."

"It's loik a sae-cret." Alice's tone had completely transformed from discouragement to excitement.

"Yes," Miss Miller said. "Exactly like a secret. Dressing in fancy clothes and speaking like a Londoner doesn't change who you are inside. It's rather like wearing a disguise."

Hearing footsteps in the corridor behind him, Charles startled.

Mrs. Snowden curtsied when she saw him, giving no indication that she though it odd to encounter the lord of the house listening at the schoolroom doorway. She must be here to fetch Alice to dress for supper.

Charles motioned for the nanny to continue on, not giving her a chance to ask a question that he would have to answer and that would give away his presence. Miss Miller would certainly have something to say about his creeping through the corridors and spying on her. And although he couldn't explain to himself why, her finding him here made him feel vulnerable, as if it would somehow give her the upper hand. He preferred to meet with the woman—and every woman, for that matter—on his own terms.

Mrs. Snowden stepped into the schoolroom, waiting just inside the doorway.

"It looks as though our time is at an end," Miss Miller said. "Before we meet again, please practice using your smile-fighting muscles. And I should like you to come up with an excellent pirate name."

Alice laughed. "Aye-aye, Miss Miller."

The sounds of chairs scooting across the wooden floor was Charles's signal to leave. He heard Miss Miller bid Alice and the nanny good evening as he hurried down the corridor, past the staircase and into his grandmother's sitting room. It was strange to be in the room without her. The curtains were drawn, and no lamps were burning. Peeking through the door's crack, the resemblance of his position to that of Miss Miller's in the marquess's smoking room was obvious, and he smirked at the memory.

Miss Miller came down the corridor. She paused, her hand on the railing as she studied the portraits arranged at the head of the staircase, Charles's being the largest.

He left the sitting room, striding toward her and leaning against the opposite rail in an exaggerated pose. "I expect you'd much rather admire the original."

Miss Miller jumped. Seeing him, she scowled, then flushed. "What are you doing here?"

He grinned, pleased that he'd thrown her off. "As I told you yesterday, it's my house."

Miss Miller gave a small curtsy and started down the stairs.

Charles followed. "How was Alice's lesson?"

Miss Miller paused, waited for him to catch up, and descended much more slowly. The stairs were wide, and she stayed close to the rail, leaving plenty of space between them. "She is frustrated," she said. "Not surprisingly. What she's doing, altering something so fundamental, is very difficult. It's not the same as learning a different language. It's relearning one's own, which is much more challenging. She'll need to think each time she speaks, about each individual sound. It becomes exhausting. But she will do it. Alice is quick-witted and hardworking."

"Of course she is," he said. "She's a member of the Chatsworth family."

Miss Miller stopped at the bottom of the stairs. Her eyes flicked to him, holding a question, but she did not ask it.

Charles knew exactly what she assumed. But he didn't clarify. A part of him wished to protect his father, even knowing the type of man he'd been. Charles already knew of Miss Miller's disdain for him, but he was reluctant to see the same sentiment directed at anyone in his family. It was childish, of course. The truth would come out eventually. Most of high Society already suspected the former earl of such dalliances and much worse, and rightly so. But still, Charles guarded his father's name.

"If you'll excuse me, my lord," Miss Miller said. She started toward the kitchens and the servants' entrance.

Feeling vulnerable again, Charles searched for something to say that would restore his advantage. "Where are you off to in such a hurry? I suppose to make some more signs to protest the upcoming vote." He rested an elbow on the newel post. "I came up with some ideas you might wish to use in future placards: Lord *Bad*-bury, Lord *Tightfist*-ol—for Bristol, of course—and Lord *Penny-Pinch*-Hennesy or Hennesy-Pinch, if you prefer."

Miss Miller fixed him with one of her flat looks, which let him know he was sufficiently irritating her.

"That last one is rather bad, I admit." Charles raised a hand. "But it has potential. Also, might I offer a recommendation? When the camera is directed at you, smile. It provides the broadsheets with a much more pleasing photograph."

Miss Miller's eyes narrowed. She put her hands on her hips, sticking out her chin. "I don't need advice from a person who has never felt deeply about any cause in his entire life."

"Nonsense." Charles stood straight and smiled. "I feel deeply about a great many things."

"Such as matching your waistcoat to your shoe buckles, no doubt," Elizabeth said.

Charles gasped, pressing his hand to his breastbone. "Shoe buckles? In 1874? Surely you jest."

She huffed and stalked away as she said, "Good evening, my lord."

"Remember that *Bad*-bury one," he called. "I imagine it with white letters. It would look smashing with *bad* painted in a different color, such as red or black, for contrast. You still have the *Rock*-heart sign, I imagine. If you decide to continue with the theme of black lettering, they will complement one another—but don't give up the idea of white letters on a dark background . . ."

Miss Miller had stomped from the entryway long before Charles had finished. He smirked, but it felt forced. He didn't know why Miss Miller didn't respond to his banter with blushes and giggles like other young ladies did. Was that why he kept pushing her? Out of a desire to impress her? Or make her laugh? Or did the reason have more to do with her dislike of him and how it bothered him more than it ought to?

He was unable to shake the disconcerting feeling that he'd teased her more than he should have. But the alternative would have been to talk about something important or uncomfortable, and Charles didn't trust anyone with those topics—except for his grandmother, of course.

"Charles?" Alice's small voice came down the stairs. She stood at the top in a dinner dress, holding a large picture book.

He had promised they would read together before supper. "There you are," he said. "I'm glad you remembered." He climbed the stairs, thinking of what he'd overheard in the schoolroom and the insights it had given him about both Alice and Miss Miller. The speech lesson had left him with quite a bit to ponder.

CHAPTER 7

THE SPACE THAT SERVED AS an assembly room at the Spitalfields School for Girls was a large area that took up nearly half of the main floor. It had, at one time, served the workhouse as a men's dormitory. A fresh coat of paint on the walls and repairs to the wooden floor had worked wonders, transforming the room into a cheerful space large enough for all the students to gather together. The windows were still barred, but they were large, and they let in enough light that the lamps were necessary only in the late afternoon or occasionally on cloudy days. At the far end was a raised platform Elizabeth hoped would one day be used as a stage for dramatic presentations. Throughout the few months since the school had opened, the assembly room had hosted weekly special-guest presenters, from scientists to police inspectors. It had been used as a dance instruction hall, an art and science exhibition gallery, and even an auditorium for physical exercise when the weather was too cold for the girls to go outside. But today the chamber had been repurposed into a make-believe hospital.

Elizabeth and the other teachers stood around the edges of the room, watching the girls who were playing the parts of injury victims. They were laid out on mats, groaning and pretending to weep in pain as their partners wrapped strips of cloth around imagined injuries. Most of the girls had chosen the head as the source of their patient's wound, and many of the injured took on the appearance of Egyptian mummies by the time their nurses had tended to them.

Hazel Thornton, wearing her nurse's uniform, moved among the students, giving advice and complimenting the girls' wrapping efforts. Her fiancé, Dr. Jim Jackson, walked among them as well, making the occasional suggestion, his white coat giving him an air of authority.

Once each pair of girls had been reviewed, Hazel and Dr. Jackson returned to the front of the room. Dr. Jackson took Hazel's hand, assisting her as she stepped onto the stage, then joined her.

Hazel clapped to get the students' attention. "Excellent work, every-one." Her voice was soft, but it still managed to carry through the room. "Remember, it is very important that the soiled bandages are replaced regu-larly. And you must wash them in clean water and make certain they are entirely dry before reapplying them to the wound."

Dr. Jackson nodded. "If you are uncertain whether the washing water is sanitary, boil the dressings." His gaze moved around the room, as if he were making certain the students were all listening.

He needn't have worried. The girls were in awe of the American doctor and his stories of serving as a medic in various conflicts throughout North America and Europe. Hazel was every bit as interesting, having worked in the International Red Cross Hospital in Spain. For children who had never journeyed more than a few miles from where they were born, the idea of the dangers of war and the adventure of travel held them spellbound.

"Now, young ladies," Hazel said, joining her hands in front of her apron. "It is the other partner's turn to be the patient."

The girls moved around, changing places so the other lay on the mat. They waited quietly for Hazel to reveal the new patients' injuries.

"This time, instead of an abrasion," Hazel said, "I'm afraid you have been burned. You drew too close to the hearth, and your skirts caught fire."

A ripple of excited noise moved through the students as they discussed this latest affliction. Some held their legs, wincing in pain or crying out. Nelly Provost blew on her skirts, as if to extinguish a fire.

Dr. Jackson cleared his throat, and the room went immediately quiet. "Now then, what is the first thing you do?"

Dora Fisher raised her hand. "Stop the fire."

"Exactly," he said, giving the girl a pleased nod. "Nurses, your patients will be frightened. Don't let them run about, or the fire will spread. Drop them to the floor and smother the flames."

"Now, let us imagine the patient's ankle has been burned," Hazel said, speak-ing quickly before the girls began dropping one another to the floor. "Nurses, carefully remove any stockings or shoes. They retain heat and will make the burn worse."

The nurses took off their patients' boots and stockings as the patients writhed in imagined pain.

Elizabeth watched, smiling at the bare feet that were exposed and pam-pered with such care by nurse and patient. Hazel and Dr. Jackson gave fur-ther instructions about severity of burns and when to seek medical help. They talked about salves and dressings, and then the nurses got to work bandaging. Most of the new nurses left their own bandages where they were, choosing fresh strips to administer to their patients. By the time the medical presentation ended, nearly every girl had some part of herself bound with dressings.

Elizabeth came to the stage. She thanked the special guests, and the students and teachers gave an enthusiastic round of applause before being excused to return to their classes.

"Looks like there's been a battle," Dr. Jackson said, motioning with his chin to the girls who were limping through the door, some holding a shoe and others their bandaged body parts.

"Providing such important information while keeping a room of sixty young girls entertained takes a special skill," Elizabeth said. "Thank you." She squeezed Hazel's hand. "Both of you."

"We were delighted to come," Hazel said, squeezing back. "The girls are very sweet, and we enjoyed ourselves, didn't we, Dr. Jackson?"

"Absolutely," he agreed. "Few come willingly—or happily—to see a doctor. It was a pleasant change from tending to the sick."

"I can't imagine it's all bad," Elizabeth said. She stepped off the stage and started gathering the mats with Mrs. Boyle. "Surely there are good moments at the Royal London Hospital."

"There certainly are," Dr. Jackson nodded, picking up bandages and folding them. "Being able to alleviate a patient's suffering, seeing a person who came to you ill or injured leave healthy, is very gratifying." He glanced at Hazel. "And the hospital's proximity to the women's hospital is an advantage I cannot overstate."

Hazel's gaze met his, and she blushed. "The weather is so pleasant today," she said, looking down at the mats she was straightening. "Perhaps you could join us, Elizabeth, for a stroll in the park before supper?"

"I'm afraid I can't," Elizabeth said. "I have a tutoring appointment after the school day is ended." Even if she could have left school early, she thought the pair would prefer to stroll alone. "But I'll see you both at Sophie's supper this Saturday?" She opened a cupboard at the back of the room, and they stacked the mats inside.

Mrs. Boyle excused herself.

"Yes, we'll be there," Hazel said. "And we are coming to see John Maskelyne's performance as well."

Elizabeth and Dr. Jackson glanced at Hazel. Her discomfort among crowds could at time grow into a panic spell, and the Egyptian Hall was known for throngs that nearly burst from the door with each performance. The newspaper office regularly received tickets from such venues in hopes of a review in the broadsheets, and considering this Saturday evening would be John Maskelyne's debut, Sophronia had extended the invitation to her friends and their significant others to attend. But they had all assumed Hazel and Dr. Jackson would take their leave once dinner was finished and avoid the illusionist's act entirely.

"I will sit on the aisle," Hazel said defensively, "with quick access to the exits. And I intend to enjoy myself, thank you very much."

"Of course." Elizabeth grinned. "We will all be very happy to have you there."

"How could I miss a show where people actually levitate?" Hazel asked.

"I should like to learn how to make people vanish," Elizabeth said. "It could come in quite handy, I think."

Dr. Jackson shook his head. "I shall remember not to get on your bad side, Miss Miller."

"That is wise," Hazel said, taking his arm. She winked at Elizabeth and gave her fiancé a warm smile.

Once Hazel and Dr. Jackson had departed, Elizabeth walked back through the entry hall to the stairs. She was pleased with the lesson and even more pleased with the affection between the presenters. Dr. Jackson was an excellent match for Hazel. In spite of Elizabeth's initial skepticism when it came to the man—or any man—Dr. Jackson had shown himself to be just as he appeared, with no ulterior motivations. And Hazel was enormously happy in his company. When Hazel had brought him to assist with the presentation, Elizabeth had worried that he, as the more qualified medical person, would take over the whole thing entirely. But he had done the opposite, allowing Hazel to lead and offering only the occasional comment, which pleased Elizabeth even more.

The diverting part of her day finished, she climbed the stairs, dreading the work that awaited her. Mrs. Boyle was an excellent assistant, but there were duties that only the headmistress could perform. Writing letters of thanks to the school's patrons, keeping them abreast of the latest happenings, and securing funds for the coming year was time consuming, but it was her job alone.

When she entered her office, Elizabeth discovered the neat pile of correspondence on her desk was strewn across the floor, and in its place, the cat slept in a sunbeam.

"Gaffer! Just look at this mess."

The cat peeked through one eye, then returned to his nap, apparently unconcerned by the disapproval in her words.

Elizabeth sighed and picked up papers and quills. Luckily she'd tightened the lid on her inkpot, which had rolled beneath the table in the corner of the room. She found her ink blotter under the cat's cushioned chair. She set down the pile on the desk by the cat and pulled back her own chair, crawling underneath the desk to retrieve even more of the wayward correspondence. When she drew back, she rose too quickly, banging her head. "I've 'alf a mind to give thee a roit cork-aiver, Gaffer," she ground out, threatening the animal as she rubbed her head. "Y'am a bleedin' nuisance."

The clearing of a throat stopped her just as she sat. She looked up, and heat rushed to her face when she saw Lord Chatsworth, arms crossed, leaning against the doorframe.

With effort, Elizabeth took on a calm expression, blinking slowly and resisting the impulse to smooth her hair. She could feel that she'd knocked loose some of her hairpins and the entire arrangement was unstable. "What are you doing here?"

"Is that how you intend to greet me always?" His mouth pulled into a mocking smirk as he came into the room. He put his hat on the hat rack, lifted a chair from the table and set it in front of her desk to sit in it. "I must say it is rather rude. If you keep it up, I am going to start believing you don't enjoy my company."

Gaffer glanced at the newest interruption to his afternoon nap and rolled over.

Elizabeth lifted the cat from her desk, setting him on his cushioned chair, and reminded herself that Lord Chatsworth was a patron of the school and, against her better instincts, admitted he should be treated with respect. "I beg your pardon," she said, sitting back in her seat and arranging the contents of her desk into a more organized display. "You came upon me in an inopportune moment." Was he always to catch her at a disadvantage?

"Yes, so it seems." He glanced at her hair.

Elizabeth held her head still, not daring to move it and have her coiffure topple. She could only imagine how she must look, crawling around on the floor, her hair and office disheveled as she admonished a cat.

She inhaled, straightened her shoulders, and gave a polite smile. "To what do I owe the pleasure of your *unannounced* visit, Lord Chatsworth?"

The corner of his mouth twitched. Why did she always get the impression that he was laughing at her? "I wanted to see the Spitalfields School for Girls for myself."

"Oh. You've come for a tour?"

"I did invest a large amount of money into the place," he said, resting an ankle on his knee. "I thought a firsthand view of the school and its workings were in order."

"Of course." She rose, and he stood as well. She motioned to the room around them. "As you can see, this is my—"

"Oh, Miss Miller, can you believe it!" Mrs. Boyle rushed in, carrying her usual armload of papers and files. "Another note from the Chancellor of Exchequer, demanding even more—" She held out a folded paper and looked up, freezing when she saw Lord Chatsworth. "Oh, I beg your pardon. I didn't realize you . . ." She looked at the mess on the desk and at Elizabeth's hair, then back at the earl standing in front of her.

"Lord Chatsworth, this is Mrs. Boyle, my assistant." Elizabeth leaned across the desk, snatching the letter, and holding it behind her skirts. Her thoughts were spinning. Another taxation notice? How could the school possibly owe more taxes?

"How do you do, Mrs. Boyle?" Lord Chatsworth said, giving his famous smile, complete with dimples.

"Such a pleasure, my lord." Mrs. Boyle curtsied, and her cheeks went red.

Elizabeth sighed. "His Lordship has come for a tour of the school." She glanced down, trying to read the letter without moving her head or allowing Lord Chatsworth to see what she was doing.

"How wonderful!" Mrs. Boyle said. Her cheeks were still flushed and her eyes bright as she looked at their visitor with adoring eyes.

"Perhaps you would show him the library?" Elizabeth motioned toward the doorway with a small lift of her chin.

"Yes, of course." Mrs. Boyle set down her pile of papers and moved with her typical quick steps to the doorway. "Right this way, Your Lordship."

"Do you plan to come as well, Miss Miller?" Lord Chatsworth asked.

"Yes, I will join you in a moment."

His gaze dropped to the letter in her hand, and she pushed it behind her.

Lord Chatsworth looked back up at her face, gave a polite nod, and followed Mrs. Boyle from the room.

Elizabeth dropped into her chair, looking over the invoice. The exchequer was requisitioning another two hundred pounds. But the school had paid so much in taxes already. Where would she find another two hundred pounds? She put her head in her hands, feeling the knot in her hair give up and fall out. Hairpins clattered to her desk.

Elizabeth rubbed her eyes. It must be a mistake, she decided at last. What other explanation could there be? She would send Mrs. Boyle to the exchequer's offices first thing in the morning with the taxation receipts to straighten it all out.

She pulled her hair back up, smoothing it and pinning it into place as well as she could without a mirror, and straightened the papers on her desk, setting the taxation notice back on her assistant's pile before walking down the corridor to the library.

Mrs. Boyle was showing Lord Chatsworth the school's newest acquisitions: copies of Louisa May Alcott's *Little Women* and *Hans Brinker* by Mary Mapes Dodge. "Both are American authors," she told him, "but Mr. Grismore at the British Library recommended them all the same."

Lord Chatsworth studied the books politely before returning them to their shelf. "The pupils enjoy literature, I take it?" He nodded to Elizabeth when she joined them.

"Very much," Mrs. Boyle answered. "For these children, the chance to ice skate on a canal in Holland or celebrate Christmas in a Massachusetts town can be done only through stories. Books give them experiences they can only dream of."

"The same is true for any of us, I'd say," Lord Chatsworth commented. "Although, I do get your meaning. Some of us have a better prospect of seeing the world than others."

"Education provides our pupils with that prospect," Elizabeth said. "Or at least increases their chance of it."

"I am in agreement with you in that, Miss Miller," Lord Chatsworth said. "One's circumstances are often limited by birth. Education opens doors that would otherwise be closed."

Elizabeth studied him, realizing that, in this one topic, they were in complete agreement.

He studied her in return, and a wisp of warmth uncurled inside her. She held his gaze, concentrating on not allowing even the slightest hint of color to touch her cheeks.

"The remainder of the upper floor is just storage, a cloakroom, and an infirmary." Mrs. Boyle's voice broke a silence that was starting to feel heavy. "I imagine you'd like to see our chemistry laboratory as well as the classrooms, my lord."

"I certainly would, Mrs. Boyle," he said. "Lead on."

She did, and Elizabeth and Lord Chatsworth hurried their steps to keep up. When they reached the ground floor, Mrs. Boyle opened the door to the assembly room, allowing him to admire the gathering area, and then led them into the laboratory. Since there was no class being held in the room, Lord Chatsworth took the opportunity to examine the equipment.

"The quality is far superior to what we worked with in Eton," he said, leaning down to look through a series of glass globes. His eyes were magnified by the effect.

"The laboratory is outfitted with the most current technology," Mrs. Boyle boasted.

"At Lord Benedict's insistence," Elizabeth clarified. She didn't want Lord Chatsworth to think she had been extravagant with donated funds. "This equipment was all provided by His Lordship and Lady Covington."

"I should have known." Lord Chatsworth nodded. "Lady Covington is a research assistant for Professor Clifford Wallis at Oxford, I believe."

"Yes." Elizabeth smiled, pleased that he knew of Vivian's achievements in scientific circles. She would have thought the doings of the Blue Orchid Society members were beneath the notice of Lord Chatsworth, but now that she considered it, Vivian was married to Lord Benedict. Perhaps Lord Chatsworth had heard it from his friend.

"Professor Wallis and Lady Covington presented a scientific demonstration for the students," Mrs. Boyle said proudly. "The school regularly welcomes special guests who are experts in their particular field."

"Indeed?"

Elizabeth couldn't tell whether Lord Chatsworth was speaking seriously or if he was mocking, which she considered more likely.

"You may notice, as we pass the classrooms," Mrs. Boyle continued, "that many pupils are wearing bandages on their extremities. Today they attended a medical demonstration. A doctor and nurse instructed the girls in emergency care and allowed them to practice their techniques on one another."

"They must have enjoyed that," Lord Chatsworth said, glancing through the laboratory entrance.

Taking his brief look as an invitation to continue the tour, Mrs. Boyle motioned for them to follow as she walked through the doorway.

Lord Chatsworth set down the beaker he held, and he and Elizabeth followed.

They walked past the schoolrooms, and Mrs. Boyle spoke in a softer voice, telling him the ages of the students in each particular class.

"Alice would have loved the medical discussion," Lord Chatsworth said, slowing to walk by Elizabeth and making his words heard only by her. They looked into a classroom. "It sounds very diverting, as well as educational."

"I believe children should enjoy their learning," Elizabeth said. She nodded to Mr. Wilkie as they passed his class. "If a lesson can be made amusing, children are more likely to pay attention and remember."

Lord Chatsworth nodded to the teacher as well. He rubbed his mustache with the side of his finger, looking as if he were considering her words, or perhaps he was coming up with an argument.

"I shall tell you the next time the school hosts a guest presenter," Elizabeth said. "You are very welcome to bring Alice." They had reached the front doors of the school. "Shall I send Mrs. Boyle for your hat?"

"Thank you." He looked more clearly at her, as if he'd made up his mind about what to say. "There is one other thing I came for. If I may speak with you alone for a moment?"

"Oh, yes," Elizabeth said. "Of course."

"Thank you for a delightful tour." Lord Chatsworth flashed his smile at Mrs. Boyle.

"You are very welcome, sir." She patted her hair and blushed, looking flustered from the attention.

Elizabeth thought His Lordship must enjoy very much the power he had over women, which firmed her resolve never to allow his attentions to go to her head. Their relationship was strictly related to business.

She led him back up the stairs to her office, noticing with relief that Gaffer hadn't redistributed the items from her desk. She gestured to the chair Lord Chatsworth had sat in before and returned to her own seat.

He closed the office door before sitting, and a pang of panic shot through Elizabeth's insides at the thought of being truly alone with him. She clasped her hands on her desk and kept her expression even, although every muscle was tight, braced.

"Alice is unhappy," he said.

"Did she tell you that?" Elizabeth asked. She relaxed slightly, in spite of her determination not to let her guard down.

"Not in so many words," Lord Chatsworth said. "I am rather an expert on knowing whether a member of the female sex is content." A touch of arrogance returned to his voice. "And this one is most certainly not."

"I do not know Alice's history, but I believe she has only recently come to stay with you, correct?"

He nodded.

"Perhaps she misses her . . . mother?" Elizabeth guessed.

"Her mother is dead," Lord Chatsworth said.

"That could account for some melancholy," Elizabeth said. She couldn't decipher his expression. Was he saddened by the girl's mother's death? Did he even know her?

Lord Chatsworth tapped his finger on the arm of his chair. "I plan to take Alice to Sussex. My family's estate is there. There is a forest she can explore, and lovely gardens, and springtime there is completely splendid."

"That is an excellent idea," Elizabeth said, pleased with his solution. Country air and exercise were very likely exactly what Alice needed. "But you did not need to come personally to tell me of a change to Alice's tutoring schedule. A message would do just as well."

His finger tapping stopped, and he clasped his hands together between his knees. "I would like you to come with us."

"I?" She stared at him, trying to make sense of what he'd said. "Travel to Sussex?"

"Alice would enjoy having you there. She likes you very much."

She stared at him. Was this a trick?

"Naturally, I don't expect you to look after the girl the entire time. Her nanny will accompany us, and the housekeeper, Mrs. Foster, will be delighted to have a child to tend to."

"But I can't simply leave," Elizabeth said. "I have a school to run."

"They can manage without you for a week, I'm sure."

Was he being serious? The man had donated a large amount of money to her cause, and part of her reasoned that she shouldn't be denying him anything he asked, but her insides rebelled at the idea. She would not be bought by Lord Chatsworth. "A week? Impossible. There is far too much to do. I have letters to write, and there are records and attendance and—"

"There is a very lovely desk in the morning room at Ashbury Park," he said, cutting off her argument. "Perfect for a lady's correspondence. And, as for the rest, you seem to have a very capable assistant in Mrs. Boyle."

"She is capable," Elizabeth admitted. "But she is not the head of the school. There are decisions, ledgers—things that only I can do. And what if a problem should arise? I must be here."

Lord Chatsworth was silent for a moment. "Please?" he said at last.

Something in his voice stopped her arguments. His teasing, flippant tone was entirely gone, and he spoke earnestly, simply. The sound made her insides behave inexplicably, her heart delaying its next beat, then making up for it by hammering in rapid succession and making her head light. Elizabeth looked away from his gaze, embarrassed and frustrated that she was behaving like every girl Lord Chatsworth came across. He knew he could get whatever he wanted and would use his appeal to do just that. It was an attribute she despised, and Elizabeth prided herself on remaining impervious to his charms. She wasn't simply going to go to Sussex with a man she barely knew just because he asked her nicely.

She calmed her thoughts, considering what he was asking and his reasons. She didn't believe Alice knew many people outside of Stourbridge. She had tutors, of course, and her nanny, but from what the girl had said, it didn't seem as if Charles's sister Kathryn was particularly kind to her. And if Lord Chatsworth was keeping Alice's presence in his house a secret, the girl likely had no friends. Elizabeth thought of the students in the classrooms beneath them. Their giggles as they'd bandaged one another and the happy chatter when class was dismissed and they all started for home. The students at the Spitalfields School for Girls were children from the poorest families in the city, but at this moment, it was a young girl in a grand mansion Elizabeth felt the most sorry for. While Lord Chatsworth provided the girl with every comfort she could wish for, Alice was lonely.

"I will go."

Lord Chatsworth's smile unfolded like a flower coming into bloom, starting at one side of his mouth and expanding until his teeth shone and his eyes sparkled. She'd seen the smile before, across a ballroom when he'd been flirting with one lady or another—for heaven's sake, images of it were in the gossip columns—but the full effect had never been directed at her.

She could have sworn she forgot the art of speech entirely. She stumbled to make a noise, opening and closing her mouth and trying to restart her mind.

Her efforts only made Lord Chatsworth's smile brighter, his dimples deeper, and one corner of his mouth turned up in the teasing expression she recognized all too well. "I knew I could persuade you."

The words brought her back to reality, and anger filled the empty space where her mind had deserted her. Her face was hot, and her pulse beat at her temples. She stood quickly, nearly knocking over her chair as she did.

Lord Chatsworth jumped up and snatched his hat from the rack. "We leave Sunday on the nine o'clock train from Victoria Station."

Elizabeth opened her mouth to protest. Or at least to offer enough of an argument so he didn't think his low voice, blue eyes, or appealing smile were responsible for her decision, but Lord Chatsworth was already at her office door. He gave a bow and was gone before she could even find the words to remind him that she had agreed to go to Sussex for Alice's sake alone.

She sat back in her chair, glancing at the cat in the corner as she did.

Gaffer watched her with an expression that appeared far too perceptive for that of an animal.

"I didn't even notice his dimples," Elizabeth said to the cat. "It is entirely a business arrangement." She wasn't like all the silly young—and old—ladies who fell victim to Lord Chatsworth's charms.

Men seldom had unselfish intentions when it came to women, and she had learned never to trust a man who offered something merely out of generosity. Seemingly innocent gestures hid deceit, and she would not be trapped like her mother.

CHAPTER 8

ONCE CHARLES RECEIVED WORD THAT Lord Ruben's carriage had arrived, he put on his coat and hat, bid good evening to Nigel, and stepped out into the spring evening. Meredith had managed to procure tickets to John Maskelyne's premier performance at the Egyptian Hall, and he, Ruben, and Charles had decided to dine at their gentlemen's club before proceeding to Piccadilly for the illusionist's show.

"Good evening, gentlemen." Charles stepped into the carriage, taking a seat beside Meredith.

Seated across from them, Ruben nodded a greeting, then tapped on the roof, instructing the driver to go on.

"Good evening, Chatsworth." Meredith smiled at his friend.

Charles settled back into his seat, holding his top hat on his knee. "Fine evening for a conjuring show, wouldn't you say?"

"It is indeed," Meredith agreed. "I spent the afternoon with my tailor, fitting my costume for the masquerade."

Charles had nearly forgotten that he'd promised his friends to host the party. He made a mental note to send for his own tailor in the morning.

Ruben glanced through the window and then looked again. He squinted, as if trying to get a better view, and then, after a moment, turned to face the others, a smug-looking glint in his eye. "Why, Chatsworth, you devil."

"I beg your pardon?" Charles asked.

Ruben pointed toward the window with his chin. "Unless my eyes deceive me, that is the Lancasters' relative, Miss Elizabeth Miller, leaving Ivy House through the servants' entrance." His brows raised in a manner that suggested something untoward had taken place.

"Miss Elizabeth Miller, you say?" Charles glanced through the window himself, his unconcerned expression concealing his clenched innards. "How nice. I imagine she has been to visit my grandmother."

"She may be soliciting donations for her charity school," Meredith suggested.

"Yes, perhaps." Charles glanced at his friend. "I really have no idea."

Ruben smirked. "You wish me to believe your grandmother takes evening callers and then sends her visitors off through the back alleyway?"

Charles shrugged, doing his best to look as if he neither knew nor cared about his grandmother's business dealings. He considered what he might say to change the subject without looking as if he were changing the subject. He didn't like Ruben's insinuations, but explaining what Miss Miller had been doing at his house wasn't something he was prepared to divulge yet, especially to Ruben. Charles meant to introduce Alice to Society on his own terms.

"It's perfectly natural, you know—expected, really," Ruben said.

"What is?" Charles asked. He didn't like the way Ruben was regarding him. His friend looked both interested and self-satisfied, like he'd discovered he no longer had to follow the rules since his friends weren't.

"A little dalliance. Everyone keeps a mistress or two—usually once an heir is legitimately produced, of course. As long as one uses a bit of discretion, I see no harm in it." He winked, and Charles's stomach soured. Without meaning to, he thought of his father, and his thoughts moved right away to his mother and the pain that resulted from what Ruben deemed "a little dalliance." Charles considered the life that lay ahead for Ruben's fiancée and firmed his own resolve never to allow love to enter his future marriage.

Meredith cleared his throat, shifting in his seat. "Who's your favorite for the race on Saturday, Chatsworth?"

Charles appreciated his friend coming to his rescue. "Kaiser is a fine racer. I imagine he could win the Gold Cup at Ascot."

"Do you really?" Meredith asked, his eyes brightening as he warmed to the subject. The man had an excellent eye for horseflesh. "And what of King Lud? He seems a promising competitor."

Charles nodded, rubbing his mustache. "Beautiful animal. But . . ."

He trailed off when Ruben leaned forward so he could look back through the window, nearly putting him in Charles's lap. "Unusual choice," he muttered. "But she's pretty enough. And spirited."

"King Lud?" Charles asked. "Spirited indeed. And I suppose he's . . . pretty." It was a strange word to describe a racing stallion.

"I'm talking about your young lady." Ruben turned to face him once again, settling against the back of the bench with a knowing grin. "Hardly surprising, with her parentage."

"And what does that mean?" Charles snapped. The surge of anger surprised him. His ears heated at Ruben's widening grin. He hadn't kept his emotions in check, and he knew he sounded defensive.

"Surely you know about Mariah Miller," Ruben said. He chuckled in a way that sounded like gloating. "Meredith, you tell him the story. You were there."

Meredith shifted again. He was always uncomfortable with gossip. "I do not know what is rumor and what is true," he said. "I was very young."

Ruben rolled his hand, gesturing for him to continue.

Meredith sighed. "All I know for certain is the woman was employed as a laundress at Foxborough Hall. She was dismissed after an incident involving a complaint from the late Lord Hubbard."

"A complaint of *unseemly behavior*," Ruben said, waggling his brows.

"I don't know for certain," Meredith said.

"What else would it be?" Ruben scoffed. "A complaint of inadequately pressed sheets wouldn't result in a dismissal."

"As I said, I don't know." Meredith looked miserable at having to recount the tale. "And it would be cruel to spread gossip about the woman."

Charles remembered meeting Miss Miller in the forest near Meredith's family estate. Had she been visiting her mother at the manor house? He knew of the former Lord Hubbard. The man was outspoken and rude, with a perpetual frown that gave him the appearance of an old toad. Charles could not imagine any woman trying to get into that man's good graces, unless she hoped for some sort of arrangement. He didn't know anything about Miss Miller's mother, but the idea that she might have grasped at a fortune and been willing to do so in such a manner didn't sit well with him. He wasn't certain whether he was more uncomfortable with the rumor or the idea that the rumor might be the truth.

He wondered who else knew of this scandal, and a feeling of protectiveness grew, much like it had when he'd first met Alice. Miss Miller was no more to blame for the actions of her parent than Alice was. And he didn't like that his friend was calling the young lady's character into question. It bothered him more than it should have, making him irritable.

Fortunately, during supper, Ruben had nothing further to say about Miss Miller. Instead of talking, he seemed happy to toss back as many drinks as he could manage. The Egyptian Hall had a policy of temperance, so Ruben must have been attempting to get himself properly into his cups before they arrived. Charles and Meredith discussed the upcoming horse race as they ate, and then the group continued on to Piccadilly.

The Egyptian Hall was filled to the brim, with more attendees than seats. From his position on the upper balcony, Charles watched as men and women crowded around the edges of the room, with more continuing to pack in.

"Look there." Ruben nudged Charles. He spoke loudly, his words slurring. "Your *grandmother's visitor* has arrived." He pointed over the rail down to the lower level, his words dripping with sarcasm.

Beneath them, Miss Elizabeth Miller was making her way through the crowd. She wore a gown of dark violet and walked with a group Charles recognized as her friends. Lord Benedict was there, too, as well as a few other men Charles didn't know.

Meredith, sitting on Ruben's other side, pulled the inebriated man back before he fell into the audience below.

Ruben laughed loudly. "Did you hear what I said? Your grandmother's visitor."

Charles gave a grunt of acknowledgment but not agreement.

"You are not going to respond?" Ruben said in a voice too loud for the small space between them. "Do you intend to simply watch?"

"It is the theater, Ruben," Meredith said. He caught Charles's eye and grimaced. "Let us enjoy the show."

"We *are* the show," Ruben said, tapping himself on the chest, then tapping both Meredith and Charles in turn. "All these people"—he motioned to the hall around him—"come to gawk at one another rather than what is happening on the stage. I like to give them something to gawk at." He puffed up his chest, glancing around at the various attendees.

Below them, Miss Miller's group started along a row near the front and spread out as they moved to their seats, revealing that one of her companions was Dahlia Lancaster.

Charles glanced at his friend and saw that Ruben went still, staring at the woman he'd once been so devoted to.

Miss Lancaster, as usual, looked stunning, her hair arranged with a spray of feathers that contrasted with her dark curls. But Charles found his gaze returning to Miss Miller. She was not as fashionable as her cousin, her dress and hairstyle leaning more toward practicality than glamour. It was the way she held herself that drew his eye. A manner he'd once found to be overconfidence or perhaps even conceit now looked different. He saw in her face the same defensiveness he'd seen in Alice, as if she were constantly bracing herself for what others might say. After hearing the story about Miss Miller's mother— whether it was true or not—Charles had a better understanding of her reasons for her self-protective air.

He glanced beyond Ruben and saw that Meredith's gaze was fixed on the women below as well, his expression thoughtful. For an instant, Charles's defenses prickled, imagining his friend to be thinking about what he knew of Miss Miller's mother. But Charles didn't truly believe that to be the case. Meredith put no stock in rumors, preferring to see the best version of everyone. Perhaps he was remembering the men's earlier friendship with Miss Miller's cousin instead. He remembered Meredith and Dahlia Lancaster had had a very amiable relationship when she was connected with Ruben. He must miss her.

Not wishing to stir up further conversation or emotion about the women, Charles looked around the hall, watching as spectators continued to fill the empty spaces at the edges of the room. Two of Miss Miller's party, a dark-haired man and a fair young lady sitting on the aisle, departed, and their seats were promptly taken by another couple. Miss Miller and Miss Lancaster looked disappointed at their friend's withdrawal.

Charles realized he was watching Miss Miller again and made a deliberate choice to look in the other direction.

The theater dimmed and a spotlight shone on the stage. The audience hushed as music sounded, growing to a crescendo as a man with a bald head and wisps of white hair above his ears walked to the center of the stage.

"Ladies and Gentlemen!" His voice reverberated through the hall. "Welcome to England's House of Mystery." He lifted his hands above his head as the audience applauded. "I am William Morton, manager of the Egyptian Hall."

There was another polite spattering of applause.

William Morton kept his hands raised, using them to accentuate his words. "Tonight you will take a journey, leaving behind your conceptions of what is real and what is impossible." He drew out each word, holding the audience in rapt attention. "Illusion. Conjuring. Magic, if you will. Fantastical feats that defy belief. A journey beyond your imagination. Together we will explore the boundaries of reality." He paused, letting the words hang in the air.

The audience applauded again.

William Morton smiled, folding his hands in front of him. "Before Mr. Maskelyne takes the stage for his premier London performance, I should like to welcome a special guest. Ladies and Gentlemen, our newly elected prime minister, the Right Honorable Benjamin Disraeli. Your Lordship, you are very welcome." The theater manager gave a bow, and the prime minister waved in acknowledgment.

"We have other guests," William Morton continued. "Representatives of newspapers, journalists who will no doubt fill their front pages with praises of tonight's extravaganza!" He looked down at the rows directly in front of him, clapping as he grinned. "Welcome, one and all."

The front rows, including Miss Miller, Miss Lancaster, and their friends, applauded.

Raising his gaze to the upper levels, the theater manager scanned the faces in the audience. He held up a hand toward one side of the balcony. "I see Lord Marlborough and his new bride looking very happy together." The crowd craned their necks to see the couple. "Welcome, my lord, my lady."

The pair waved.

William Morton's gaze continued to travel over the crowd, and a mischievous smirk curled his lips. "And I see some couples who are not as happily together." He put a hand over his mouth, eyes widening playfully. "Lord Ruben is here." He held up a hand toward him. "And all the way down here, we have Miss Dahlia Lancaster." He held his other hand toward the young lady, shaking his head sadly. The audience laughed, turning to look between the two.

Ruben scowled at the stage.

Even from his seat high in the balcony, Charles could see Miss Lancaster's cheeks and neck redden. He felt a rush of pity for the woman.

A voice echoed through the theater, causing every head to turn toward Miss Miller. "That is uncalled for, sir!" She sat straight in her seat, a hand on her cousin's arm.

The theater manager's grin grew, and he pointed at her. "And I see here beside Miss Lancaster is another familiar face." His other hand pointed up toward the balcony on the far side. "This outspoken young lady is certainly not an admirer of yours, Lord *Rock*Heart."

Charles saw Lord Lockhart's eyes bulge and his face go red. Beside him Lord Tynsdale blustered, but his words couldn't be heard over the audience's laughter.

"Let us hope neither of these pairs encounter one another at intermission," William Morton said. "And if it does happen, I recommend to you reporters to have your cameras at the ready!"

Charles felt ill. He could feel the embarrassment of those the theater manager had drawn attention to. The entire scene was familiar. He had recognized William Morton's showmanship from the moment the man stepped onto the stage. Charles had mastered the same art, holding a crowd's attention, knowing when to speak and when to let a silence stretch, and at times, entertaining at the expense of heartache. Throughout the years, he'd said any number of things to get a laugh, but as time passed, he'd been chagrined to realize there were real people behind the jabs. And the teasing was simply a pathetic attempt to keep others at bay.

A moment later John Nevil Maskelyne took the stage, appearing in a cloud of smoke, and the magic show commenced.

Though the illusionist performed unimaginable feats, making a woman disappear from inside a locked cupboard and even levitating his assistant off the stage floor, Charles could feel the discomfort and embarrassment in his friend, and he could see by the set of Miss Lancaster's and Miss Miller's shoulders that they were discomposed as well. It was a relief when the show ended and they could at last leave.

He, Meredith, and Ruben exited beneath the Egyptian carvings over the main entrance and joined the crowd making its way along the street. Ruben was silent as they walked toward the waiting carriage, and Meredith's words sounded forced, as if he were making small talk simply to dispel the unease. But in truth, the theater manager's taunting words had cast a pall over the entire evening.

Ahead, Charles could hear raised voices. It sounded like a disagreement of some type was escalating into a shouting match. And as they drew near enough to see the source of the noise, Charles's stomach sank. The crowd had cleared a space around two people: Lord Tynsdale and Miss Miller.

"You pushed too far this time," Lord Tynsdale said in a loud voice that was just shy of a bellow.

Lord Lockhart stood behind him, his face a brilliant red. He was either too angry or too embarrassed to speak—likely both.

Lord Tynsdale continued his tirade. "To go so far as to publicly humiliate—"

"You are blaming me for the theater manager's words?" Miss Miller shouted back. Her eyes flashed, furious. "That is preposterous." A photographer stepped around the edge of the clearing, arranging a tripod and lining up his camera for a clear shot.

Charles's muscles tensed, and he considered his options. If he barged into the middle of the dispute, it would only garner more attention, and with Ruben's propensity for gossip, it would bring his accusations of a relationship with the young lady into the public realm. The society pages would have it in their edition first thing in the morning. Besides, he didn't think Miss Miller would appreciate him interceding, even if it was on her behalf. But remaining silent while the young woman was publicly insulted went against his principles as a gentleman. He stepped forward and then hesitated, wondering which of the arguing parties would be more angry with him for his interference. He took another step, catching himself as he realized he was stepping toward Miss Miller.

Ruben pulled him back. "What do you think you are doing?" he hissed.

Charles pulled his arm away from Ruben and moved to block the camera's shot instead.

"Of course you are responsible," Lord Tynsdale roared. "The prime minister was in attendance, and with the vote approaching . . . you are a sly one. A minx!"

The gathered crowd turned toward Miss Miller, waiting for her response.

"I had no—" Miss Miller began, but her sentence was cut off when Miss Lancaster stepped between them. The young lady looked exhausted, but she carried herself with a graceful presence and an authority that none questioned—except for her cousin, who continued her protestations against Lord Tynsdale's accusation.

"Excuse us, Lord Lockhart, Lord Tynsdale." Miss Lancaster spoke in a soft, cordial voice. She took her cousin's arm, motioning to the photographer to lower his camera. "We are leaving now, gentlemen."

"We are absolutely not leaving," Miss Miller said. "Did you hear what he . . . ?"

Without further argument, the men, including the photographer, tipped their hats, giving no objection as Miss Lancaster led away her sputtering cousin.

"Temperance policy indeed," Ruben muttered. He turned away from the scene and climbed into his carriage, sitting heavily and tossing his hat onto the seat beside him. "I've never been in more need of a drink in my life."

Charles climbed in behind Meredith.

"And what was that?" Ruben motioned toward where Lord Tynsdale and Lord Lockhart still stood. "Were you planning to step into the fray?" He knocked on the ceiling, and the carriage started off.

"I believe Chatsworth was simply doing what any gentleman—" Meredith began.

"Gentleman." Ruben snorted. He retrieved a bottle from beneath his seat, uncorked it, and took a long drag. "Chatsworth's no gentleman."

Charles had had enough. He banged on the carriage roof until it halted. "If you don't want my company, then I will bid you good night." He pushed open the door and stepped out.

"Chatsworth." Meredith looked between him and Ruben, then seemed to make up his mind. "I'm coming with you."

CHAPTER 9

Two days after the Egyptian Hall performance, Elizabeth arrived at Victoria Station at fifteen minutes before nine o'clock. Clem unhitched her traveling trunk from the rear of the cab, and just as Elizabeth turned to look for a porter, one approached with a trolley.

"Miss Elizabeth Miller?" he said as he drew up beside her.

"Yes?" Looking closer, she saw the man's uniform was different from that of the other porters. He must be in Lord Chatsworth's employ.

"Very good. If you will follow me." He lifted the trunk onto the trolley.

"'Av an enjoyable 'oliday, miss," Clem said.

"Thank you." The uncertain feeling she'd been fighting ever since Lord Chatsworth's invitation prickled at her skin. A holiday? Surely not. She was a tutor accompanying her student. But her unease didn't abate. Setting the coins for Clem's payment in his palm, she said, "And an extra penny for a meat pie."

"I thank you, miss, as does me belly." Clem patted his middle. "But don' tell th' wife, eh?" He winked and pulled at his forelock before climbing back into his cab.

Elizabeth followed the porter into the station. Lord Chatsworth had obviously sent him to meet her, but how had he described Elizabeth to ensure the man recognized her so quickly? Her cheeks went hot, and she wondered again why she'd agreed to spending a week with a person who made her feel so decidedly unsettled.

"Miss Miller!" Alice's voice carried over the noise of other voices and steam engines.

By the time Elizabeth had located the girl among the crowd, Alice had nearly reached her. The girl rushed up, grabbing on to Elizabeth's hand with both of hers. "Thee came. Oy'm so chuffed."

Mrs. Snowden, Alice's nanny, followed along after her charge. The pair were dressed in traveling clothes, including wool coats with wide-brimmed hats to protect their clothing from the coal smoke.

Lord Chatsworth came up behind them. When his gaze met Elizabeth's, he raised a brow and gave a slow, knowing smile that held a hint of a tease. He glanced at Alice. "I told you she'd come."

Elizabeth wanted to give him one of her best scowls, but for Alice's sake, she did no such thing. Best to just ignore him, as he again seemed determined to aggravate her. "Good morning, Alice," she said, ignoring him.

"Shall we?" Lord Chatsworth motioned for the others to precede him.

"It ay nearly time to goo." Alice tugged on her arm, pulling Elizabeth down the platform to a large carriage at the rear of the train that bore the Chatsworth family crest on the side.

The porter assisted Alice and the women as they stepped up into the carriage, where another woman was preparing tea. Lord Chatsworth's railway carriage was furnished with upholstered benches and tables for card play or meals. Fresh flowers were arranged in vases. There were even framed paintings on the walls—in case a person grew tired of looking out the large windows, Elizabeth supposed. Ruffled pillows and folded blankets were placed throughout, an invitation to make oneself comfortable. At one end was a red velvet curtain that gave privacy to what Elizabeth thought must be a sleeping berth and an open door that led to what she could see was a small kitchen.

She'd had no idea people traveled in such luxury. Her few train journeys had consisted of cramped seating and the odor of bodies packed together in a small, hot space. This was something entirely new, and she didn't know whether to resent His Lordship and the entire upper classes or to feel relieved that she wouldn't be squeezed between strangers on a hard bench.

Alice took a seat near a window, and Elizabeth sat across from her. Mrs. Snowden sat next to the girl, and Lord Chatsworth settled into a deep armchair nearby. Within a few moments, the whistle blew, and the locomotive started from the station with a jolt and a cloud of black smoke.

"Weem gowin' to have a bostin time in Sussex, won't we, Miss Miller?"

Elizabeth nodded. "I believe it will be quite an adventure. Have you chosen your pirate name?"

Alice stood, putting her fists on her hips. "Oy'm the dreadful scallywag Captain Sharkfin."

Lord Chatsworth laughed at her pose. "Brilliant—and, I must say, terrifying."

Elizabeth clapped her hands. "That is an excellent name indeed."

Alice had brought one of Sir Cornelius Poppleford's many publications for the journey. This volume, *An Illustrated Handbook of Deadly Predators*, was filled with drawings and, in some cases, photographs. Alice pored over each entry, recounting the most interesting parts for her fellow travelers as the train took them away from London into the green countryside. She recounted facts about Bengalese tigers, Canadian grizzly bears, and Amazonian piranhas as their party rested on the comfortable seats and took tea.

Elizabeth closed her eyes, listening to the steady sound of the rails. A thump sounded, and she opened her eyes to see that Alice had fallen asleep with her cheek against the window and Sir Cornelius Poppleford's *Illustrated Handbook of Deadly Predators* had fallen to the floor.

Elizabeth eased Alice down into a more comfortable position on the bench, putting a pillow beneath her head. As she turned, she glanced toward Lord Chatsworth and saw that he was watching her.

She turned away quickly, not liking the way her chest hitched when their eyes met, and returned to her seat.

The train drew in to the West Sussex station, and the travelers gathered their things as they exited. The porters moved about, making certain hats, gloves, and other personal items weren't left behind.

The porter who had taken Elizabeth's luggage walked with the group along the platform to the exit, pushing a trolley with a stack of trunks and bags. Even through the smoky air, Elizabeth caught a whiff of the sea and looked toward the horizon, but the buildings of the town blocked any chance of viewing the ocean.

Two carriages awaited: a wagon meant for the luggage and a grand landau bearing the gold crest of the Chatsworth family. As the group approached, they were greeted by the driver. "Welcome home, Your Lordship." He removed his top hat, revealing a head full of straw-colored hair, holding his hat in front of his chest as he bowed.

"Thank you, Davies. It's been far too long." Lord Chatsworth clapped the man's shoulder. "How is your family? Your Tommy will be three now, I believe?"

Davies beamed, and his formal facade cracked. "Yes, my lord. Three last January. 'E's a delight, that lad. Bright as a button, if I do say so m'self."

"I hope for the chance to see him while I'm at Ashbury Park," Lord Chatsworth said. "And Mrs. Davies, of course."

"We would be honored, my lord."

Elizabeth watched the interaction, surprised. Was it typical for an earl to show such courtesy to those he employed?

Lord Chatsworth stepped to the side. "Davies, may I present Miss Alice?"

"Welcome to Sussex, Miss Alice." The driver smiled at the girl.

Alice smiled shyly. "Thank thee."

"And our companion is Miss Elizabeth Miller," Lord Chatsworth said.

"How do you do, miss?" Davies inclined his head.

"Good afternoon," Elizabeth said in return.

"And here is Mrs. Snowden, Miss Alice's nanny."

"Madam." The driver returned his hat to his head and unlatched the carriage door as Mrs. Snowden curtsied.

Elizabeth was taken aback by His Lordship's gracious manners. Was this how he treated all his servants?

"Let's open her up, shall we?" Lord Chatsworth said to Davies as he patted the landau's bonnet. "It's a nice day for it, and I've not seen blue sky in months."

"Very good, my lord." Davies folded down the carriage top, and once they were settled inside, he snapped the reins, and they started off.

Lord Chatsworth waved to a few of the townspeople as the carriage rolled through the streets, and Elizabeth wondered if he noticed the curious looks he received in return. Surely everyone wondered about the child that accompanied him. She didn't like the idea of people speculating about Alice. As they passed more people, however, she realized quite a few of the inquisitive looks were directed at her. She glanced at Lord Chatsworth, wondering what he thought about the conclusion many would draw from seeing the party in the landau. But he looked entirely unbothered, so she stopped worrying about what strangers might or might not be assuming and enjoyed the ride in a very fancy carriage.

The cool air was refreshing after the hours aboard the train, and Elizabeth leaned back her head to feel the sun on her cheeks.

"'A Cal-ee-foy-na condor's wingspan can reach oohva three meters in length,'" Alice read from her book. She apparently wished to continue recounting facts of nature's predators. She turned around the large volume, showing an illustration of the bird.

Elizabeth thought it looked like a particularly ugly black turkey.

Lord Chatsworth leaned forward, looking closely at the picture. "Over three meters, you say?"

Alice nodded.

"A marvelous creature, isn't it?"

He leaned forward to read the paragraphs beside the drawing, and Elizabeth wondered whether he was just humoring Alice with his interest or whether he truly wished to learn more about the California condor.

The carriage left the town and traveled along country roads bordered with hedgerows that were just starting to open their leaves. When they crested a hill, Elizabeth marveled at the patchwork of fields. They passed charming cottages behind low rock walls and the occasional grand country home set back from the road and surrounded by manicured gardens. They even saw a ruined castle high on a green hill.

For the most part, the journey was silent, the tired travelers content to watch the scenery they passed. After a while, Mrs. Snowden's head dropped to her chest, and she began to snore.

They came to the top of a rise, and Charles nudged Alice. "See there? It's the Channel."

Alice and Elizabeth both stared out at the endless blue of the sea, and Alice sighed. "Beautiful. Oy've never seen th' sea."

"Neither have I," Elizabeth admitted. She was spellbound. It appeared as if the sky and water joined together on the horizon and the world beyond disappeared.

Alice squinted. "Oy can't see France," she said, looking disappointed. "It should be just ovah there on th' othah side of the wotah."

"There is a bit of mist out on the sea today," Lord Chatsworth explained, "or you would certainly see it. You will have another chance during our visit. Perhaps you and I shall even visit France one day. If you continue to improve with your French lessons."

"Oui, oui!" Alice's grin was wide, and her face shone with wonder. Much like Elizabeth, Alice had never considered that she might one day see a place as distant as France.

A lane led away from the main road, and the carriage followed it, passing through a pair of ornate iron gates that were set into stone towers.

A man waved from the gatehouse as they went by, and Davies, Lord Chatsworth, and Alice waved in return.

The lane led over a meadow and through the cool shadows of a forest before emerging to reveal a stunning vista. Ahead, beyond a large pond, stood the most imposing structure Elizabeth had ever seen. The building was ancient, of that there was no doubt—likely hundreds of years old. It was built of honey-colored stone, its roofline irregular and covered in chimneys. A stone wall led off each side, perhaps concealing private gardens. The windows were tall, and there were so many of them. Elizabeth counted three stories and possibly an attic above them.

"There it is," Lord Chatsworth said to Alice. "Ashbury Park."

"This is yoor 'ouse?" Alice asked. Her eyes were wide as she tried to take it all in.

"Yes, and it's your house too," he said.

"But it is too big. Oy will get lost inside."

Lord Chatsworth chuckled. "Trust me. Within a few moments, you will feel right at home. Mrs. Foster will see to that."

Elizabeth smiled at the girl's innocence. But inside, she held some of the same fears. How did one find her way around such an enormous place? Perhaps the housekeeper would provide a map.

Davies followed the long lane as it curved in front of the manor house, where a row of servants waited to greet their master.

When Lord Chatsworth stepped from the carriage, the women curtsied and the men bowed.

Elizabeth recognized many of their uniforms: maids, a housekeeper, a cook and her staff, footmen, a butler . . . but there were many more that she was unsure of. The Lancasters' country home was fully staffed, but it did not have a fourth of the employees that managed Ashbury Park. To think, all this was for just one family. There were probably rooms Lord Chatsworth and his relatives had never set foot in and never would. The inequality between this wealthy noble family and Elizabeth's students, who slept packed in drafty, windowless houses, three families to one small room, were so blatant that she felt queasy at the excess.

The woman Elizabeth assumed to be the housekeeper stepped forward. She was slender and wore a cap over her white hair and an apron over her dress. Based on the wrinkles around her eyes, Elizabeth guessed her age to be near sixty.

"Welcome home, Your Lordship." She curtsied, jingling the ring of keys that hung from her waist.

"Mrs. Foster, how good to see you." Lord Chatsworth gave a warm smile.

Mrs. Foster looked him up and down and shook her head, tsking in disappointment. "You've grown so thin, my lord. Are you not eating in London?"

Lord Chatsworth laughed. "I'm eating plenty, but I do miss Cook's shepherd's pie."

The woman who was most certainly the cook to whom he referred smiled, and her cheeks turned pink. "Then, you shall have it, my lord. Tonight, if it pleases you."

"Splendid." He turned, holding a hand out to Alice and motioning for her to join him.

She stepped forward shyly, her head cast down and to the side.

"This must be Miss Alice," Mrs. Foster said. "You are very welcome."

"Thank yooou." Alice spoke the words slowly, enunciating with tight vowels as she and Elizabeth had practiced.

Elizabeth felt a swell of pride and silently cheered for the dreadful scallywag Captain Sharkfin.

Lord Chatsworth introduced Mrs. Snowden and Elizabeth, and Mrs. Foster got to work. With a few orders, she sent all of the staff back to their duties and directed the footmen on where to deliver the trunks.

His Lordship conducted Alice and Mrs. Snowden to their sleeping chambers, and after the flurry of activity died down, Elizabeth was left alone with Mrs. Foster.

"Come along, dear," the housekeeper said with a warmth that surprised Elizabeth. "I'll show you to your room."

"Thank you." She followed the woman inside, and two footmen swung the enormous doors closed behind them. Once she was inside, Elizabeth could do nothing more than stare. The entry hall was lit with a chandelier that looked as if it had come straight from a medieval castle. The modern inhabitants must have adapted it for gas lighting. It hung above a round table that held a large vase filled with flowers.

Wainscotting covered the walls and ceilings in a rich oak. Gold-framed portraits hung on the walls, and plush sofas sat at intervals between statuary and potted trees.

The stairway ahead of her was built from dark wood with a thick carpet running down the center. It led up to a landing and split into two flights, each leading in a different direction. Railings with thick carved balusters ran along the sides, and a pair of bronze cherubs stood on the newel posts, aiming their arrows at the sky.

Elizabeth's uncle had made his fortune in the steamship industry, and the Lancasters' homes were considered some of the finest in the kingdom. But Ashbury Park was something else entirely. It was old and time-honored, belonging to a family with traditions and heraldry that passed through generations. It seemed as ancient as time.

"The manor house can be a bit overwhelming," Mrs. Foster said kindly.

Elizabeth knew she must look like a child, gawking wide-eyed with her mouth open. She smiled at the housekeeper. "I'm rather out of my element here."

Mrs. Foster chuckled. "Well, that is a pleasant change," she said. "Most of the manor's guests are very much *in* their element, and few take the time to really appreciate the extraordinary beauty of Ashbury Park." She started up the stairs. "I shall be very happy to give you a tour once you've rested. It was built in the sixteenth century, you know. And there are a great many surprises in this old house."

"Secret tunnels, I hope," Elizabeth said, walking beside the older woman. "And a dungeon with skeletons."

Mrs. Foster chuckled again. "Unfortunately, it is just a damp cellar used for storage."

They paused on the landing. "The family resides in the east wing." The housekeeper gestured at one set of stairs and then led Elizabeth up the other. "And guests in the west. His Lordship tells me you are Miss Alice's tutor?"

"Yes," Elizabeth said.

"I found some of Lady Kathryn's old things," Mrs. Foster said as they walked down the wide corridor. "Ribbons and costume jewelry. A few dolls. I hope Miss Alice enjoys them."

"I'm certain she will," Elizabeth said. "She is a very amiable child."

"And how could she not be?" the housekeeper said. "Her brother is the kindest, most sincere man I know—and I've known him since his birth." She stopped at a door.

"Her brother?"

Mrs. Foster opened the door. "You're right, of course. I wouldn't call *Leonard* particularly sincere, though he is a good boy. But Charles . . . he's a special one."

Luckily, the housekeeper had already entered the bedchamber and was adjusting the curtains when realization dawned on Elizabeth. She was certain she wouldn't have been able to hide her surprise if the woman had been watching her face.

Lord Chatsworth was Alice's brother. It made sense, of course. Everyone knew of his father's reputation with the ladies. It would come as no surprise to anyone that he had fathered a child outside of his marriage.

Elizabeth schooled her expression, stepping farther into the bedchamber. The room was beautiful, with a large bed piled with pillows. She might need a stool to climb into it. There was a hearth directly opposite the bed, and on the far wall, a large window that looked out over the pond and the forest beyond.

"Molly will be up to unpack your trunk promptly," Mrs. Foster said. "And I'll send tea in . . . an hour?"

"That will be lovely, thank you."

Once she was certain Elizabeth was comfortably situated, the house-keeper left her to rest.

Elizabeth took off her hat and unbuttoned her traveling cloak. *His sister.* If Alice had grown up in Stourbridge, it was possible the family had not known of her existence until recently. What had changed? Why had Lord Chatsworth brought the girl to live at Ivy House with his family?

Elizabeth sat in front of the window, staring out at the scene as her mind turned over this new piece of information. In such cases, she knew, a child like Alice would typically have been kept a secret. Perhaps her mother would have been given a sum of money to guarantee a reasonably secure life. But in no instance had Elizabeth ever heard of a nobleman bringing an illegitimate child into his family. And, from what she'd seen, Lord Chatsworth was providing Alice with every opportunity for a better life, even at the expense of his family's reputation.

This latest revelation about the man made Elizabeth's heart feel as if it were being filled with sunshine. In spite of her questions about the situation, she was unexpectedly pleased with Lord Chatsworth. Pleased indeed.

CHAPTER 10

CHARLES TUCKED HIS NOTEBOOK AND spyglass into his pockets as he strode out of the manor house and into the forest. Only a few hours of daylight remained, and he was eager to catch up for the months he'd been away.

Right away he heard the chirps of house sparrows and saw a pair flitting through the garden. They may have a nest nearby. He walked along the path beside the wall, looking into the low shrubs and listening. He would typically spot a blue tit or a blackbird here near the garden, but today he saw neither. He would remind the gardener to fill the birdbaths and stock birdseed in the feeders.

Charles heard a rustle in the shrubbery and paused. A chaffinch took flight, flashing the bright white of its wings and outer tail feathers. It was a male, with a blue-gray cap and rust-colored chest. The bird landed on the wall, letting out a string of agitated twitters. It was obviously displeased at being disturbed. Charles stood stock-still studying the bird. Though it was a common species, it was one of his favorites. He scribbled in his book, noting the variety of colors, the olive green above the bird's tail, the stripes on its wings, the charcoal-gray beak.

Charles continued on, scanning the open sky as he walked toward the forest. He hoped to spot a honey buzzard or a falcon flying over the fields, but he was disappointed.

When he entered the forest, the cooing of wood pigeons met his ears. He slowed, stepping quietly over the spongy ground as squirrels and finches chattered above him. The sound of an industrious woodpecker met his ears, and Charles slowed even further, scanning for a dead tree or a rotten log where the bird might be pecking for insects.

He saw the creature, finally, on the trunk of a dying hawthorn. Crimson crown, black and white bars on its wings . . . the lesser spotted woodpecker, much rarer than its larger relative. It was the smallest woodpecker in all of Europe. Charles studied it through his spyglass, watching as the bird pecked the tree, its knocks echoing through the forest as it searched for wood larvae. He made a note in his book before leaving the woodpecker behind and continuing on.

Ahead was a majestic beech tree. Charles looked through his spyglass, studying the forks of the tree where he might see a nest and the branches where an owl might be sleeping away the last hours of daylight. He'd seen both tawny owls and barn owls in the forest through the years and even the occasional short-eared owl in the winter months, when they migrated from the snow in Scandinavia and Russia.

But the rarest of all, the lesser horned owl, he'd seen only once, here, in this very tree. As small as a starling, with amber-colored eyes and fluffy ear tufts, the owl had looked exactly like a drawing of a character from a fairy-tale book. It had blended so completely into the tree that Charles wouldn't have seen it if the bird hadn't chosen the exact second that Charles's gaze was on his branch to blink its large eyes. Even knowing where it was, Charles had had a difficult time making out its form through his spyglass. As he'd stared, the owl had stared back, fixing him with a regal gaze that had given the impression that it was much wiser than the other inhabitants of the forest. Lords of the manor included.

They'd watched one another for a long moment, and then, without warning, the owl had lifted off into the air, moving on silent wings. Though it had been years, Charles still thought of this as the owl tree, and each time he passed, he hoped the lesser horned owl or one of its relatives would be there.

He looked closely at every branch of the beech tree but only spotted a pair of nightingales carrying twigs and grass to build their nest. He would have to check back before returning to London to see if any eggs had been laid.

He looked at his pocket watch, disappointed to see that, as usual, the hours had passed much more quickly than he would have liked.

He started back, taking a different path in hopes of spotting different species. Each year Charles told himself that once Parliament recessed for the summer, he would have months of leisure time to spend doing the thing he most enjoyed—searching for birds, documenting the various species, and studying their habits. His father had always scoffed at what he'd considered to be a pointless hobby. But Charles felt more himself when he was among the birds. Flight represented freedom, and he was drawn to these creatures, fascinated by their endurance, their instincts for survival, and their ability to soar.

A screech sounded overhead, but Charles couldn't see its source through the trees. If he adjusted his route, he would come to a clearing with a better chance of seeing whether the cry came from a kite or a harrier. It could even be a goshawk, but that was unlikely. Charles had only ever seen a few, when he was young. The species were nearly extinct in Britain, thanks to their main enemy: gamekeepers.

The hope of spotting the rare bird sent him moving more quickly, his footsteps muffled by the spongy covering of dead leaves and pine needles, but seeing a flash of color through the trees, Charles slowed. As he came closer he saw it was Miss Miller sitting on a fallen log in the clearing, her face turned upward to catch the last rays of sunlight.

Charles watched her, much as he had watched the birds, studying her form and behavior. In appearance she was much like any other young lady of her age. She was pretty—beautiful, even. Especially with her head tilted back and the golden light illuminating her face and glinting off the lighter strands of her hair.

It wasn't only Miss Miller's beauty that Charles found remarkable. She was outspoken and passionate about causes dear to her. The way she cared for her school, for Alice, for her friends, was admirable indeed. But there was much more, a depth he rarely encountered with young ladies in Society. Miss Miller was quick to anger, but she was also quick to defend a friend. Through her uncle she had the opportunity to indulge herself, to live the life of a high-Society debutante, and yet she'd used her situation to improve the lives of the less fortunate. She was intelligent and fiery and determined. Miss Miller was, for lack of a better word, *interesting*. And interesting was a quality Charles had encountered but rarely.

Seeing the opportunity to catch her off guard, he found a long thin stick and stuck a clump of moss on the end. He crept toward the young woman, whose eyes were still closed, placing his feet carefully on the forest floor and holding his breath. When he was close enough, he reached the stick forward to tickle the moss beneath her chin.

Unfortunately, he'd overestimated the distance and poked the young lady in the throat.

She gave a shriek, clutching at her neck as she pulled away and flew backward over the log.

"Miss Miller!" Charles dropped the twig and rushed to her.

She flailed in the dirt and pine needles, holding her neck. "Something jumped on my throat," she said, her voice panicked. "I think it bit me." She thrashed, trying to crawl away, but her boot had pushed into a crack in the old log, and it was stuck fast.

"Stay still," Charles said. He put a hand on her stockinged knee, holding her leg still so she didn't twist her ankle.

Miss Miller continued to pull, scrabbling with her foot and hands, but she was no longer twisting. Charles put his other hand beneath her leg, turning her heel and easing her foot out.

Once it was free, she scrambled back, hand at her throat. Strands of her hair had fallen loose, and bits of foliage were caught in them. "What was it? Is it gone?" She darted her wide-eyed gaze around the clearing. "Whatever it was, it flew at me. Could it have been a bat?"

"It's gone," Charles said. Guilt sat like a lump in his belly.

She sighed in relief and pushed a lock of hair out of her face. "Thank goodness you were here. You must have frightened it away." She looked at her fingertips, as if expecting to see blood. "If not for your level head, I think I should have quite lost myself in a panic."

Charles helped her stand. "Miss Miller, you are quite safe." He stepped back over the log and retrieved the stick. "This is your attacker, or I suppose *I am*." He grimaced, watching her expression change from frightened to confused.

"You *stabbed* me?"

"It was more of a poke than a stab," Charles said. "And, in my defense, it was meant to be a tickle."

Her confused expression turned stormy, and her lips flattened into a line. She snatched the stick from him without breaking eye contact.

Charles jumped when she snapped it in two. "I apologize, miss." He reached toward her to inspect her neck, but she swatted his hand away with a piece of the stick.

"Why would you do that?" Miss Miller's voice trembled as if she were fighting to hold back tears or fury or both.

Her question caught him off guard. Did he have a reason for his action? "I . . . well, I don't exactly . . . I thought you'd like it."

"You thought I'd like being stabbed in the throat?" Her voice rose both in volume and pitch.

"Poked," Charles reminded her. "And, as I said, it was meant to be a tickle. Just a little tease to surprise you. And I was aiming for your chin, not your throat."

"And you assumed I'd enjoy being teased? That I like surprises?"

He shrugged. "Most young ladies do."

"You know nothing about me." Miss Miller threw down the sticks and stomped away toward the house, her hair and skirts covered with pine needles and dirt.

"That's not true." Charles stumbled over the log in his hurry to catch up. "I know you're intelligent and determined."

She huffed and increased her pace to the point that she was nearly running.

"And you care about people," Charles called after her. "You care about the vote, the poor of London. You have dedicated your life to those less fortunate."

Miss Miller slowed, then stopped, spinning around. She came toward him. He noticed her face hadn't softened, but at least she was no longer running away. "Someone must care for them, Your Lordshi—"

"Shh." Charles held out his hands and cocked his head. "Did you hear that?" He could have sworn . . .

Miss Miller put her fists on her hips. "Is another stick returning to—"

He cut her off, putting his fingers over her mouth to silence her. "There it is again." He heard it for certain this time. Charles's heart started to race. If he was right about this . . .

She swatted his hand away none too gently. "Another game? What on earth makes you think I would—"

Charles grabbed her hand, pulling her behind him as he rushed toward the sound. "Come along. Hurry!"

"What are you doing?" She slapped at his hand. "Stop pulling me. I told you I don't like these games."

"Trust me," Charles said, pausing, the excitement of sharing the experience with her making his pulse race. "This is not a game. You *will* like this. Please come with me?"

Her expression was still doubtful, but she stopped pulling away. He guessed it was as close to agreement as he would get. He kept hold of her hand, and they hurried between the trees, Charles's ears straining as he followed the call. The shadows were deepening, and if they didn't hurry, night would be fully upon them. He paused again to listen and then took off in a slightly different direction. The nightingales, blackbirds, and crickets were just beginning their evening songs, making it more difficult to single out the sound he sought. If only he could convince the rest of the creatures to remain quiet.

Away from the paths, the ground was uneven with thick roots and clumps of underbrush impeding their course, but he pushed on, scrambling up hills and stepping over fallen trees.

Miss Miller followed, her hand still joined in his. He didn't know whether she was simply curious or if she didn't wish to be left alone as night fell, but she kept pace with him. Once he judged they were close, he stopped and put a finger in front of his lips. He crouched, pulling her down next to him and taking out his spyglass.

Miss Miller knelt on a mossy patch. She remained quiet, and he could feel her eyes on him.

When Charles located the source of the call, he nearly cried out and did a dance of joy. "You must have a look," he said in a quiet voice. He gave Miss Miller the spyglass and pointed toward the top of the tree in front of them. "It's there."

She took the spyglass, giving him a suspicious look before putting it to her eye. "What am I meant to see? The little orange bird?"

"That's not just any bird." Charles had his notebook out and was writing as quickly as he could. "That, Miss Miller, is a red-backed shrike." He grinned. "More commonly known as a butcher bird. And I'm certain we're the first to see one this year, or I'd certainly have heard about it." He chuckled. "Mrs. Wembley-Pratt will be spitting with envy."

Miss Miller handed him back the spyglass. "If this is another game, it's even less appealing than the stick poke."

"A red-backed shrike is extremely rare in this part of Europe," Charles said. He looked through the lens, squinting in the twilight to study the details of the bird. A dove-gray head, a black bandit mask across its eyes, a white throat, and a beautiful russet-colored back. "Listen to its song," he said in a low voice. "You may never hear it again."

Miss Miller moved, but she didn't settle. She appeared ready to jump up and leave at any moment. She looked up at the bird and then at Charles. She still looked skeptical, as if she still believed this was all another joke. "Why is it called a butcher bird?" she asked at last.

Charles looked back up at the bird, which had gone quiet now that night was closing in. "It is so called for its practice of impaling its prey—insects and small reptiles—on thornbushes. Rather a gruesome habit, I'm afraid."

"Perhaps it means to simply tickle them and it goes too far," Miss Miller said.

Charles turned more fully toward her, letting out a laugh. "I believe that was a jest. Are you teasing me, Miss Miller?"

She shook her head, letting out a huff. But a smile tugged at the corner of her mouth.

Charles looked back up to the top of the tree, but either it had grown too dark for them to see the bird, or the shrike had flown away. "I really must apologize again," he said. "Not only for the very gentle and hardly noticeable poke to your throat but for all the teasing. It is a habit, I suppose, to treat people thus. It's in my nature to keep things playful, and I don't always take into account people's feelings. I recognize it as a fault. Not every person enjoys it." In the anonymity of darkness, he'd spoken more freely than he'd intended, and his apology had turned into something of a confession.

Miss Miller was quiet. When she spoke at last, her words came slowly, as if she were thinking as she said them. "Teasing makes me feel as if I'm being mocked. I have endeavored my entire life to be taken seriously. I don't enjoy being laughed at, even when the intent is not malicious." She sighed, pushing out her breath as if she were frustrated, and folded her arms across herself. "It is a fault of mine to harbor suspicion, especially of men. I should not have allowed myself to grow so angry at you."

Her face was hidden in shadows, but Charles could sense her discomfort in revealing something so personal. There was more behind what she said, but he did not push his luck by inquiring further. "We should return." He rose, put away his notebook and compressed his spyglass, then helped the young lady stand as well. They started off through the darkening forest, Charles in the lead. "The staff is used to me losing track of time and arriving late to supper when I'm bird-watching, but I shouldn't wish for Alice to eat alone." He offered a hand to help her down an incline. "And if I can help it, I never miss Cook's shepherd's pie."

"Is that why you were out here today? Looking for birds?" she asked.

"It is." Charles skirted around a large beech tree and helped her avoid the roots bulging beneath. "And what about yourself? What drew you to the forest?"

"The quiet," Miss Miller said. "The smells of fresh air and trees. The sounds of creatures . . . it is very restorative. A bit of peace can put one's worries into perspective."

"I agree fully," Charles said. He wondered if she was speaking generally or if Miss Miller had something in particular concerning her, but he felt like he shouldn't pry. "I hope Alice will feel the peace in the nature here as well."

"She has shown an interest in animals," Miss Miller said. "I wonder if she might enjoy joining you on a bird search."

Charles nodded, though he didn't believe she could see the motion in the shadows. "I hope you might join us as well, if you're so inclined."

"I?"

"Of course. Alice would enjoy having you there." A skip in his heartbeat told him that he would enjoy it as well. He was being a coward. Why couldn't he simply invite her for his own sake instead of using Alice's affection for her teacher as an excuse? "Tomorrow morning?"

They emerged from the forest and started toward the house.

"Very well, then."

He smiled, pleased that he'd convinced her. It wouldn't have surprised him one bit if she swore off his company altogether after this evening.

Miss Miller pushed her loose hair back into its arrangement as they walked.

The two were met at the garden door by Mrs. Foster, who hurried them inside the kitchen. "Did you find something interesting?"

"A red-backed shrike," Charles said, blinking at the light.

"How wonderful," Mrs. Foster said in the same voice she'd used when he'd come into the house as a boy excitedly describing the various birds he'd seen on his excursions. "And it looks like he's convinced you to tramp around in the woods searching for his little feathered friends as well, Miss Mill—oh gracious! Your throat!"

Charles winced at the sight of a dark-red scrape on her fair skin.

Miss Miller glanced at Charles, then looked back at the housekeeper. "I was poked by a twig," she said, touching the mark carefully. "But it must look worse than it is. It doesn't hurt at all—just a little tickle."

CHAPTER 11

THE NEXT MORNING ELIZABETH ROSE at first light—Lord Chatsworth had insisted upon an early start, telling her the birds were most active in the early-morning hours—and she dressed in clothing she considered appropriate for exploring the woods. She'd hesitated to pack the plain dress but had reminded herself that she was not taking a holiday but was here as Alice's tutor. Simple clothing was much more practical, even if Lord Chatsworth would be present. She wasn't here to impress him, after all. And besides, after her tumble in the woods last night, she needn't bother. He was most certainly not impressed.

At the memory, her cheeks flushed hot. Why was it that every time she encountered the man, it was in a moment of mortification? To be fair to herself, yesterday's awkward situation was his doing. She had been entirely composed, enjoying the late-afternoon ambiance of the forest, when he'd come upon her. What had the man been thinking, jabbing her throat like that?

She had been terrified and furious and embarrassed, and she'd certainly let him know it. His remorse for his action and its result had been sincere, or at least it had appeared to be.

One of the maids, Molly, arrived to help her dress, but seeing that Elizabeth was already clothed, she offered to arrange her hair instead.

A few moments later, coat in hand, Elizabeth made her way down the main staircase.

Mrs. Foster met her in the entryway, taking her coat. "They are meeting in the breakfast room."

Elizabeth thanked her and hurried in the direction the housekeeper had indicated, hoping Lord Chatsworth and Alice hadn't waited long.

As she came to the doorway, she heard a mixture of unfamiliar voices and paused. Had she come to the wrong room? She peeked inside and found several strangers sitting at the table and clustered at the sideboard.

Elizabeth was just about to leave when she caught sight of Lord Chatsworth, seated at the head of the table.

He saw her at the same time and stood, waving his arm. "There you are!"

Her stomach fluttered, and she nearly convinced herself the reaction could be attributed to the smell of bacon, rather than His Lordship's smile.

Alice waved from her seat next to his. She was eating with one hand and turning the pages of a book with the other.

Lord Chatsworth left the table and came to Elizabeth. He motioned toward the sideboard. "I'll introduce everyone once you have your breakfast."

Elizabeth filled her plate, and Lord Chatsworth accompanied her to the table, where he pulled out the empty seat on his left side, across from Alice. Elizabeth sat as he scooted her chair in for her.

"Charles is taking us in search of birds," Alice said, her lips and cheeks tight as she pronounced the words with slow precision.

"Yes" was all Elizabeth could think to say in response. Had she misunderstood their plan? Who were all these other people?

Alice held up her book: *A Guide to Birds of Britain.* "Charles gave it to me." Her eyes shone as she looked at her brother.

Elizabeth bit into a piece of toast and glanced around the table of strangers. Aside from herself, His Lordship, and Alice, there were five others. They were a varied collection of people differing in age, gender, and from what she could see of their clothing, social class. A curious gathering made all the stranger by their location in Ashbury Park's breakfast room.

Lord Chatsworth pushed back his chair and stood. At his nod, a footman removed his plate and left a fresh cup of tea. "Continue eating, please," he said. "And with Mrs. Wembley-Pratt's permission, shall we commence our meeting?"

An elderly woman with a hooked nose, frizzled white hair, and eyes magnified by round spectacles gave an assenting nod.

"Welcome, all of you." Lord Chatsworth held out his arms, palms up. "I am so happy to once again be among the West Sussex Order of the Friends of Fowl and Feather."

"Hear! Hear!" A tall gentleman with a tweed jacket and a black necktie lifted his teacup in a very proper-looking toast.

A rather grubby-looking man with patches on his jacket and greasy dark hair and red cheeks raised his cup as well. He heaved an approving grunt and pushed a sausage into his mouth.

Two middle-aged women dressed in matching gowns with blue-and-white-striped bodices clapped softly.

"Before we formally begin, I should like to introduce my guests: Miss Alice and her tutor, Miss Elizabeth Miller." He gestured to each in turn.

"Ladies, please meet the members of our order: our president, Mrs. Wembley-Pratt . . ."

The spectacled woman inclined her head graciously.

"Mr. McDuff," His Lordship continued.

"Welcome to ye," the floppy-hat man said, wiping his mouth with a dirty handkerchief.

"Mr. Fitzwaring . . ."

The tweed-wearing man lifted his teacup again. "A pleasure, ladies."

"And, of course, the Misses Leavenworth."

The women, who Elizabeth could see were twins, gave identical smiles. "How do you do?" they said in unison.

Elizabeth smiled at the collection of mismatched individuals. "It is very nice to meet you all."

Alice gave a shy smile and waved.

Lord Chatsworth sat in his chair and took a sip of tea.

Elizabeth watched him, expecting a look of frustration or a hint that he'd gathered this group together out of obligation, but his countenance spoke of the exact opposite. He seemed . . . eager, happy, comfortable.

She realized she was again staring and looked down at her toast. Here sat one of the most powerful men in the kingdom, and he appeared entirely at ease among the motley band. She bit into her toast, as her surprised thoughts tried to make sense of it all.

"Let us call the meeting to order," Mrs. Wembley-Pratt said, putting down her teacup with a clink. She took a notebook from her handbag. "Welcome to our visitors, and, Your Lordship, it is always a delight when you are in residence."

"And providin' grub," Mr. McDuff said.

Mrs. Wembley-Pratt opened her notebook, taking a pencil from between its pages. "Yes, the meal is very appreciated, Your Lordship." She spoke in a businesslike tone, writing something and then underlining it. Elizabeth thought she must be a teacher. "Mr. Fitzwaring, would you like to lead off?"

Mr. Fitzwaring opened his own notebook and sat, if possible, even straighter. "I've embarked upon two excursions to Shoreham Beach this spring and have documented the usual cormorants, gulls—both herring gulls and their black-headed cousins—as well as a pair of oystercatchers."

"No turnstones?" Mr. McDuff asked.

"Rather early in the season for them, I believe," Mr. Fitzwaring said.

Mr. McDuff picked at something in his teeth, looking as if he were considering Mr. Fitzwaring's words, then nodded. "Right you are, ole chap."

"Last year we spotted a kingfisher at Shoreham Beach, don't you remember?" One of the Misses Leavenworth leaned forward, speaking in an excited voice.

"Indeed." Mr. Fitzwaring nodded at the woman. "A thrilling day, to be sure." His austere expression remained, but his eye twinkled.

"Lord Chatsworth, you were there," the other Miss Leavenworth said.

"One of the best days in my memory," he said warmly, bringing a smile to the older woman's face.

Elizabeth was astonished at his easy manner. She'd never have imagined him to associate with such company, let alone behave as if they were on friendly terms. She hardly recognized London's most charming flirt.

Alice was turning through the pages in her book.

Lord Chatsworth leaned close to the girl. "Kingfisher," he said in a quiet voice. "It begins with *K*."

"And Mr. McDuff?" Mrs. Wembley-Pratt said, making another note in her book. "What is your report?"

"Wading birds are nestin' in Pevensy Marsh," Mr. McDuff said. "Seen warblers, redshanks, lapwings, a few harriers, o'course, and teals."

"Any herons?" Mr. Fitzwaring asked.

"Not as of last Tuesday," Mr. McDuff responded.

"We will certainly plan an excursion to the marsh soon," Mrs. Wembley-Pratt said, writing in her notebook. Once the others had given their reports, she faced the far end of the table. "And Your Lordship?"

He took a small notebook from his breast pocket. "I have been in the country only since yesterday, but I did manage to tramp about in the woods a bit." Lord Chatsworth motioned with his chin toward the window in the direction of the forest as he looked at the page in his notebook. "Blackbirds, finches, the typical woodland birds." He made a show of running his pencil down a list. "Oh yes," he said, as if just noticing a last entry. "One red-backed shrike."

Gasps sounded, and every member of the West Sussex Order of the Friends of Fowl and Feathers jolted as if they had been electrocuted.

Mr. McDuff let out a low whistle.

Mr. Fitzwaring jumped to his feet. "You are joking!"

"Are you certain?" The Misses Leavenworth leaned forward.

Even the apparently unflusterable Mrs. Wembley-Pratt appeared flustered. "I've not seen a shrike in Sussex for years," she said.

Lord Chatsworth dropped his flippant demeanor and grinned excitedly, raising his brows.

Elizabeth's stomach fluttered again.

"Miss Miller can confirm," he said.

His words caught Elizabeth off guard, and all eyes turned to her. "Oh yes. I saw the bird." She looked at Lord Chatsworth, and he nodded for her to continue. "There was a black stripe over his eyes, like a mask, and he had a gray head and rust-colored feathers on his back and tail."

"'Ow did 'e sound like?" Mr. McDuff squinted suspiciously.

"Ah, well . . ." Elizabeth rubbed her brow and looked at Lord Chatsworth. "Let me think."

He gave an encouraging smile.

"It was something like, 'Twee! Twee! Ruk ruk ruk.'" She felt ridiculous.

Mr. McDuff looked at Mr. Fitzwaring. "Sounds like a red-backed shrike."

"It certainly does," Mr. Fitzwaring said.

"And you say it was here, in your forest, yesterday?" Mrs. Wembley-Pratt asked, looking toward the windows.

"Yes," Lord Chatsworth said. "Which is why I petitioned last night to change the meeting location." He gave an eager grin.

"Well then." Mrs. Wembley-Pratt snapped her notebook shut and put it in her handbag. "If there is no further business, and with Your Lordship's permission . . . shall we?"

Moments later, hats, coats, and gloves donned, the West Sussex Order of the Friends of Fowl and Feather tromped up the garden path in their sensible footwear. Their heads darted about as they scanned the skies and looked beneath shrubs and up into trees. The group looked even more mismatched in their outerwear, if that was even possible. Lord Chatsworth led the way in a straw boater hat, fitting for a gentleman on a country stroll. Mr. Fitzwaring had put on a pith helmet that would look at home in the Indian jungle or on an African safari, while Mr. McDuff's hat was made of floppy felt.

The females' headpieces were equally dissimilar. Mrs. Wembley-Pratt wore a practical hat with a wide brim that would shade her face, the Leavenworths sported flower-covered bonnets, and Alice wore a flat-topped straw hat with a ribbon. Elizabeth did not know why she'd fretted about which hat to bring to the country. She could have chosen any style of clothing or accessory from the past few decades and not looked out of place among this group.

Alice carried a small rucksack over one shoulder. "Charles gave it to me," she told Elizabeth, lifting the flap. Inside was the guidebook as well as a small spyglass. The girl appeared every bit as eager to explore as her older brother was.

As they stepped deeper into the wood, any earlier conversation was muted. They were listening.

Elizabeth pulled her coat tighter around her shoulders. The early-morning air was chill, and even more so in the shadow of the trees.

"Ye 'ear that, Miss Alice?" Mr. McDuff cupped his hand behind his ear. "'S a robin's call." He squinted into the trees and pointed. "'Ere they are—a pair o' them, carryin' grass for their nest."

Alice looked through her spyglass as she walked, and Mr. McDuff held his hand near her elbow so he could catch her if she tripped.

Lord Chatsworth pointed Mrs. Wembley-Pratt toward where he and Elizabeth had seen the bird the day before, leaving the elderly woman to lead the party, and he came to the rear, falling into step with Elizabeth.

"What do you think?" He spoke in a quiet voice, lifting his chin to indicate the group.

"I don't know what to think, my lord." She glanced at him and then toward the others. "You seem different here."

"It is the only place I feel truly at ease," he said. His voice was still soft, sounding introspective. "I do not have to pretend to be anything other than myself."

Elizabeth hadn't considered that a man of Lord Chatsworth's standing would feel the need to conceal his true self behind a facade of any kind.

As they walked through the forest, she watched His Lordship and his birding friends motion to one another when they found a bird and creep together for a better view, whispering and using hand signals to communicate. They marched through the forest, happily discussing breeding habits, migration, and plumage, then remembering to shush one another when their conversation grew too loud.

Elizabeth tried to picture Lord Chatsworth describing a red-backed shrike enthusiastically at a London Ball or any of the other noblemen and debutants crouching with him on a forest floor or watching a nest being built through a spyglass, but she could not envision any such scenario.

Lord Chatsworth was indeed different here in the forest, and if this was the genuine man as opposed to the flirt he was reputed to be, she was both sorry that he felt he had to conceal this part of himself and pleased that there was more to His Lordship than she'd believed. She thought of her conversation with Alice, when Elizabeth had explained how it felt to show the world what she wanted them to see while her true self was kept secret. In this Lord Chatsworth was not so very different. And knowing he'd allowed her to see him thus felt like a privilege. He had trusted her with something dear to him.

Her heart caught at the realization, beating with more force. But it lasted for only a moment. She knew why His Lordship had no qualms about allowing her to know his truth. It was for the same reason he'd not hidden it from the housekeeper. He did not care what Elizabeth thought of him. He did not hope to impress her. She was not his special friend, but an employee. Hardly more than a servant. Why should the lord of the manor care one way or the other for the approval of a child's tutor? She shook herself, angry that she'd let her sensibilities be carried away by fantasy.

The group stopped again, clustering around to look up at a branch. "It's a red-winged thrush," Lord Chatsworth whispered to Elizabeth when she caught up to them.

She looked up at the bird, brown stripes and a blush of red feathers on its sides.

"'Its diet consists of berries and soil inver . . . invertebrates,'" Alice read from her book. The girl was enjoying herself immensely. The group had taken her under their proverbial wing, helping her find the correct pictures in her guidebook and allowing her to guess at the species.

After a few moments the bird flew away, and they started off again.

Lord Chatsworth didn't hurry ahead with the others. He walked next to Elizabeth.

"Is this a regular occurrence?" Elizabeth asked. Her thoughts from a moment ago embarrassed her, and she spoke about the most nonpersonal topic she could find. "Do you often come together with the bird society?"

"They meet weekly, sometimes more often, especially during nesting season. I join them when I am able." The wistfulness in his words told her he was not able as often as he wished to be.

"And this is what you do?"

"Yes, exactly. Isn't it wonderful?"

His smile tugged at her heart, the reaction making her realize that again she'd imagined more to their friendship than she should have. His brows pulled together, and the smile dissipated. "I hope you don't find it dull."

"Not at all." Elizabeth did not like to be responsible for the disappearance of his smile. "As I said yesterday, I enjoy the forest." She glanced at him and then at the others. "I am just surprised by it all."

"Ah." He gave a playful smile and leaned closer, whispering directly into her ear. "Miss Miller, I am full of surprises."

The warmth of his breath sent a current of heat through her, making her fingers and toes tingle. She didn't dare look at him.

"Oh! Look there!" Alice said, managing to somehow shout in a quiet voice.

It gave Elizabeth an excuse to step quicker. Her skin burned. Lord Chatsworth was playing again. She must force herself not to react.

When she reached Alice, Mr. McDuff and Mr. Fitzwaring were beside her. "Another robin," Mr. Fitzwaring said. "You 'ave excellent eyes, miss."

They soon came to the tree where the red-backed shrike had sat the evening before, but the bird wasn't there. Elizabeth glanced to the mossy spot, remembering the feel of Lord Chatsworth's hand around hers.

They searched the area, listening and looking among the branches, and finally the West Sussex Order of the Friends of Fowl and Feathers admitted defeat. They had been in the woods for hours without one glimpse of the red-backed shrike.

"We saw some very special birds today," one of the Misses Leavenworth said, trying to reassure the group.

"Miss Alice spotted near to twelve robins," Mr. McDuff said, patting Alice on the back.

They started back toward the manor house, and Lord Chatsworth walked with Elizabeth again. "You will all stay for luncheon, I hope," he said.

There were grateful agreements at the invitation, but Elizabeth could feel the group's disappointment. "I wish we could have found it," she said, feeling disheartened herself. Lord Chatsworth had been so eager to show the bird to his friends.

"It happens more often than not," he said. "Birds don't stay in one place, and that's what makes it challeng—"

"Shush!" Elizabeth cut him off. She tilted her head, trying to catch the sound again.

"I appreciate the effort," he said, "but—"

She put her fingers over his mouth to quiet him and looked in the direction of the sound. "Do you hear it?" she whispered almost soundlessly.

His lips moved into a smile beneath her fingers, but the call came again and he stilled, tipping his head.

Their eyes met, and they both grinned.

"This way," Elizabeth said quietly. She started off toward the sound as he alerted the others to follow.

Her heart pumped hard, and she knew it was not fully from the thrill of hearing the shrike's call. She balled her hands. Her fingers still felt the waxed bristles of Lord Chatsworth's mustache and the softness of his lips. Who would have known a man's lips would be soft? She shook her head, trying to dislodge the thoughts and focus on the bird's call. It was louder now, and based on the whispers from those behind her, the others heard it too.

Elizabeth walked slower as she got near the sound, not wanting to scare the bird away. She located the tree from which it came and stopped, scanning the branches. The others clustered around, spyglasses moving like antennae.

Mr. Fitzwaring pointed, and the eyes and spyglasses turned to focus in the direction he indicated. There was a flurry of whispers and the scratch of writing in notebooks.

Lord Chatsworth held his spyglass out to her, and Elizabeth accepted it and squinted through it. When she finally spotted the bird, her shoulders dropped and she frowned. This bird was more simply colored. They hadn't found the red-backed shrike after all. She handed back the spyglass, feeling as if she'd let the group down. "It's not the same bird."

Lord Chatsworth smiled and leaned close to whisper, "She's a female." He motioned back to the bird.

A commotion started among the birding group. Some whispered loudly, pointing. Others shushed them. Spyglasses moved back and forth.

Lord Chatsworth tapped her shoulder and pointed. The bird she recognized from the previous day flew toward the tree, its mouth filled with long grasses. Once it landed, the female joined him.

"Thair buildin' a nest," Alice whispered, slipping back into her country speech in her excitement.

From where they stood, the group had a clear view of the birds as they brought more building material, then shaped it into a suitable nest. They watched for nearly an hour before their stomachs started to complain and they deemed their birding adventure complete for the day.

This time the trek back had a different energy. The group chatted about the shrikes, excited to see the eggs and fledglings throughout the spring.

"I'll need to return with Alice," Lord Chatsworth said, coming to walk beside Elizabeth.

"She will like that." She squashed down the hope that she might accompany them as well. She had responsibilities in London and couldn't just run off to Sussex to check on a bird family. Besides, she would be deluding herself if she believed Lord Chatsworth would wish to bring her again. It was a silly thought.

She could feel him looking at her but didn't turn her head, concentrating instead on maintaining her footing on the forest floor.

Mr. McDuff joined them, and Elizabeth slowed, letting herself fall behind so the men could talk. "I'd never o' believed it, Yer Lordship. A red-backed shrike. Right 'ere in Sussex."

"I was surprised myself," Lord Chatsworth said.

"She's a good-luck charm, 'at one." Mr. McDuff glanced back at Elizabeth and smiled.

Lord Chatsworth looked back as well. "My good man, I believe you are right."

His smile lit up the forest, warming Elizabeth's skin and making her heart do a slow roll. She smiled back—it would be impossible not to—but part of her ached, and another part of her was furious at the aching part for allowing this to happen at all. She knew better than to let herself develop feelings for someone like Lord Chatsworth. But, apparently, her heart had other ideas.

CHAPTER 12

CHARLES ROSE FROM HIS DESK after spending an entire morning reading through tenement contracts. He had known, of course, that leaving London for a few days didn't mean he could forget about his obligations entirely. And he still had a masquerade party to plan. The work had taken longer than he'd expected, and with the spring sun shining, he was restless to be outside.

He walked to the window, looking down over the garden, and smiled when he saw Miss Miller sitting with Alice on a blanket beneath a willow. The girl was reading aloud from her guidebook.

Five days had passed since they'd found the red-backed shrike's nest. The three of them, occasionally accompanied by a member of the Order of the Friends of Fowl and Feather, had returned each morning to monitor the status of the birds' nest. Although it was too high up in the tree for them to see inside it, Charles was certain there were eggs. The last two days the female had remained on the nest the entire time they were near while the male chirped and flapped around them, trying to draw their attention away.

The day before, Elizabeth had looked through the spyglass. "I know where the nest is, but I still have such a hard time seeing it."

Alice had taken the opportunity to tell them about camouflage, explaining that the reason the female didn't have the same bright plumage as the male was to make it more difficult for predators to discover her when she sat on the nest. Charles could not have been more pleased at her love of animals. Neither of his other siblings had shown the slightest interest in birds, but Alice had taken to birding as if she were meant to do it. Charles smiled, watching as the girl showed Miss Miller a page in the guidebook.

Miss Miller nodded, pointing at something on the page. Charles didn't know if she was truly interested or simply being kind. Either way, he approved.

Miss Miller had been the perfect companion for Alice on their adventures. And he'd found he enjoyed her company quite a lot as well.

Over the past days Charles, Alice, and Miss Miller had traveled to the marsh with Mr. McDuff, finding ducks, warblers, and sandpipers. They had explored the meadows of the downs, seeing larks and soaring hawks.

Mrs. Snowden had been invited to join their excursions, but the nanny had claimed her body was not capable of trekking through the wilderness for hours at a time. It was no matter. Charles preferred it with just himself, Alice, and Miss Miller. The three of them got along well together.

Outside, beneath the willow, Alice lay down and Miss Miller leaned back on her hands. They looked up through the willow's branches, and Alice pointed at something. She expanded her spyglass and looked up through it.

Although he could not see her face in the shade of the tree, Charles knew Miss Miller was smiling at the girl. Her mannerisms were becoming familiar to him, he realized.

He remembered the feel of her fingers on his lips in the woods. He'd done the same to her before, covering up her mouth, but at the time, he'd been thinking of nothing besides quieting her so he could listen to the bird's call. Her touch had been sudden, sending a thrill through him that had caught him so off guard, he'd almost forgotten what they were doing in the forest in the first place.

He brushed his finger over his mustache. It hadn't been the actual touch as much as the way her eyes had brightened and her cheeks flushed in excitement when she recognized the call of the red-backed shrike. Seeing it, his impulse had been to kiss her, which had jolted him as much as hearing the bird.

He'd had similar reactions to young ladies before, but this felt different somehow, more genuine. Perhaps it was because the moment had come about naturally instead of being manufactured by elegant decor, music, and flirting. But it couldn't be because he was developing an affection for the lady. That idea was preposterous. She didn't even like him, though he was nearly certain she no longer despised him. And they assuredly moved in different social circles, which made an affection for her impractical.

But as he walked down the stairs and across the garden to join them, Charles couldn't keep the memory from returning, and it was made even stronger when Miss Miller looked up, saw him approaching, and waved.

Alice had fallen asleep, spyglass in one hand.

Charles's heart warmed. He eased down onto the blanket next to Miss Miller. The view of the gardens from this spot was marvelous. Tulips, daffodils, and lilacs already bloomed, and overhead, trees were in various stages of blossom. "Lovely morning, isn't it?" he said quietly so as not to disturb Alice.

"It is lovely," Miss Miller agreed. "This garden, the woods . . . I was thinking how very pleasant your childhood must have been here."

A memory came into his thoughts: Mother sitting in the garden, painting, while he and Leonard chased one another along the paths and Kathryn slept in a pram in the shade. "It was, for the most part." He couldn't remember his father spending time with the family at Ashbury Park, and what Charles had later discovered of him had tinged all the earlier memories with an ache that hadn't been there when he was a child. He hadn't noticed until much later that his mother's smiles had always been sad.

"I've never asked about your family," Miss Miller said. "I've met your grandmother, of course. You also have a brother and a sister?"

"Two sisters," he said, pointing at Alice. "You are already acquainted with the youngest." He didn't miss the flash of curiosity in Miss Miller's eyes, but he didn't pause to explain. "The other is Kathryn. She is seventeen years old and preparing for her debut into Society. My brother is Leonard. At twenty-four, he is closer to my age." He looked again at Alice, then at Miss Miller. "And what of yourself? What of your family?"

"My childhood was rather lonely," she said. "I have no siblings, and my da' died when I was four. After that it was just Mother and me. She was typically away working."

"And what did you do while she was away?" His earlier curiosity about the girl in the woods rekindled.

Miss Miller shrugged. "I took care of our room, cleaned the floor, dusted the furniture, and helped Mrs. Porter, the owner of our boardinghouse. She must have felt sorry for me, spending so much time alone, and sent me on errands to the woodbox, the market, the apothecary."

"You attended school?"

"When I was older. There was no girls' school within walking distance a child could manage." She glanced at him. "But Mother made certain I was always learning. When she had a respite from work, we visited the lending library in Wolverhampton. She was determined I should read as much as possible to make up for my lack of schooling." Miss Miller scrunched the woolen blanket in her hand and then pressed it flat as she spoke. "Things were always difficult financially, but Mother still put away the money she earned, saved all she could to send me to school. She told me my da' wished for me to be educated, to have a chance for a better life, away from the factories."

"And now you provide the same opportunity for the girls in Spitalfields. That is very admirable."

She looked at him, a small smile on her face.

The idea of kissing her came into his thoughts again. Charles turned back toward the garden.

"I have you to thank for that," she said. "For supporting the school. And your grandmother and everyone who funded the endeavor. Especially my uncle and Dahlia. I could never have managed it on my own." She let out a breath, grimacing. "I hadn't meant to share so much. I apologize."

"No need for an apology." He bent a knee, resting his arm on it, and faced her more completely. "I am interested in what you have to say. Please, continue. Tell me about your uncle. I confess to knowing him only a little."

Miss Miller looked down at where her hands rested in her lap. "He has been sick for as long as I can remember. And lately he's been growing worse. Dahlia wishes he would go to a sanatorium—there is a doctor in Switzerland who claims he can heal tuberculosis—but Uncle Eldon doesn't want to leave us all to die alone in the mountains."

"I'm sorry to hear it. A difficult time for the family, surely. Miss Lancaster must be very happy to have you there with her."

Miss Miller looked up at the willow. She breathed in and out, swallowing hard. "She and my group of dear friends have been—" Her voice cracked, and she swallowed again. "I suppose I do have sisters after all," she said softly. Her eyes were bright when she looked at him, her smile gentle.

A tear looked close to spilling over, and Charles fisted his hand to keep from wiping it away. "You certainly take care of Miss Lancaster, from what I've seen. She is lucky to have you as a defender."

Miss Miller's head tipped. She looked confused for an instant, and then her face cleared as she realized to what he was referring. "The conjuring show. You were there." She scowled. "How dare that horrible man embarrass her like that!"

"He was very out of line, pointing her out so publicly," Charles agreed.

"I am speaking of Lord Ruben."

Miss Miller's face had darkened, her eyes flashing and her expression the complete reverse of what it had been only a few seconds earlier. And, surprisingly, it caused a similar reaction inside him. The depth of Miss Miller's emotions was intoxicating.

"I know he is your friend, so I will hold my tongue, except to say that he treated Dahlia very badly, and the insult is still felt to this day."

"I agree with you," he said. He thought of the affection Ruben and Miss Lancaster had shared a year earlier. The man had been in love; Charles knew it. Everyone knew it. But in the end, Ruben had chosen a title, alliances, property over sentiment. And he was miserable for it. "Miss Lancaster did not deserve such treatment."

Miss Miller's expression hadn't softened. She scowled even tighter, pulling up her knees beneath her skirts and putting her arms around them. "Men like them . . . Lord Ruben, Lord Lockhart . . . they are reprehensible."

Charles was glad not to have been included in the list, but still, her words were harsher than he'd expected. Especially toward Lockhart. "I understand your dislike of Lord Ruben, but why Lord Lockhart? Has he offended you personally? Or is it his politics you detest?"

"He is the head of the committee evaluating and reporting the needs of London's poor to the House of Lords—which, of course you know—and he has a record of voting against any measure that will improve government-assisted programs in their behalf." She glanced at him, then went back to glaring at the garden. "He has shown himself to be completely apathetic to the suffering of people who need him."

Arguments flooded into Charles's thoughts, but he did not give them voice. The issue was a complex one, and Miss Miller was not in the state of mind to have her opinions changed with reasoning. Besides, in a way, she was right. Lord Lockhart did consistently vote in opposition to poor relief. But Charles didn't believe it to be cruelty on his part or a desire to keep taxes low for the middle classes. In reality the man was overanxious to please, which made him vulnerable to pressure from men, such as Lord Tynsdale, who used less assertive men as their pawns.

Charles realized Miss Miller watched him, waiting for a response. "You are correct about his voting record," he said. "But do you think publicly shaming him the best way to convince him to reevaluate?"

"I did write letters," she said. "But they made no difference." Still, she looked less certain. Seeing him watching her, she schooled her expression into a scowl. "I should have made a bigger sign."

He laughed. "Your point was made quite succinctly."

She allowed a small smile.

She seemed calmer, so Charles thought she might listen now. "Lockhart may be the head of the committee, but Tynsdale's the one you should watch out for. He is cunning and vengeful. Lockhart is all bluster. Politically, he is still trying to find his footing. His elder brother died suddenly, and he wasn't prepared to take on the title and its accompanying duties. If he'd had his way, he'd have remained in academia. If I remember correctly, I believe he was involved in some type of scientific experimentation at the university."

"I did not know that." Miss Miller blinked, and her brows lifted. "I have never thought of him as anything but a cruel tyrant. Perhaps my sign was a bit hostile."

Charles was surprised by her concession. "You are angry," he said. "And understandably so. These are the people you associate with on a daily basis, and you hope for an improvement to their lives."

She nodded, laying her knees to the side and leaning on one hand. "How would you go about it if you were in my position? How would you change the minds of men who don't understand? How would you get through to them?"

Charles pondered for a moment before answering. "Being associated with both high Society and the poorest residents of the city, you have a unique perspective. Your advice would be useful to Lord Lockhart's committee."

"But he won't listen to me." She blew out a frustrated huff. "None of them will."

"You've injured his pride," Charles pointed out. "That will be difficult to repair." He rubbed his mustache. "In my experience, people are more willing to listen when they feel as if they are appreciated."

She drew in a quick breath, but he held out a hand before she let loose her argument.

"I don't mean you should flatter him or pander to his ego. Lord Lockhart is moved by the same things that move us all. Feeling wanted, feeling important. Human beings crave love."

Her eyes went wide, and her lip curled as she stared at him. "You think I should *love* Lord Rockheart?"

Charles chuckled at the horror on her face. "Not romantically, of course. But he may be less inclined to be oppositional if he felt he weren't constantly under attack. Lord Lockhart navigates a wider river than you know. Offer him a bridge."

Miss Miller studied him as if trying to see whether there was more to his words than he was saying. In truth, Charles didn't fully understand why her cause suddenly felt so important.

"I would think inheriting a peerage would be enough to make a person feel appreciated," she grumbled.

"You might be surprised in that." Charles pursed his lips, thinking of his friends, of the young ladies in Society, with their false compliments and fawning. None of it ever rang true.

"In what way?" Some of the fire returned to Miss Miller's eyes. "Lord Lockhart is a man. Not just a man but a powerful one with wealth and connections. Surely it is enough and he doesn't need to be reminded that people are fond of him."

"Would it be enough for you?" Charles asked. He thought again of Ruben. His marriage to Lady Lorene would connect two of the wealthiest estates in the country. He would own more land and assets than nearly anyone in the kingdom. But land did not make a person happy. Assets did not return affection. "Would it be enough to have money and power but no relationships to make life worthwhile?"

"I don't know," she said, "but I wouldn't mind trying it."

Charles remembered his mother's sad eyes. "Our connections, the people we love—they are everything. A poor man with love is wealthier than a lonely king."

"I feel like I've upset you." She looked confused at the direction the conversation had taken. "It wasn't my intention. I let my frustrations—"

Charles kissed her. And everything else fell away. He hadn't intended to do it. It had happened without him even thinking. As soon as he had, it felt right, as if it were the culmination of everything he'd wanted. This touch. This woman.

He pulled away, feeling vulnerable, exposed, as her gaze took him in while a myriad of expressions moved over her faze. Expressions he couldn't interpret. Was she angry? Offended? His heart dropped. "I beg your pardon. I shouldn't have—"

Miss Miller leaned forward, closing the distance between them, her mouth on his. The smell of her filled up his senses, and the feel of her lips was the only thing in the world. He slipped a hand beneath her ear, his thumb brushing her cheek. She leaned against his palm, tipping her head to the side, deepening the kiss and sending heat flowing through him.

Without warning, she suddenly went still, her body rigid.

He blinked himself back into awareness as she pulled away.

Alice stirred and rubbed her eyes. "Oh, Charles, is it time to check the nest?" She yawned. "Where is your spyglass?"

"I must have forgotten it," he said. His thoughts were moving slowly. He glanced at Miss Miller, taking satisfaction in the flush that covered her skin and the dazed look in her eyes.

"No matter." Alice stood. "You can share mine."

Charles rose, offering a hand to Miss Miller.

She took it, standing, and then bent to pick up the blanket.

Alice looked toward the woods. "Are you coming, Miss Miller?"

"I just remembered some correspondence I need to see to," Miss Miller responded. She shook out the blanket, folding it over her arm. "You'll tell me all about it when you return?"

"Of course we will," Alice said. She took Charles's hand.

Miss Miller bid them farewell and started toward the house.

Charles and Alice continued in the other direction. He glanced back toward Miss Miller, and their gazes met for just an instant. But it was long enough for something to pass between them. A feeling that was both thrilling and comfortable, a longing and a dizziness. A feeling that made Charles fear that he may have accidentally fallen in love.

CHAPTER 13

RAIN POURED DOWN, EXTINGUISHING ANY hopes of visiting the forest. Elizabeth stared from the window of her bedchamber, picking at her breakfast tray and watching the drops slide on the glass with unfocused eyes. Lord Chatsworth had kissed her the day before. He had *kissed* her. Lord Chatsworth, the flirt, the cad, the man who never allowed a serious thought to take up residence in his mind, whose smile was worshiped by London Society, the man who teased relentlessly. He had kissed her. And what was more, she had kissed him back.

She was still attempting to sort her thoughts on the matter. Was it possible to be both drawn to a person and repelled by them at the same time? She knew she shouldn't have allowed the kiss. She should have stopped it, been furious, accused him of being a scoundrel. But in the moment, she'd wanted nothing more than to be close, to feel his lips on hers. Was she so lonely? Or were her earlier opinions of Lord Chatsworth so very changed? She couldn't tell. Everything felt so muddled, and whenever she thought of their kiss, her heart swelled and she wanted to sigh or throw something or perhaps swoon.

She chided herself. It was all foolishness. Lord Chatsworth certainly thought nothing of it. He probably kissed every woman he could when the opportunity presented itself. It was likely simply a habit of his and she merely a conquest. Her cheeks burned as she thought of him writing her name on a list as he did with the different bird species. Was she simply a tally in his book?

Humiliation spread, hot in her belly. Well, if that was the case, she would not let him see that the kiss had meant something more to her. She would make a list of her own. So far there was only his name, but Lord Chatsworth didn't need to know that.

Above all she wouldn't allow him to see that the kiss had affected her. Holding her head high, she left the room and made her way to the library. As she'd expected, Alice was inside, reading to Mrs. Snowden, who sat beside her, knitting.

The girl's face lit up when Elizabeth stepped into the doorway. "Good morning, Miss Miller." She was making such progress with her speech that Elizabeth could hardly make out any trace of her Black Country accent.

"Avast!" Elizabeth said. "Is that Captain Sharkfin?"

"Aye," Alice said. She brandished an imaginary sword, raising it into the air, then pointing it toward the sofa. "Sit down, scurvy dog! And I will read to you about the cape penguins of South Africa." She lowered her booming voice. "They are very charming." She turned around the book, showing an illustration. "See here? They look as if they are wearing dinner coats."

Elizabeth greeted Mrs. Snowden and sat on the sofa, settling in for what she knew would be a barrage of facts about the animals and their behaviors, habitats, and characteristics.

After an hour Mrs. Foster came into the room, carrying a tray of sandwiches. "Ladies, the luncheon meal will be delayed today. His Lordship received word this morning informing him that Lady Kathryn and Mr. Seaton plan to arrive early this afternoon." She set the tray on the low table in front of them. "In the meantime, I thought you might need something to tide you over."

"Thank you," Elizabeth said.

"Where is Charles?" Alice asked, picking up a sandwich.

"He rode to the train station with Mr. Davies to greet his brother and sister."

"Lady Kathryn is very elegant, Miss Miller," Alice said. "She is to have her debut this year and has purchased heaps of gowns and stockings and hairpieces for all the balls she will attend."

Elizabeth tried to decipher the girl's expression as she spoke of Lord Chatsworth's sister—*her* sister. She obviously admired the woman, but a nervousness tightened her smile.

"I will be very happy to meet her." Elizabeth knew nothing about Lady Kathryn, but she had seen Mr. Seaton occasionally, though they had never been introduced. He was often featured in the society column as a particular friend of Prince Leopold's. The young man was apparently a patron of the arts and literature as well as quite adept at chess. It was no wonder the prince sought his company. The two were reputed to be very much alike.

They heard the carriage pulling up below an hour later, and Elizabeth and Alice glimpsed the company's arrival through the library's blurry windows.

Davies stopped the carriage in front of the manor, then jumped down to open the door.

Footmen hurried out, holding umbrellas for the members of the Chatsworth family. "Kathryn and Leonard," Alice told Elizabeth as the woman and man hurried inside. Lord Chatsworth remained outside a moment longer, speaking to the carriage driver before the man returned to the driver's seat and drove away.

Elizabeth's heart apparently hadn't understood her resolution not to react to him, and she pressed the inside of her wrist against her breastbone in an attempt to calm her heart's rapid beating.

Soon after, Mrs. Foster returned, announcing luncheon would be served.

Alice took Elizabeth's hand as they walked down the staircase. The girl seemed anxious, and Elizabeth couldn't tell whether she herself was nervous or excited by the new arrivals.

Voices were already coming from inside the dining room.

"The dress shops in London have nothing but the same dull, ordinary gowns everyone will be wearing." A young woman was speaking—Lady Kathryn, Elizabeth assumed. "I will surely find some unique items in Brighton. Charles, you simply must come with me. Leonard knows nothing about fashionable cuts or which feathers one must wear in her hair."

"You're right about that," a man—probably Mr. Seaton—responded.

Elizabeth and Alice came into the dining room, and the men stood from their seats at the table.

Kathryn glanced at the new arrivals but did not show any interest.

"I'm so glad you could join us." Lord Chatsworth held Elizabeth's gaze an instant longer than was polite, and her heart tripped. He motioned toward the table. "Leonard, Kathryn, this is Miss Elizabeth Miller, Alice's diction tutor. Miss Miller, please meet my sister, Lady Kathryn, and my brother, Mr. Leonard Seaton."

"I am very pleased to meet you." Elizabeth dipped in a curtsy.

Kathryn glanced at her again. "A pleasure."

"How do you do, Miss Miller?" Mr. Seaton inclined his head, looking only slightly more interested than his sister, but Elizabeth got the impression that he was distracted rather than unfriendly.

Lord Chatsworth's mouth tightened. He cleared his throat as if to remind them of something. "And it is very nice to see Alice, is it not?"

The siblings greeted Alice with noticeable indifference.

Lord Chatsworth's mouth tightened further.

Alice took a seat beside Lady Kathryn, and Elizabeth sat across from her, next to Mr. Seaton. The meal was served, and the smell of hot steak pie filled the room. A perfect meal for a dreary, cold day.

"As I was saying, Charles," Kathryn said. "You really should come to Brighton. Lady Lorene's favorite dressmaker has a shop there, and I simply must find some new gowns. We could stay at the Grand Hotel and drink iced lemonade on the pier."

"I'm sorry, Kathryn." His Lordship cut into his pie. "I am obligated to return to London."

Kathryn blew out a frustrated breath that sent the curls on her forehead bouncing.

"Alice, shall we tell them about the birds we found this week?" Lord Chatsworth said, smiling at the girl.

"Oh yes!" Alice spoke carefully and clearly. "We have found a red-backed shrike nest and visited it every day. And Mr. McDuff took us on an expedition to the marsh. A pity we couldn't go to the seaside today to find shorebirds."

"It is a pity indeed," Lord Chatsworth replied. He took another bite of his pie.

Alice watched Kathryn from the corner of her eye, dabbing her napkin on her lips exactly as her half sister did.

"But Charles says we will return soon," Alice said. The girl seemed much more confident with her speech and eager to show it off.

Kathryn darted a look at Lord Chatsworth, and the young lady's face fell.

Elizabeth didn't think His Lordship noticed. She looked between the sisters, one desperate to please the woman next to her and the other longing for the attention of her elder brother. Instead of resentment for Lady Kathryn, Elizabeth felt sympathy. It seemed Alice's arrival had displaced her. No wonder she showed such disregard for the younger girl.

"And how have you enjoyed Sussex, Miss Miller?" Mr. Seaton said.

"I've enjoyed it very much," Elizabeth replied. She was surprised the man had remembered her name. He'd certainly not seemed to be paying her any mind when they'd been introduced. She wondered again if he was preoccupied. "The forest is beautiful, and I have enjoyed the gardens very much."

Mr. Seaton nodded as if he'd done his polite duty in making conversation and could now let his attention return to his former thoughts.

"We have been very fortunate to have Miss Miller's company, have we not, Alice?" Lord Chatsworth said.

Elizabeth felt heat rising up her neck as their eyes met again. He seemed to have no qualms about fixing her with his gaze.

"Yes," Alice replied. "Miss Miller is the one who found the nest in the first place."

Kathryn was scowling at her food. But as Alice spoke, she looked up at Elizabeth. "Miss Miller—is that what you said your name is?"

"Yes," Elizabeth said.

"Oh, I believe I have a letter for you." She called for a footman, directing him to fetch her handbag. "The conductor was going to send it off with the postman, but when he learned Davies was to bring us to Ashbury Park . . ." She took the bag the footman brought, opening it and digging inside until she found what she was looking for. She handed the letter to Elizabeth.

The return stationery and Mrs. Boyle's handwriting indicated it was from the school. Not unsurprising. But when Elizabeth turned it over, the word *URGENT* jumped out at her from the paper.

Something was wrong. The steak pie churned in her stomach. "I am very sorry to be rude, but I think I need to read this now." She pushed back her chair and stood.

The men stood as well.

Lord Chatsworth's brows furrowed at her abruptness, but he didn't inquire.

Elizabeth hurried up the stairs, moving into the library, where the sun was beginning to break through the clouds, warming the room through the large windows.

She cracked the wax seal, opening the letter. According to the date, it had been written four days earlier.

My Dear Headmistress,

Upon inquiry into the absences of many of our students, we learned that the factories in Spitalfields have reversed their policies in regards to the girls' work shifts. If they do not work every day, their employment will be revoked. The teachers and I have been unable to gain audience with the foremen. And since they've lost their former arrangement of half-time employment, the girls are unable to attend school.

I beg you, for the children's sake, to return promptly.

Yours,
Ethel Boyle

Elizabeth sat hard on a chair. Her insides felt heavy. *It is so unfair.* Over the past nine months since she'd opened the school, she'd been met by obstacle after obstacle. Was it always to be this way? She thought of the girls—*her girls*—threading looms, climbing into and beneath dangerous machinery, working with toxic chemicals, when they should be in school, reading, learning arithmetic, preparing for a life full of opportunities. She never should have left them.

As her thoughts solidified, she started to plan. Of course she must return to London immediately. She did not know the train schedule, but she could surely leave today, or tomorrow morning at the latest. She would speak with the factory foremen, and if they were unwilling to talk, she would appeal to whomever the foremen reported to. Lord Benedict would know the noblemen who owned the factories. And he would undoubtedly petition them on her behalf.

She folded the letter and started off to find Mrs. Foster, rushing out of the library.

"Miss Miller?" Lord Chatsworth's voice came from behind her.

Elizabeth turned.

"What has happened?" He came toward her, clasping her elbows. "Is it your uncle?"

She shook her head. "It is the school." Anger and frustration clogged her throat, making her voice catch. She swallowed hard against the lump.

"My dear, you are pale." Lord Chatsworth led her back to the library. "Come, sit down and tell me what has happened." He spoke gently, and the sound made the ache inside her grow until it cracked as they sat together on the nearest sofa.

"The girls—the students—are gone." Her voice turned into a sob, and there were tears. She wiped them away, embarrassment making her emotions even more volatile. "They have to return to the factories."

He produced a handkerchief, pressing it into her hand.

Elizabeth took it, dabbing her damp cheeks. "It is so unfair." She choked on the words. "By law, boys can attend school and work half time with no penalty, but . . ." She squeezed her eyes closed. "Why must the world always be more difficult for girls?"

"But the students had been working half time," he said. "What changed?"

"Nothing that I can think of." She was glad he thought through the problem logically. It gave her something to hold on to when she felt like she was drowning. "I left, but I don't see how that—" She stopped as the truth became clear. "Lord Lockhart," she said.

Lord Chatsworth brushed a finger over his mustache as he watched her. His brows drew together. "What has he to do with this?"

"Don't you see?" The more Elizabeth thought about it, the more certain she was that it must be so. "He did this. First with the excess taxes and now the factories. It must be him." She jumped to her feet, nearly knocking him backward with the movement.

Lord Chatsworth shook his head. "This isn't Lord Lockhart's doing. Tax increases are not new. And all businesses are feeling repercussions from the rise in interest rates. It is a byproduct of the word's economy, not a scheme meant to sabotage a girls' school. Come, sit down, and I'll send for tea." He stood, too, and took her arm, pulling her gently back to the sofa.

Elizabeth slapped his hand away. Lord Chatsworth wasn't taking her seriously. He was mocking her. Heat flooded through her, and her body went tense. "You could not possibly understand." She shot the words at him like darts. "I don't need tea. You men think you can fix everything. You can't know what I need." Her angry tears were back, but she didn't brush them away this time. "I have fought for every single gain in my life. And men like Lord Lockhart have impeded me each step of my way." She rubbed her hands over her face. "Men make every decision, and women are always on the losing end. My entire life was controlled by one man of title. The *Most Honorable* Marquess Lord Hubbard's delicate sensibilities were hurt by my mother's rejection of his advances. And he executed his revenge on a poor widow, taking everything from her—from us—in one fell swoop. His action changed our courses forever. It destroyed my mother, and she never recovered." She shook her head against the memory. "And now that I've finally found a way to give women a chance to claim their own futures, it is happening again."

"I'm sorry." He spoke quietly. "I know what it is to lose a mother. It is devastating. I understand—"

"You *don't* understand." Elizabeth was working herself into a fury, her voice rising as years of pent-up anger was released. "You will never understand. How could you, sitting here in your grand manor house with your imported-silk handkerchiefs?" She shook the handkerchief and motioned with a wave of her arms at the house around them, at the shelves of books, each costing more than her mother's yearly wages. "You've no idea what it's like to lose everything on one man's whim. You don't understand, because you were fortunate enough to be born male. Not only that, you were born here, to this family, this wealth, this perfectly marvelous life." She motioned around again. Her words came out as sobs, and she sniffed, wiping her dripping nose on the imported-silk handkerchief.

"I know what it's like to feel trapped," he said. His face had lost every bit of charm as his mask fell away, leaving behind something Elizabeth recognized. Pain.

"From the instant I was born my life was determined—my duty, my future. Every tutor, every playmate, the very clothes I wore were decisions made for the good of the Chatsworth estate, for the good of the family, for the future earl. Not for Charles. Never for Charles." He waved his hands in the same manner she'd done a moment earlier. "No decision was made based on my personal happiness, even as a child, only on what would improve my ability to serve as head of the family, to protect the estate, to ensure future generations. Unlike you, Elizabeth, I had no choice in my life's direction." He worked a muscle in his jaw and swallowed. "I don't own this house. It owns me."

His words and the emotion behind them surprised her. But Elizabeth was far too agitated to allow them to have their desired effect. She breathed heavily, and they stood watching one another, vulnerable, as their words hung heavy in the air.

Elizabeth wanted to rush into his arms, to let him hold her, to ease his pain while he soothed hers. But she couldn't. The wounds she'd hidden away were exposed, but she wasn't willing to allow anyone, least of all a nobleman, to soothe them. Doing so would require both trust and letting go of her own pride. And she couldn't do that. Her pride was all she had.

So she left.

CHAPTER 14

THREE DAYS AFTER RETURNING TO London, Charles walked through his London dining room and crossed the entry hall to the drawing room, astonished at the changes that had been made in such a short time.

The woman beside him exuded an air of competent organization, making notes in a notebook and giving instructions to the workers still rushing around as she showed him the decor for the masquerade soiree.

The Planner of Events, Parties, and Peculiar Festivities had come highly recommended, and from what he could see, the endorsement was entirely justified. The rooms had been entirely transformed into an Egyptian oasis, complete with black-and-gold pillars, draped linens, and potted palmetto trees. Chairs were arranged in one corner for the musicians. The drawing room furniture had been cleared away, leaving only seating around the edges and a dance floor in the center, and the dining room table was decorated with greenery, black linens, painted parchment, and urns of various shapes and sizes. And there was even a wall of painted scenes and hieroglyphics.

"Mrs. Hopewell, you have quite outdone yourself," Charles said.

"Thank you, Your Lordship," Mrs. Hopewell said, turning a page in her notebook and making a mark. "Your costume was delivered this afternoon." She glanced at the pocket watch that hung from her neck. "If you'll excuse me, I should check on the food. Your guests will arrive within the hour."

Charles thanked her again and started up the stairs to don his costume, wishing he felt more enthusiastic about the upcoming festivities. The soiree had sounded so diverting at the time he'd suggested it. But, even with Mrs. Hopewell's assistance, the planning had taken hours, which, along with his regular parliamentary meetings and estate duties, had made him feel neglectful of Alice. He'd hardly seen the girl since returning. Luckily, grandmother had returned from Bath and was delighted to spend time with Alice again, which did ease his guilt somewhat.

When he reached the top of the stairs, he paused on the landing, remembering meeting Miss Miller in this very spot after Alice's first speech lesson. How was it possible that everything reminded him of the woman? It was as if his mind were trying to torment him.

Miss Miller had managed to avoid him when she'd come for Alice's tutoring the day before. And he'd avoided her as well. Their last interaction had left him unsettled. He'd attempted to be understanding, chivalrous, even. But his behavior had been misunderstood—she'd thought him patronizing, and the situation had only devolved from there. He'd been angry by her response and hurt at her lack of trust. But in her anger, she'd also confided in him. She'd been vulnerable at the very same time that she was shutting him out, which had left him confused and—as was becoming habit when it came to Miss Elizabeth Miller—frustrated.

She had left for London that evening, without a farewell.

He rubbed his forehead as if the action could erase his thoughts. Everything had become complicated when he'd allowed his emotions to get involved. He was Charles Seaton, eleventh Lord Chatsworth. His duty was to increase the prestige of his lineage by aligning himself with a noblewoman who brought with her a sizeable dowry and thereafter to produce an heir. It had always been thus. Letting himself develop feelings for a teacher had been a mistake.

His valet assisted him in dressing, brushing the woolen coat with its war medals. As a final touch, he settled a white wig over Charles's hair.

The man stepped aside, and Charles studied the ensemble in the mirror. When the tailor had suggested the costume of George Washington, Charles had thought it a brilliant idea. He turned to the side, admiring the epaulets on his shoulders and running his fingers over the silk sash that crossed his breast. Charles had to admit he cut quite a dashing figure dressed in the uniform of the first president of the United States during his time as general of the Continental Army.

He thanked the valet and went to his grandmother's sitting room. He had enough time to bid her and Alice good night before the guests arrived.

When he stepped inside, he chuckled, once again grateful that his grandmother had returned. She and Alice sat on the floor, lounging on cushions. A tablecloth was spread over the carpet, with finger foods arranged on small plates.

"Have I stumbled into a sultan's palace?" Charles asked.

Grandmother's brows rose when she saw him. "Oh my. Aren't you a handsome General Washington?"

Charles rested a hand on his sword's hilt and posed.

Alice clapped.

Grandmother motioned toward a pile of cushions. "Won't you join us?"

"Please, Charles, do," Alice said.

Charles sat on the sofa near them. "I'm afraid I can't tonight," he said. "But I shall give instructions for the party decor to remain, and tomorrow we shall dine in an Egyptian palace."

"Shall I wear a costume too?" Alice asked.

"I think we must." Grandmother shrugged as if there were no other option.

"May I watch the guests arrive, Charles?" Alice asked. "I will hide away on the landing where nobody will see me."

"You certainly may," he said.

Grandmother offered a plate of hothouse berries to Alice. "I am so pleased with your speech, my dear. You sound like a true lady."

"Actually, I am a pirate," Alice said.

"Oh yes?" Grandmother gave the girl an amused smile.

"It is a game she and Miss Miller devised," Charles explained.

"Ah, I see. Perhaps we shall find a pirate costume for supper tomorrow," Grandmother said.

"I should like that very much indeed." Alice spoke the words precisely, demonstrating her pronunciation.

Charles rose. "If you will excuse me, ladies . . ."

"Oh, I nearly forgot." Alice jumped up. She handed him a folded piece of fabric. His handkerchief. "Miss Miller asked me to give it to you," she said.

Charles stared at the handkerchief. It was folded carefully, and cleaned, he thought, since the last time he'd seen it Miss Miller had been wiping her face with it. His imported-silk handkerchief that she'd thought so extravagant. The corners of his mouth tugged as he remembered her words, and at the same time, the ache in his heart surprised him.

He cleared his throat, giving his head a little shake and tucking the handkerchief into his pocket.

"Charles?" Grandmother watched him with a look that was rather too perceptive for his peace of mind. She held out a hand, seeking his assistance.

He took it, helping her stand.

"I shall return in just a moment, Alice," Grandmother said. She took Charles's arm, walking with him out of her sitting room and toward the staircase.

Charles waited for her to speak.

When they reached the landing at the top of the staircase, she stopped, turning to face him. "You are very much like your grandfather, Charles." She smoothed his lapels. "You know you have his smile, his playful manner, his ease among company." She sighed. "But that was only the side of himself he allowed others to see. Privately, he was less . . . jovial." She looked toward the portrait of her late husband that hung among all the other Lords Chatsworth. "It is a heavy responsibility you bear as the earl. And I know you feel it. My Edward felt it as well."

"How did he manage it?" Charles asked. He stared at the portrait. Grandfather's eyes were soft and kind with a twinkle of mischief. Charles wished he could remember his grandfather.

"Edward knew what kind of man he wished to be," Grandmother said. "He hoped to live a life he could look back on with a smile. Understanding that informed the earl he was, the husband he was, the father he was."

Charles's eyes moved to the portrait of his own father, whose features were hard, impatient, greedy. He looked away, his gaze settling on his own portrait. What type of man did he wish to be?

"I think you know," Grandmother said, answering the question he hadn't asked aloud. She patted his cheek, her eyes shining.

The bell rang, and servants scuttled around below.

Alice came from the sitting room, eager to see the guests in their costumes.

But Charles remained where he was. He held his grandmother's gaze for a moment longer. She nodded, giving a proud smile that made a lump grow in his throat. He swallowed hard, looking down the stairs to where Nigel stood, ready to open the door.

Alice crouched in the shadows, hands on the balusters as she looked between them.

Grandmother joined her, kneeling on the floor.

Charles nodded to Nigel. He glanced at Grandfather Edward's portrait once more, and then he started down the stairs for his party.

The guests arrived, filling the rooms with color and excited chatter. The costumes varied from butterflies and fairies to French hussars and Roman senators.

Meredith stepped through the entrance, his heavy boots thumping on the floor. He wore a long leather coat, a stiff felt hat, and a kerchief around his neck in the guise of an American cowboy.

"Welcome," Charles greeted his friend, surveying his ensemble. "This suits you."

Meredith pulled at the brim of his hat, smiling. "Good evening, General."

The Darling Debs arrived, each wearing a costume representing one of the seasons.

Charles was surprised to see that Lorene had come with her friends rather than her fiancé. But Lord Ruben arrived soon after, wearing a doublet and hose and carrying a skull, his costume representing Prince Hamlet.

Charles greeted Marie Antoinette, a Scottish laird, and a woman wearing Turkish-style clothing, making small talk and easing into his role of smiling host. Benedict and his wife, Lady Covington, arrived, costumed as Napoleon and Josephine Bonaparte. She looked stunning, tall, and slender, wearing a cream-colored gown with an empire waist, in the style popular during the Regency era.

"I am delighted you could come," Charles said, patting his friend's shoulder.

"Thank you," Benedict said.

Charles pretended to push his friend out of the way. "I was, of course, speaking to Lady Covington." He took her gloved hand, bowing over it. "You look splendid this evening, my lady."

"Thank you." She flushed. "And thank you for the invitation. It is very diverting to dress in costume."

The few times Charles had met the former Miss Vivian Kirby, she had seemed shy and unsure. And while he still sensed her hesitance to say something that might be misinterpreted, she seemed to be more at ease with herself and her position.

Charles watched the couple walk through the entry hall. Lady Covington took her husband's arm, and he gave her a warm smile. The woman was a friend of Miss Miller's, and Charles wondered if Her Ladyship had told her friend about the party. Perhaps Miss Miller had made a recommendation about her costume.

Having greeted everyone, he nodded at Nigel, who closed the door. He peeked into the dining room, saw that the table was in order, and continued across the entry hall, where the guests were gathered in the drawing room. Footmen carried trays of hors d'oeuvres and wine. Charles wondered what costume Miss Miller might have chosen for herself. He ruled out fairies and butterflies. She would not want something so whimsical. His gaze traveled around the room, ruling out each costume in turn. Miss Miller would have selected something with meaning; he was sure of it. She would wish to represent someone important. A Dickensian character, he thought. Or Abraham Lincoln. He let the image of the young lady in a stovepipe hat and beard take shape in this thoughts and chuckled.

"And what brings such a smile to your face, my lord?" Lady Priscilla had come up beside him without his noticing.

"I am simply enjoying the view, my lady." He gestured at the gathering.

"Any view in particular?" She had moved much closer, the daffodils on her bodice brushing against his sleeve.

Charles looked down at her. Lady Priscilla's eyes were wide, her lips pouting prettily. There was a time he would have loved this game, this flirtation. But today it felt artificial, hollow. Out of habit, he smiled.

She smiled in return, taking his arm. "Come, you must circulate. As the host, it is your duty."

The word stung his ears, but he kept his pleasant expression. The pair moved through the room, stopping to exchange the occasional pleasantry. Charles was glad to see that everyone seemed to be visiting happily.

"Oh, Lady Tynsdale!" Lady Priscilla did not release her hold on Charles's arm but pulled him toward where her friend was visiting with a group of ladies. "What a marvelous costume. Let me guess. You are Titania, Queen of the Fairies."

"Yes," Lady Tynsdale said. She turned toward them and inclined her head carefully so as not to dislodge her floral crown. Her gown was made of layer upon layer of colorful diaphanous fabric, and attached to her shoulders was a silk cape, embroidered with vines, that the other guests were taking precautions not to step on. "Lord Chatsworth." She inclined her head again at Charles, then turned back to his companion. "You look splendid as well, Lady Priscilla." She gestured at the costume. "Having seen Miss Gray, Lady Lorene, and Miss Rothschild, I believe you complete the set. You are spring."

In response Lady Priscilla swished her flower-covered gown and gave a curtsy.

"And is Lord Tynsdale dressed as King Oberon?" Lady Priscilla craned her neck in an attempt to see over the crowd.

"He is, yes," Lady Tynsdale said. "I hoped he would consent to wear a donkey's head and assume the role of Bottom." She sighed. "But, as you are no doubt aware, His Lordship is not inclined toward humor."

Charles chuckled, sharing a knowing smile with the woman. Lord Tynsdale didn't have a playful bone in his body.

Lady Tynsdale looked over the crowd as well. "He is here somewhere, likely talking to Lord Ruben or Lord Hastings about some business matter or another. He wears antlers, so it should be easy to spot him . . ."

Charles saw Mrs. Hopewell giving a prearranged signal at the doorway. He excused himself, easing his arm from Lady Priscilla's hold, announced that dinner was ready, and requested they please follow him to the dining room.

As per the event planner's recommendation, there were no place cards, and guests were free to sit wherever they chose. It was a modern convention that she assured him was the latest trend. There was giggling and shifting around as places were chosen, and further shifting as stools replaced chairs in order to accommodate the more complicated costumes. At last, the company was seated and the meal was served.

Charles sat at the head of the table, Meredith on one side with Lady Covington and Benedict next to him. Ruben and Lady Lorene sat across from them, but the couple rarely acknowledged one another throughout the meal. Lady Lorene appeared much happier to converse with her friends, while Ruben discussed horse racing at length with Meredith.

As the meal continued, Charles participated now and then in the horse-race conversation, but he was more interested in observing, which was unusual for him. He was typically the center of attention at such events. Tonight he didn't feel like performing.

As Lord Ruben filled his glass, Meredith took the opportunity to turn to the lady beside him. "I hear you are going to America, my lady."

Lady Covington dabbed a napkin over her lips before replying. "Yes, to Philadelphia."

"Vivian was invited to demonstrate her mechanized velocipede at the Centennial International Exhibition," Benedict said from her other side. He beamed at his wife. "It is an enormous honor."

The lady's cheeks turned pink, but her eyes sparkled. "It is two years away yet. Professor Wallis has helped me modify the design," she said.

"But the engine is your creation, my dear. There is no need for modesty."

"That is wonderful," Meredith said, grinning. "I saw the bicycle at the Crystal Palace exhibition," he said. "A lad was riding it, if I'm not mistaken."

"My cousin," Lady Covington said. The color in her cheeks deepened. "If you ever care to attempt it, the ride can be quite diverting."

"It drives very fast," Benedict said with a teasing smile. "I'm sure Meredith wouldn't be interested."

"On the contrary." Meredith tossed his napkin onto the table. "I should very much like to try it." He looked at Charles, tipping his head toward the couple. "What about you, Chatsworth? Fancy a ride?"

Before Charles could answer, a burst of laughter from the far end of the table drew everyone's attention. The company was becoming more boisterous. It was time to adjourn for games and dancing.

Following Mrs. Hopewell's advice again, Charles dispensed with the gentlemen's after-dinner port, and the men and women left the room together. On cue, the musicians started to play, and by the time Charles arrived in the drawing room, couples were already moving around the dance floor. The lights had been dimmed, their glow sparkling on the gold paint of the columns and hieroglyphics.

He saw Lady Priscilla coming toward him, and on pretense of catching someone's eye, Charles waved and nodded and hurried off in the other direction, moving around the edge of the room until he came to a cluster of palmetto trees and stepped back into their shadow. The lady's attentions and assumptions about the pair of them were exhausting and only served to make him less likely to seek her out. From his place in the shadows, he scanned the room, searching to find a young lady who was not dancing.

"The Brookline Group is not dead, no matter what you've heard." A shadow wearing antlers was speaking. Lord Tynsdale. Charles hadn't even seen him in his haste to escape Lady Priscilla, but the man was speaking with a shadow wearing the high feathered hat of a French hussar. Lord Hastings, Charles believed.

"But what of Everleigh?" Lord Hastings said.

Hearing the name, Charles's breath caught. Lord Everleigh had been an owner of the Brookline Group, attempting to reopen a tunnel beneath the Thames for a new railway line. But his dishonest dealings had turned into criminal acts. Charles had assumed the rail-line proposal had died with the man's imprisonment.

"Everleigh was not subtle," Lord Tynsdale said. "He made mistakes, but do not fear. The obstacles preventing the rail line from going forward are being dealt with as we speak."

"The school?" Lord Hastings asked. "Surely you'll receive no support for the demolition of a charity endorsed by the future Duke of Ellingham, especially when tensions about the Poor Relief Laws are already high."

"Trust me," Tynsdale said, his antlers dipping as he lowered his head toward Lord Hastings. "It is being taken care of. Lockhart's injured pride is the perfect incentive. With just a bit of encouragement, he's done more to forward the cause than even Everleigh managed, and without even knowing he's doing it."

Charles backed up farther, moving behind the pots and coming out on the other side, near the musicians. His heart was racing. If he understood the men's conversation correctly, Miss Miller's school was at risk. Not only that, but she'd been correct about the source of the trouble. He winced, remembering his patronizing tone when he'd discounted her theory about Lord Lockhart, and considered how he could make it up to her. He and Benedict wielded a tolerable amount of power in Parliament, but they wouldn't get far if they started making accusations with no more than an overheard conversation as their evidence.

Charles wondered if Miss Miller had made any progress with the factories. Likely not, if Lord Lockhart had given the owners a threat or another incentive to keep the girls from school. He rubbed his mustache, thinking as he continued on around the room.

His mind was so occupied that he bumped into someone and caught her before she could fall. "I beg your—oh, it is you, Lady Priscilla."

She clung to him more tightly than was necessary. It was hardly more than a small bump.

Charles sighed. "I am so glad I found you," he said, making his words sound pleasant. "Would you care to dance?"

As the couple stepped around the dance floor, Charles somehow managed to make conversation, though his mind was engaged elsewhere. How could he help Miss Miller? And, more worryingly, would she accept his help? He caught sight of Benedict and Lady Covington, Miss Miller's friends. He'd start with them.

CHAPTER 15

ELIZABETH PUSHED OPEN THE DOOR of the Exchequer and Audit Department, stepping out into the cool afternoon air. She held the door for Mrs. Boyle, making a concerted effort not to slam it behind them, and then the women walked down the steps to where Clem's cab waited.

They had already been to the Trade Commission today, as well as the Standards Department, but each office had referred them to another, and it had become a ridiculous trail of paperwork, waiting rooms, and irritable clerks. They were no closer to an understanding or a resolution of their tax increase than they were last week.

Clem stood beside his horse, rubbing his hand over her neck and talking in a quiet voice. When they reached him, he frowned. "Ye ladies look as though ye've lost yer puppy."

Elizabeth tried to smile at his attempt to cheer them, but the expression wouldn't form.

Mrs. Boyle climbed into the cab, sighing as she sat in the seat.

Clem looked at her, then at the government building the women had come from, and finally at Elizabeth. His expression was somber. He knew as well as any what these failures meant for the school. "Where to now, Miss Miller?"

Elizabeth sighed as well. "Back to the school, if you please, Clem."

He nodded but stopped her with a hand on her arm as she turned to climb into the cab. "When trials arise, it's only them what loses hope who fail." He took off his hat, revealing stringy hair barely covering his pate, and shuffled his feet. "'At's whot me mum used to say." He looked back at Elizabeth, his manners awkward, as if speaking so personally made him uneasy. "Ye mustn't lose hope, miss." He gave an encouraging nod, his brows raised.

"Thank you, Clem." Elizabeth's throat choked. She patted the hand that rested on her arm and climbed inside the cab, sitting beside her assistant. The women didn't speak during the ride back to the school. There was no need to. Over the past week they had visited an exhaustive number of factories and government offices. Those who would speak with them told them the matter was out of their hands. But most hadn't so much as given the women audience.

Elizabeth and Mrs. Boyle had even visited some of their students' homes, but their parents had all said the same thing. The girls' income was needed, and schooling wasn't as important as eating. Elizabeth couldn't fault them for that.

"There is only one thing left to do." Mrs. Boyle sounded as discouraged as Elizabeth felt. "We must appeal to our patrons. Many have connections in Parliament and some in the factories. If they are unwilling . . ."

Elizabeth nodded. She held no delusions that those who had already contributed so much would be willing to give more as well as use their influence for the benefit of a charity that couldn't manage to operate successfully for even six months. If they were unwilling to help, she would have no choice but to close Spitalfields School for Girls. The thought made her physically ill.

She imagined how she would go about appealing to the patrons. She could show them ledgers, explain how the financial obligations had been so many more than anticipated, but she didn't think that would be of concern to them. They would view it as her making excuses for her inability to manage the funds they'd trusted her with. Most—save those like Lady Chatsworth and Lord Benedict—saw the school as no more than another charity to which they could contribute and feel reassured that they were doing something to assuage the problem of London's poor population. They would simply move their philanthropic interests elsewhere.

Most had never been to the school or known the effect it had on the girls, the confidence and skills it gave them.

"If only they could see," she muttered.

"What was that?" Mrs. Boyle raised her voice over the sound of the carriage. "What did you say?"

Elizabeth held up a finger, asking her friend to wait a moment as a notion took shape, growing in her thoughts until it was the barest framework of a plan. It would not be simple, and she would most definitely need help. But if it had its intended effect . . .

She twisted in her seat until her knees bumped into her assistant's. "Mrs. Boyle, I believe I may have a way to save the school."

"Indeed?" The woman's eyes were wide. "How?"

Elizabeth smiled for the first time in a week. Her mind was still spinning, but she recognized the spark of intuition and wanted to trust it. The idea was a good one. Now she simply had to make it work. "I am yet contemplating the details . . . but I think it may be just the thing." In her excitement she took her friend's hand. "But we cannot do it alone. It is time to rally our troops."

The next morning said troops rallied in the school's assembly room. Aside from Elizabeth and Mrs. Boyle, there were in attendance the school's two teachers, the other four members of the Blue Orchid Society, three elderly widow patrons, one police inspector, one doctor, one cabdriver, and a tabby cat who scrutinized each new member of the gathering with an imperious gaze from his seat beside the school's headmistress.

They sat in a circle of mismatched chairs gathered from the different classrooms and offices. Elizabeth made introductions, pleased when the noblewomen greeted the members of the working class with the same grace they employed with one another. The very notion of the women even being in this part of the city was extraordinary, and seeing Lady Chatsworth speaking cheerfully with a visibly uncertain Clem was the reassurance Elizabeth needed. She'd gathered the right people.

Once she deemed that they were all present—aside from Lord Benedict, who'd sent word with Vivian that he would arrive late—Elizabeth stood, and the company faced her, silent with attention. "Thank you, everyone, for coming today on such short notice." She looked around the circle, feeling her heart lighten at the sight of her friends. With them the impossible task felt much more possible. Now, if she could only convince them.

She took a calming breath and continued on. "As many of you are no doubt aware, the school is in crisis." Elizabeth winced as she said the words. Hearing them out loud made the desperation of the circumstance much more real.

"If you require more funding, you have only to ask," Lady Mather said kindly.

Elizabeth gave Sophie's grandmother an appreciative smile. "I am very grateful for your generosity. But it's not simply a matter of money." Realizing she was tapping her fingers against her skirts, she clasped her hands together. "The foremen of the local factories have altered their policies. They are requiring the girls to work daily to maintain their employment. At the moment, the Spitalfields School for Girls has no students."

Her pronouncement sent the group muttering to one another. To most, this information was new. Dahlia pressed her lips tightly together, shaking her head. She'd heard every evening for a week of her cousin's unsuccessful efforts in contacting those she'd thought could help. Clem and Mrs. Boyle looked grim. The others' expressions varied from surprised to angry. Elizabeth waited for a lull in the muttering so she could continue but was stopped when Lord Benedict entered the assembly room.

Lord Chatsworth accompanied him.

The sight of him derailed Elizabeth's thoughts and sent her heart into a spin. Why was he here? She looked away, certain the others had seen her reaction. She and Lord Chatsworth hadn't parted on good terms. His claim of understanding the difficulties of a common-born woman and her struggles to find her footing in a man's world was nearly laughable and had infuriated her. He may have acted sympathetic to her during their time in Sussex—affectionate, even—but when she'd actually been in need of a friend, she'd seen the person that from the beginning she'd known him to be: a presumptuous aristocrat who had laughed off her worries. He'd certainly not given a second thought to the plight of the school. *Or to me.* This last thought brought her up short, sending a flush up her neck. She cleared her throat and looked only at Lord Benedict as she spoke. "Welcome, Your Lordship."

"I am so sorry for interrupting," he said. "And I hope you don't mind that I brought a friend. Lord Chatsworth, as you know, has a vested interest in the school as well."

"Of course." Elizabeth put on a mask of calm. "Please, have a seat." She looked back at Lord Chatsworth and tilted her head, asking a silent question. *What are you doing here?*

In answer, he shrugged, his lips moving into a lazy smile.

Elizabeth looked away, using all of her strength to suppress any sort of reaction. That smile had power, and he knew it.

The men brought empty chairs, and the company shifted to make room in the circle. Elizabeth was glad for a moment to compose herself.

Once they were situated, Lord Benedict gestured to her. "Again, I apologize for interrupting. Please continue."

"Yes, thank you," Elizabeth said. She wouldn't allow herself to be distracted by Lord Chatsworth's presence. It was easy enough not to look in his direction. She would continue on as if he weren't here. "As I was saying," she continued. "With their employment as it is, the girls cannot attend school."

"It shouldn't be difficult to convince the factory administration to change their minds," Vivian said. She tipped her head toward her husband and his friend. "We have connections with influence in that regard."

This was an avenue Elizabeth had considered but discounted. "I know it would be simple enough to ask them, even intimidate them into changing the policy." She shook her head. "But, in my opinion, the result would be short-lived. Another obstacle will arise preventing the children's attendance and returning us back to where we are now."

She didn't say it aloud, not wanting Lord Chatsworth to renew his mockery of the idea, but she was certain Lord Lockhart and his friends were behind the school's difficulties. If Lord Benedict spoke to the factory foremen, the school's enemies would simply find another way to interfere. It was rather like an infestation of ants. She'd made the comparison the night before when she'd explained it to Dahlia. One could stomp on each ant in turn, but they would persist. The only way to put an end to their incursion was to destroy the ant hill. Stop them at the source.

"What would you do, dear?" Sophie asked. She squinted her eyes, studying Elizabeth shrewdly. "I recognize your look. An idea is brewing."

Elizabeth winked at Sophie, pleased with her friend's assessment. "I believe if everyone could see for themselves how the school is run and how education will improve employees, communities, and families, their presuppositions will be changed."

"What did you have in mind?" Hazel said.

"I'm so glad you asked." Elizabeth retrieved a large board from where it leaned against a wall. She turned it around, resting it on her chair.

Mrs. Boyle held it steady from her chair next to Elizabeth's.

The others leaned forward for a better view.

Tacked to the board was a diagram of the school. "The Spitalfields School for Girls will host a public event," Elizabeth announced. "The community, the girls' employers, families, and of course patrons and . . . prospective patrons will all be invited."

She glanced around the group, assessing their reactions. Overall, the response was positive, though a few looked confused. She avoided meeting Lord Chatsworth's gaze altogether, worried she'd see his mocking grin. "I want to give the girls an opportunity to demonstrate what they've learned," she continued. "To allow myself and the teachers a chance to answer questions about the importance of female education and the opportunities it will provide and to give those who may doubt the chance to see firsthand how extraordinary this school is. If it is successful, I hope it will become a yearly event. I am aspiring for a carnival-like atmosphere, a celebration for the community, where the girls can be proud of what they've accomplished."

She looked around the company again. "I welcome any suggestions, but here is what I have devised thus far. By law, the factories are closed on Saturday afternoons, so I propose we hold the event one week from this Saturday." Using a pencil, she tapped the diagram in the area indicating the front doors. "Tours of the school will be provided by Mrs. Boyle to any interested parties."

The secretary nodded her agreement.

Elizabeth tapped another section. "The teachers will host guests in their classrooms, answering questions and allowing the girls to read for their families or otherwise demonstrate their knowledge of a particular subject. I will leave it up to you how best to display the girls' learning."

The teachers nodded, Mrs. Podmore looking eager and Mr. Wilkie thoughtful.

"Some may have questions about what types of occupations might be available to a girl who can read and do arithmetic," she told the teachers. "Please help them understand the futures the girls might expect and how their education will prepare them for those positions. Sophie"—she turned to her friend—"I hoped you might advertise the event."

"Naturally," Sophie said. Her eyes were bright as she spoke. "And I shall print handbills to distribute through the tenements."

"Most of the residents won't be able to read them," her husband, Inspector Jonathan Graham, reminded her.

"You are right, my dear." Sophie pulled her lips to the side, thinking. "Illustrations, then," she said. "Signs in shop windows. And word-of-mouth advertising is the best way to go about it, I think." She took a notebook from her bag and opened it, writing inside. "I will send word to other news agencies to advertise as well as send their own reporters to the event." She continued to write. "And I will print formal invitations for patrons, if you would like."

Elizabeth hadn't thought of that. The upper-class patrons would expect something more elegant than a handbill. "That is a wonderful idea. Thank you. Mrs. Boyle, will you provide Sophie with a list of our supporters?"

The secretary nodded, holding the board steady with one hand and writing in her notebook with the other.

Elizabeth pointed to the diagram again; this time her pencil tip touched the rectangle labeled *Assembly Room*. "Vivian, I hoped you would present a science demonstration of some type."

Vivian sat up straight. "Absolutely."

"I'm certain anything you do will be impressive," Elizabeth said. "And perhaps we might enlist Professor Wallis as well?"

"If he is available, I know he will be delighted to come," Vivian said. "He enjoys teaching the girls very much, as do I."

"And I shall take my customary place, manning the fire extinguisher," Lord Benedict said, referring to the copper vessel of compressed air and pearl ash that Professor Wallis had insisted upon when they had demonstrated the properties of a hydrogen balloon.

The others in the company chuckled, and Lord Benedict smiled fondly at his wife.

Elizabeth smiled at Lord Benedict's jest and continued on. "Hazel and Dr. Jackson," she said, turning to the couple. "I hoped you might give a demonstration about germ theory with an emphasis on hygiene for a person's overall wellness. Such a thing is much needed among many of these families."

"We would be happy to," Hazel said shyly.

"With one condition," Dr. Jackson cut in. "We're going first. None of the attendees will stay around to hear about the importance of handwashing after Lady Covington's chemical explosions."

The others laughed, and even Vivian grinned.

Elizabeth was thrilled that her friends were getting into the spirit of the thing.

"We will oversee the decorations," Lady Mather piped up. She motioned to her companions, Lady Chatsworth and Mrs. Griffin.

"You will need a police presence," Inspector Graham said. "In spite of what my wife and you young ladies seem to believe, this part of London is prone to crime." He gave Sophie an exasperated look, which she returned teasingly. "An event like this will draw pickpockets and other unsavory sorts," he continued. "I'll station some of the lads throughout the school that evening."

"Thank you." Safety was another thing Elizabeth hadn't considered.

"In the main hall we should have refreshments," Dahlia said. "I volunteer to arrange catering."

"I thought you would," Elizabeth replied. If there was one thing her cousin did well, it was host a party. "But I hoped you might look in a different direction than the caterers you typically enlist. This is a Spitalfields school. Our support should go back to the local businesses." She took a step toward the cab driver, who had watched the entire proceedings in silence. "I was hoping Clem could help us in this. He knows the best street vendors. Perhaps the two of you could work together to arrange the food."

At that proposition, Clem's eyes grew wide and darted to Dahlia as if he feared she would protest. "Miss, I—"

"An excellent idea," Dahlia said without a pause. She traded places with Lady Chatsworth, putting herself next to the cab driver.

The company separated into smaller groups, discussing their assignments and sharing ideas. The air in the room was charged and optimistic. Elizabeth moved her board, returning it back to the wall.

When she turned, Lord Chatsworth stood before her. "Oh." She took a step back. He had startled her, but she also needed distance between them if she was going to keep her emotions out of things.

"You didn't assign me a task," he said.

He appeared entirely at ease, which irritated her. "Why did you come? Our arrangement is not connected to the school." She folded her arms. "I will continue to tutor Alice whether or not the school succeeds or fails." Frowning was a good way to disguise the pain of what she was saying.

"You were right," he said. "*Are* right. Lord Lockhart is responsible for the school's hardships."

Elizabeth's breath caught. It was one thing to suspect a man, but to hear her suspicions confirmed dropped a cold stone inside her belly.

"Benedict and I have made inquiries with the factories," he said. "Apparently the Brookline Group has a significant amount of influence with the landowners in Spitalfields."

Elizabeth remembered the Brookline Group from Sophie and Inspector Graham's investigation. "Are they still hoping to build a railway line through Spitalfields?"

Lord Chatsworth nodded grimly. "Directly through here, if their strategy is successful." He made a sweeping motion with his hand, as if a train were speeding past. "It is much easier to condemn a building if it is not housing a charity school."

Elizabeth let his words sink in. She'd been right. And, in agreeing with her, Lord Chatsworth was agreeing that he had been wrong. "I knew Lord Lockhart was vindictive, but this . . ."

"It is not he alone," Lord Chatsworth said. "As I told you, Lord Lockhart has not the disposition of a politician. I do not believe he fully understands the effects of his actions. The Brookline Group is using his lack of experience for their own benefit."

She tried to picture Lord Lockhart in this light—a man plunged into a life he hadn't asked for, acting under the influence of experienced men he trusted, with his anger toward Elizabeth spurring him on.

"Benedict and I are in a position to make an accusation," Lord Chatsworth continued. "We have called upon Sir Stafford Northcote, and it is clear that the school's property has been mis-designated with the exchequer's offices."

Elizabeth narrowed her eyes, feeling a rush of anger. Naturally the men had met with the chancellor of the exchequer himself while she and Mrs. Boyle had been relegated to junior clerks. It would have been simple enough to discover the mis-designation themselves if their complaints had only been taken seriously. For Lord Lockhart to have gone to such measures, surely what he'd done was illegal—an abuse of his position. Her anger grew, making her twitch in her impatience for justice.

Lord Chatsworth leaned closer, his tone becoming more somber. "We have the evidence necessary if you intend to pursue a claim."

Elizabeth blinked, looking up at him. He and Lord Benedict had spoken with all of the people she had endeavored all week to even have an audience with. He had the power and the evidence to take the matter to the courts, to accuse Lord Lockhart officially. But he hadn't. Not without her approval. He was deferring to her.

Knowing that he trusted the decision to her, she calmed her thoughts, considering what he'd said. A scandal such as this would ruin Lord Lockhart entirely. He would lose credibility in every facet of his life if it were known that he'd taken out his petty revenge on a charity school for girls. Her heartbeat sounded in her ears. She'd felt helpless for months as the most important thing in her life—her school—was slowly being taken away, and at last she had the means to put things right, to prosecute the person responsible, and to validate her own competence. She hadn't failed as headmistress; the fault was another's, and she could place the blame where it belonged.

Her fury pulsed inside, feeling like a living thing, tingling in her fingers and making her head hurt. She wanted compensation, vengeance . . . but with the anger she recognized another emotion that surprised her. Pity. She felt sorry for Lord Lockhart. Thinking of the man who'd been thrust into a world he'd not wanted nor been prepared for, she could not help but feel compassion. She thought of Lord Chatsworth's words beneath the willow tree: *"Lord Lockhart is moved by the same things that move us all. Feeling wanted, feeling important."* Was it really so simple?

"We did not wish to do anything without your permission," Lord Chatsworth said. "How should we pursue the matter?"

She considered for only a moment more before making up her mind. "I do have an assignment for you, Your Lordship. If you please, will you make certain Lord Lockhart attends the school event next Saturday?"

Lord Chatsworth raised his brows, surprised. "Certainly I will." He spoke slowly, as if he were confused. His eyes narrowed, looking suspicious. "Miss Miller, what do you plan to do?"

Elizabeth grinned, pleased to be the one holding the cards for once. "I plan to offer Lord Lockhart a bridge."

CHAPTER 16

As it turned out, convincing Lord Lockhart to attend the school event was unnecessary, as Charles discovered three days later. He had watched the man throughout the parliamentary sitting and timed his own exit from Westminster Hall so they would meet in the doorway.

"Lord Lockhart, how are you this fine afternoon?" Charles greeted him.

Lockhart's waistcoat was tight across his belly, and his trousers were rumpled from sitting. He was pushing a disorganized jumble of papers and files into a portmanteau as he walked. He looked surprised, glancing around, as if suspecting Charles had approached him by accident. "Good afternoon, Lord Chatsworth." He tilted his head in an awkward acknowledgment and continued on through the gothic-arched doorway and along the path toward the palace grounds.

Charles kept pace with him. "I was wondering if you'd heard of the event at the Spitalfields Girls' School on Saturday."

Lockhart hesitated. "I have," he said after a moment. "I received an invitation." He kept walking, head down, legs moving quickly, as if he wished he were anyplace else.

"Wonderful," Charles said. "I hope you plan to attend. I should be very happy to see you there."

Lord Lockhart shot him an apprehensive look, as if suspecting himself to somehow be the butt of a joke. "I intend to accompany Lord Tynsdale and Lord Hastings."

Hearing who his companions were, Charles suspected an ulterior motive to the plan. But instead of voicing his suspicion, he gave a cheery grin and clapped Lord Lockhart's shoulder. "Excellent."

They parted ways, and Charles continued on, pondering what he'd learned. Did the Brookline Group intend to sabotage the event? Or were they simply attending to gather information about the school? He would make certain the others, particularly Inspector Graham and his constables, knew to keep a watchful eye on the men throughout the evening. They would certainly not attempt something so publicly, and if they did, Charles pitied them, especially when Miss Miller's friends found out.

On Saturday afternoon, Charles arrived at the school. He was pleasantly surprised to see a crowd on the steps and carriages lining the street. The local residents looked out of windows or peeked out from alleyways, likely uncertain what to make of the disturbance in their neighborhood. Charles stepped out of his own carriage, then reached back inside to assist Alice.

She climbed down, standing on the paving stones and looked excitedly at the pennants hanging from the windows and the crepe buntings draped around the doorway.

A photographer set up a tripod for a shot of the crowd and the decorations.

The crush of guests was a curious mixture of locals and upper-class patrons, though the two groups were not mingling. They were in separate bunches, eyeing each other with curiosity and suspicion. Or simply pretending they weren't there.

Charles took Alice's hand and joined the queue to enter.

As they went inside the school, he nodded at the constables stationed on either side of the doorway. The entry hall was filled, smelling of people and food. Banners were hung over the classroom doors, and tables were arranged around the edges of the space, holding an array of refreshments Miss Miller's friends were helping serve to the attendees.

Children chased one another through the crowd. Some wore paper carnival masks, and most held a sticky Chelsea bun or other confectionary treat.

Even in this small space Charles noticed the members of each class remained decidedly segregated from one another.

He glanced over the crowd, hoping to find Miss Miller.

"Good afternoon, Lord Chatsworth." Mrs. Boyle came toward him with quick steps. "A fine turnout, isn't it?" The woman's practical attire had been replaced by a dress of black-and-green plaid with lace trim. Her hat bore feathers that had, unfortunately, been dyed a bright-red color, preventing Charles from assessing their species of origin.

"It is indeed," Charles said. He drew Alice forward. "Please allow me to introduce my sister. Mrs. Boyle, this is Miss Alice."

"How do you do?" Alice spoke the words precisely and curtsied.

"A pleasure to make your acquaintance, Miss Alice," Mrs. Boyle said warmly. "Perhaps you would wish to go to the library. There is a puppet show underway."

"Oh!" Alice tugged at Charles's hand. "May we?"

"Of course we may," Charles said. "But we should find Grandmother and Miss Miller first, don't you think?"

"When I last saw the headmistress, she was meeting with one of the factory foremen in her office," Mrs. Boyle said. She pointed to a far corner of the entryway. "Lady Chatsworth is there, distributing bonbons."

Charles and Alice bid Mrs. Boyle farewell and made their way through the crowd.

Grandmother and her two friends were beneath a banner painted with the colorful letters *SUGAR CANDY* as well as pictures of various confectionary delights. In front of them was a table covered with glass jars filled with every color and variety of sweets imaginable, which they scooped into small drawstring bags for the gathered children. The women wore aprons over their elegant gowns and looked as if they were having the time of their lives.

Charles had assumed nothing his grandmother and her friends did could yet surprise him, but he was once again proven wrong. He stepped around the table, kissing Grandmother's cheek and greeting Lady Mather and Mrs. Griffin. "I have never met such enchanting confectioners," he said, reaching into a jar for a licorice stick.

The women beamed at his teasing and greeted Alice.

Grandmother swatted his hand away. "You shall have to wait your turn like everyone else." She motioned to the children.

Alice went to the rear of the queue.

"You three seem to be enjoying yourselves." Charles leaned his shoulder against the wall as he chewed his pilfered licorice. He scanned the entry hall but saw neither Miss Miller nor Lord Lockhart.

Lady Sophronia Graham was directing a photographer as he captured a shot of the candy table, and Charles imagined what fun reporters would have with the headline.

"I've not had such a diverting time in decades," Lady Mather said, leaning forward to present a bag to one of the children. The boy thanked her, doffing his felt hat and bowing deeply.

The others concurred. "There is really nothing quite so gratifying as making a child happy, is there?" Mrs. Griffin said, dumping a scoop of tiger balls into a bag.

When Alice's turn came, she stared wide-eyed at the colorful confection-ery jars. After much deliberation, she chose her favorite treats, accepting her bag with a grin. "We are going to see a puppet show," she told Grandmother.

"Oh, won't that be amusing?" Grandmother said, waving her fingers. "Do enjoy yourselves, my dears." She leaned forward to assist the next small customer.

Charles snitched another licorice stick. He took Alice's hand, and when he turned around, Miss Miller stood on the staircase. She was dressed in a gown of midnight blue, one hand resting on the railing. The window behind illumi-nated her silhouette and haloed her hair. Charles was captivated.

Their eyes met, but he could not make out the details of her face. He hoped she was pleased to see him.

She tilted her head, looking down to his side, and seeing Alice, Miss Miller came down the stairs. She looked tired but happy.

"Welcome, Your Lordship." She dipped in a curtsy, but before Charles could answer, she had already turned to his companion. "Alice! I'm so glad you've come! Is this a new dress?"

Alice curtsied. "Good afternoon, Miss Miller." She looked down at her pink-satin gown, holding out her skirts to show the layers of ruffles. "Grandmother bought the dress especially for today." She turned her head so Miss Miller could see the matching bow in her hair.

"Beautiful," Miss Miller said. She bent down until her face was close to Alice's and winked. "You look lovely in pink, Captain Sharkfin."

"You look lovely as well," Alice said. She tugged on Charles's hand. "Doesn't she?"

"Very much so," Charles said.

Miss Miller flicked her eyes at him as she stood straight, her expression friendly but not warm. He wished he knew how to return them to their former easy rapport.

"You've a considerable assemblage gathered," he said. "You must be pleased with the turnout."

"I am pleased," she said. "Employees from various factories have made an appearance, patrons, news agents, and so many students have come." She smiled at this last part. "I hope they enjoy themselves." She turned back to Alice. "You must see the puppet show. Many of the girls have gathered there."

The three turned and climbed the stairs together.

"Is he here?" Elizabeth asked Charles in a low voice. There was no need to clarify whom she spoke of.

"I haven't seen him," Charles replied. "Not yet. But he said he was planning to attend."

"He must," she said.

As they walked down the corridor toward the library, they could hear the sounds of Punch and Judy as well as the children's laughter when Judy inevitably whacked her puppet husband with a bat.

Charles and Miss Miller remained in the doorway while Alice went inside. She found a space next to a group of girls, greeting them in a whisper as she sat on the floor beside them.

One of the girls said something Charles couldn't hear, and Alice faced forward to watch the puppets.

"Mrs. Boyle told me you've spoken to one of the factory foremen," Charles said now that they were alone.

"A few," she replied. "It is not so easy to avoid me when they are in my school." Her eyes flashed.

Benedict had told Charles of the factory administrators' unwillingness to meet with the women. Charles's immediate reaction had been one of anger. He'd insisted on going down himself and having a word with the men and the clerks of the various government offices who had dismissed the women as well. But Benedict and his wife had discouraged this course of action, and in retrospect, Charles had realized the wisdom of their advice. This was not his battle to fight, nor would Miss Miller appreciate his interference. Not if she didn't specifically ask for it. His intervention could be seen as a lack of faith in her ability to do it for herself.

"It's a lesson one learns with difficulty when one is dealing with an independent woman," Lord Benedict had said. "It is so much easier to simply solve the problem, but such assistance is not always welcome."

"Do you feel your meetings were a success?" Charles asked Miss Miller.

"I do not know yet," she said. "But we are closer than we were a week ago."

He nodded, absently watching as Mr. Punch found himself pursued by a hungry crocodile. Charles looked down to where Alice was sitting, noticing now that she sat in the center of a wide space. Had the other girls moved away for a better view of the show? Why hadn't Alice moved with them?

"My uncle Eldon sponsored this." Miss Miller lifted her chin toward the puppet theater. "He was unable to attend, but he still wanted to contribute." She glanced over her shoulder, and seeing Mrs. Boyle bringing a group of patrons up the stairs, she took her leave, joining the tour group. They spoke at the top of the stairs and then came toward the library.

Charles stood aside to allow a better view, nodding as they passed and exchanging brief greetings with them. He knew a few of them, but not well.

When the group moved out of the way, Alice came through the doorway, taking his hand.

"Had enough of the puppets already?" he asked.

She didn't look up. "Can we return to Miss Miller or Grandmother?"

Charles studied her. He wasn't certain whether something had happened with the other children or Alice was simply being timid. "Shall we see if Grandmother has any more licorice sticks?"

As they descended the stairs, he saw a group of noblemen enter the school. Lord Tynsdale came in first, his shrewd gaze taking in the crowd. Directly after him, Lord Hastings entered. He whispered something to his friend, and the men went toward one of the classrooms, avoiding Mrs. Boyle entirely. Lord Lockhart followed behind. He took off his hat, running a hand over his disheveled hair and, as usual, looked as if he wished he were anywhere else. Charles wondered if the man were ever truly relaxed.

When he reached the bottom of the staircase, Charles looked for Inspector Graham. He'd informed the police inspector of the men's intention to attend the school's event, and he wanted to notify the inspector that they'd arrived.

Alice tugged his hand, pulling him toward the candy table. He followed along without paying attention to his trajectory as he scanned the crowd. Where had Inspector Graham gotten to? When he did glance forward, he stopped short, nearly colliding with Lady Priscilla and Miss Charlotte Grey, who wore an elaborate hat with an entire stuffed Labrador duck on it. No wonder the species was close to extinction.

"I beg your pardon, ladies."

"Oh, there you are." Lady Priscilla took his arm and shot a look behind her. "I am glad to see there is one reasonable person here. Our grandmothers have decided to masquerade as shop keepers, if you can believe it. It is as if they are intent on humiliating—" She started to pull him away but stopped when she realized there was a child attached to his other hand. Lady Priscilla's forehead wrinkled. "Who is this?"

Charles had known Alice would be subject to scrutiny. He had worried about bringing her, but he'd thought it might be an opportunity to start making her known to people in his social circles. His defenses rose into place, but he smiled graciously. "My lady, allow me to introduce my sister."

He drew Alice forward gently. "Alice, this is Lady Priscilla and Miss Grey." Alice curtsied. "How do you do?"

The women exchanged a surprised glance.

Neither replied to the girl.

"Your sister?" Lady Priscilla looked from Alice to Charles and back. One brow rose and her nose wrinkled. "Well, this is indeed a surprise."

Charles could see the calculations behind the lady's eyes. The girl's age, the potential for scandal, how many others knew of her existence. Would Lady Priscilla be the one to divulge the fresh on-dit among Society? Panic edged into his thoughts, but he'd known this would happen, and he would protect Alice from the repercussions.

Alice watched Lady Priscilla and Miss Grey as well, her cheeks reddening. The women's disgust wasn't lost on the child.

Over the heads of the children waiting at the candy table, Charles caught his grandmother's eye. He tipped his head toward Alice.

Grandmother took in the scene with a perceptive glance. She beckoned to Alice.

"See there?" Charles said to the girl. "Grandmother requires assistance at the confectionary table."

Alice hurried away to join Grandmother just as another flock of children came down the stairs. The puppet show must have ended. The children went directly toward the candy, pushing past the adults. Miss Grey gasped.

Lady Priscilla clung tighter to his arm. "There are so many of them," she said, moving away from the children. "When I agreed to support my sister, I'd not planned to spend the day among the great unwashed." She sniffed, then put her fingers in front of her nose.

"Really, this is too much," Miss Grey agreed.

Miss Miller moved through the crowd, and seeing Charles, she started toward him. She stopped to speak with a group of women, pointing toward the assembly room. The women went in that direction, and Miss Miller came toward Charles and Lady Priscilla. Her gaze took in their linked arms. If Charles hadn't been watching for it, he wouldn't have seen the slight tightening of her eyes. "The main presentation is nearly ready to begin," she said when she stood before them. "We are directing people into the assembly room. Is Alice—"

"She is with my grandmother," Charles said, wishing he could think of a polite way to disentangle his arm. The lady's grip was surprisingly robust.

Miss Miller glanced at their joined arms once more before hurrying away.

Lady Priscilla looked in the direction the crowd was moving. Her nose wrinkled again. "The smell will be even more potent confined to one room."

Miss Grey gave a disgusted snort.

Despite the ladies' protestations, the three of them joined the company walking toward the doorway.

Charles looked toward the candy table, wondering if he should save a chair for Alice, but it was impossible to see the girl or their grandmother through the throng of people. As he looked back, a movement caught his eye. Lord Tynsdale was climbing the stairs. The man glanced behind him and hurried upward, apparently counting on the confusion of the crowd moving in the opposite direction to conceal him.

Charles pulled his arm away. "I beg your pardon, ladies. If you'll excuse me for a moment . . ."

"Where are you going?" Lady Priscilla looked personally offended.

"There's something I have to do," Charles said. He turned the women around, giving them a little push toward the door as he glanced toward the stairs. Lord Tynsdale was nearly at the top. "I'll meet you inside."

Without waiting for a response, he rushed after the man, coming upon him just as he was stepping into Miss Miller's office. "Hullo, there, Tynsdale!" Charles called.

Lord Tynsdale jumped back, bumping into the desk and disturbing the cat that was curled up atop it.

The cat hissed.

"Oh, Chatsworth, it's you." He looked both angry and guilty.

"The festivities are downstairs," Charles said. "You must have lost your way." He stepped back, opening the door wider and giving his friendliest smile. "Allow me to show you."

Lord Tynsdale shot a glance toward the pigeonholes filled with papers and files that lined one side of the room before stepping through the door. The cat followed. "I was just looking for . . . I thought perhaps I might find a water closet."

Charles closed the door behind them and clapped the man on the shoulder, leading him toward the stairs. "No plumbing in this section of the city," he said. "I'll wager you'd find a privy shed in the garden."

Lord Tynsdale's face blanched. "Out of the question," he said. "I will simply . . . wait."

Charles clapped his shoulder again, keeping his hand there until they were at the bottom of the stairs. The majority of the crowd had left the entry hall, leaving only a few remaining guests and some of the police officers. Charles caught Inspector Graham's eye, darting a look from Tynsdale to the stairs.

Inspector Graham nodded and spoke to a pair of constables, directing them to the upstairs corridor.

One potential crisis was averted, but Charles couldn't rest easy. Who knew what else the Brookline Company had in store?

CHAPTER 17

ELIZABETH WAS SEATED ON THE assembly room stage, looking out over the gathered spectators. Children sat on the floor in the front, and adults sat behind them in rented chairs or stood along the back and sides of the chamber. A group of news reporters stood to one side, pencils poised above notebooks. The room was filled completely with hardly any space to move.

She looked at Hazel, who sat beside her, worried that her friend would suffer a fit of panic at finding herself in such a crowd. "Are you all right?"

Hazel nodded. Her hands were clenched tightly in her lap, and Elizabeth could hear her taking slow, deep breaths.

"I'll clear the doorway," Dr. Jackson said from Hazel's other side. He got up and made his way toward the entrance.

"I'm sorry," Elizabeth said to her friend. "I didn't even think . . ." She reprimanded herself for her short-sightedness. She'd been so worried about the school that she hadn't even considered her friend's condition.

Hazel took her hand, squeezing it reassuringly. She lifted her chin toward the doorway, where Dr. Jackson had cleared away the crowd, making a clean exit path. He spoke to Inspector Graham at the doorway for a moment, then started back toward them, his eyes tender as he looked at his fiancée. Hazel squeezed Elizabeth's hand again and leaned closer. "I don't believe my heart will ever not react to seeing him."

Without meaning to, Elizabeth glanced to where Lord Chatsworth sat beside Alice. Her heart leapt when his eyes met hers. She fully understood the feeling Hazel described, but when her gaze moved to Lady Priscilla seated on his other side, her insides went hard, and she looked away, irritated by her own foolishness.

Seated beside Dr. Jackson, who had made it back to his chair, was Professor Wallis, looking cheerful and at ease as he studied the crowd with his intelligent eyes, and Vivian, whose gaze was every bit as intelligent but which had settled upon her husband, who had brought a chair to the side of the stage so that he might sit beside the large copper fire extinguisher. He'd set the hose within easy reach and now leaned back in his chair, sharing a soft smile with his wife.

Mrs. Boyle rose, standing at the podium and extending a welcome to those in attendance. She spoke clearly and precisely, and Elizabeth appreciated her effort to slow her typically rapid speech. The teachers and committee who had planned and carried out the event were thanked with warm applause. "And now please join me in welcoming our headmistress, Miss Elizabeth Miller." Mrs. Boyle applauded with the crowd as Elizabeth crossed the stage and replaced her at the podium.

Elizabeth set down her pages of written notes. "Before I begin, I would like to thank one person without whom this school would assuredly fall to pieces. She manages the finances, the scheduling, the enrollment; works tirelessly to keep the school operating; and does so with cheerful competence." She turned toward her secretary. "Mrs. Boyle, what would we do without you?"

The crowd applauded again, and Mrs. Boyle blushed.

Once the room had quieted, Elizabeth smoothed her papers and took a breath. The enormity of the situation settled over her once again, and panic jolted in her belly. If she couldn't convince this roomful of people of her school's value . . .

"Ladies and Gentlemen and, of course, Girls." She smiled at the children seated in front of her, seeing the faces of so many she loved. "Today we celebrate these children and their accomplishments. But, as you know, it takes more than a building with teachers and chalkboards to make a school." She spread her hand through the air, encompassing all of those assembled. "Each of you is vital to the success of Spitalfields School for Girls. But I understand many of you are apprehensive—doubtful, even—as to the necessity of such an institution. Today I hope to ease your concerns and reassure and convince you of the value of girls' education."

Elizabeth paused, scanning the crowd, trying to ascertain their reactions, and praying in her heart that her words would prove persuasive.

Lady Chatsworth appeared to be trying to coax Alice to join the other children on the floor, but Alice was shaking her head.

Lady Priscilla was whispering to Lord Chatsworth.

Lord Lockhart sat between his two associates, arms folded as he glared at her. The men at his sides glared as well.

She looked down at her notes, clasping her hands behind her back to hide their shaking. "The renowned American educator Catharine Beecher said,

'If all females were not only well educated themselves but were prepared to communicate in an easy manner their stores of knowledge to others; if they not only knew how to regulate their own minds, tempers, and habits but how to effect improvements in those around them, the face of society would be speedily changed.'"

Elizabeth did not dare look at individual faces, thinking that half the crowd would not recognize the woman's name and the other half would be disdainful at her mention. She hoped the power of Miss Beecher's words would overcome any scorn about the woman herself.

She let the silence stretch for a moment before continuing. "These children will change the face of society." She spread her hands, motioning to the girls seated on the floor before her. "There is little in life that will benefit a person more than an education. Doors open, opportunities grow, and possibilities expand. This is true in the case of boys *and* girls. Families, societies, and communities prosper when their members are able to think critically, are able to read and to understand."

Elizabeth turned her focus to the area in the back of the room where the factory foremen stood. "I do not seek to interfere with your workforce but to create more capable workers. Employees who can reason, who can read and understand, will increase the productivity of your companies."

She let her gaze travel over the crowd again, purposely not allowing it to rest on any of the Chatsworth family. Sophronia and Dahlia sat on the first row, watching with proud expressions that made her heart expand. She looked at the girls again and then back up at the congregation.

"Today we have prepared demonstrations, a sample of what is taught here. Our teachers, Mrs. Podmore and Mr. Wilkie, instruct the students in the basic subjects of reading, writing, arithmetic, and geography. But we have an additional benefit here at Spitalfields School for Girls—specialists in their fields who volunteer their time to present exclusive learning symposiums on the various topics of their expertise.

"And so, today I present for you Dr. Jim Jackson and Nurse Hazel Thornton, and after, Oxford professor Clifford Wallis and Lady Covington."

The audience applauded as Elizabeth returned to her seat. When she arrived, she found Gaffer had taken her chair, looking at her as if he were insulted by the very idea that she might sit there.

When Hazel stood, Elizabeth sat in her seat instead.

Mr. Wilkie and Clem moved the podium away and Hazel stepped forward. Her crisp white hat and apron glowed in the light of the gas lamps, as did Dr. Jackson's coat. The pair's mere presence commanded the attention of the attendees, many of whom had never been to a hospital, let alone interacted with a medical professional.

Dr. Jackson wheeled a rolling chalkboard to the center of the stage.

Hazel leaned forward slightly, speaking to the girls gathered in front of her. "Good afternoon, ladies."

"Good afternoon, Nurse Thornton," the girls repeated together.

"Dr. Jackson and I are so happy to be with you again," she said.

"Hello, girls," Dr. Jackson said in the American accent that made the girls giggle.

"Good afternoon, Dr. Jackson," the girls said.

Elizabeth took a box from beneath her seat, bringing it to Hazel at the front of the stage.

Hazel reached inside, drawing out a contraption made of brass. She held it up for the girls to see. "Who remembers what this is?"

The students raised their hands, and when she was called upon, Nelly Provost replied that it was a microscope.

"Yes, very good." Hazel set the microscope back in the box, and Elizabeth returned with it to her seat.

Dr. Jackson stepped forward. "If you will remember, when we looked into the microscope at various objects, we viewed organisms so small that our eyes could not see them without help. What were the organisms called?"

After Sarah Baker informed him that the organisms were bacteria, Dr. Jackson invited some of the girls to come forward and draw the shapes on the board. From where Elizabeth sat, she couldn't see the depictions the girls made. She watched the crowd instead. She didn't believe most of them had ever looked into a microscope—few of the women, if any, and very likely none of the Spitalfields residents. They watched the lesson closely.

Dr. Jackson and Hazel continued to discuss the bacteria with the girls, reminding them there were different types, some beneficial and some harmful.

Dr. Jackson drew something on the board that made the girls laugh. When he saw Elizabeth and the other presenters leaning forward, he angled the board so they could see. The girls had drawn long oval shapes that resembled worms or sausages. On some of them, Dr. Jackson had drawn angry eyes. One even wore a hat and had a long mustache—the quintessential penny-dreadful villain. "The harmful bacteria are responsible for infection, illness, and disease." He drew on the board again, putting smiles on some of the other sausage shapes. On one he drew a sword. "The beneficial bacteria help our bodies fight sickness. They make us healthy and strong, but sometimes they need assistance."

Hazel picked up a chalk eraser. "What things do we do to help the benefi-cial bacteria and eliminate harmful bacteria?" Seeing Emma's hand raise, she called on her.

"Wash our hands afore eatin'," Emma said.

Hazel gave her the eraser, and Emma eliminated one of the evil-looking sausages.

The girls cheered.

As the girls continued their lesson, Elizabeth watched the audience. Alice was leaning so far forward in her chair that she was in danger of falling off, but when her grandmother motioned for her to join in the lesson, she again shook her head.

Lady Priscilla and Charlotte Grey were whispering together.

Lord Lockhart leaned forward in his chair nearly as far as Alice. The presentation interested him.

Elizabeth smiled.

When Hazel and Dr. Jackson finished, the crowd applauded.

Not wanting to disturb Gaffer, Elizabeth scooted into Vivian's chair when she stood with Professor Wallis.

Hazel sat beside her.

Dr. Jackson eyed the sleeping cat suspiciously before taking the seat beside him.

Clem and Mr. Wilkie returned, carrying a table carefully to the front of the stage. On it was an array of items, including wires, coils, and rods. Elizabeth thought a glass cylinder attached to a pair of wires and filled with liquid might be a battery of some type.

Vivian arranged the items on the table while Professor Wallis stepped forward to address the crowd. She much preferred to work in the background rather than be the focus of attention.

Lord Benedict rolled the copper fire extinguisher closer and drew his chair up beside it.

Lord Lockhart stretched out his neck in hopes of a better view.

"I am so very happy to be with you again." Professor Wallis directed his words to the girls gathered at the front of the stage.

The students smiled excitedly. The professor was a favorite guest, not only for his interesting presentation but also because he had a certain air about him. He made the most mundane topic seem fascinating. Elizabeth supposed that was what made him such a sought-after teacher, his ability to hold a crowd's attention and make them feel as if they were discovering something new and wonderful.

"Who can remember what we discussed last time Lady Covington and I were here?" he asked.

Hands shot into the air. When he beckoned to one student, she stood. "We talked 'bout the states o' matter," she said. At ten, Jane was one of the older students and one of the brightest young ladies in the school.

"That is exactly correct." Professor Wallis beamed at her. "What was your name, my dear?"

"Jane Lewis."

"Miss Lewis, how did we determine whether a substance is a gas, liquid, or solid?"

"A solid object 'as a def'nite shape," she said. "A liquid can be poured. It takes th' shape o' its container and 'as a volume. Gas 'as no shape and no volume."

"Once again, a perfect answer, Miss Lewis. You may take your seat now."

Alice was again leaning forward in her seat. She looked as if she were straining to join the lesson without physically getting any closer.

"During our last lesson, someone asked a very astute question," Professor Wallis continued. "Miss Fisher, I believe it was." He motioned for Dora to join him. "Do you remember what you asked?"

"Sugar," she said, glancing at the crowd and looking down at her feet. Her face flamed red.

"Yes, sugar. You asked if sugar was a liquid, did you not?"

She nodded.

"And . . . ?" he prodded gently.

"We looked in the microscope," Dora said.

"And what did we find when we studied the sugar through a microscope?"

"Spaces," she said.

"Yes, exactly. There were spaces between the individual sugar grains, much too small to see with our naked eye—just like Dr. Jackson's bacteria." He patted her shoulder, directing her to return to her seat.

"Today we will discuss other bits of our world that can't be seen but are extremely powerful. They are called electrodes." He stepped back, motioning to the table. "Lady Covington has prepared a variety of demonstrations to illustrate the power of electrodes. But I think she will require assistance."

The girls' hands shot into the air again, but Professor Wallis was looking toward the audience. "I know just the person. He was one of, if not my most, brilliant student, and happily, he is in attendance today." Professor Wallis held out his hand, bending his fingers toward him. "Lord Lockhart, if you would be so kind."

Lord Lockhart looked stunned. His eyes were wide, and his face paled, then flushed. He stood, scooting along the row until he reached the aisle, and hurried forward.

Pencils scribbled madly on news reporters' notepads.

"Your Lordship," Professor Wallis said when he arrived at the stage. "If you would be so good as to explain to the students how a current-bearing wire operates in a magnetic field."

Lord Lockhart's cheeks were still red, and a sweat had broken out on his face.

Elizabeth worried she'd made a mistake. If this didn't work . . .

He stepped up to the table and looked over the items, choosing a few and coming back to sit on the edge of the stage.

The girls looked at him and then at one another, as if they were unsure.

Elizabeth looked at Professor Wallis, who watched his former student with a confident smile. She strained in her chair, trying to get a view of His Lordship, but the table blocked her.

Lord Lockhart cleared his throat. "I imagine you young ladies are familiar with magnets . . ." He coughed. "You may have noticed that some metal objects stick to one another." He spoke in a nervous voice, clearing his throat again.

Audience members in the rear of the room stood, craning their necks for a better view.

Elizabeth moved back to her former chair, pushing Gaffer off the seat and sitting where she could see what was happening at the front of the stage.

The cat glared at her.

Lord Lockhart held up two pieces of metal, demonstrating how they stuck together, and then when one was turned around, they repelled one another. He gave the metal to Betsy Norris, motioning for her to turn around to show the others. "Hold them close, but don't let them touch," he instructed. "Can you feel them pulling one another?"

Betsy did as she was told, bringing the metal pieces toward one another. "I feel it," she said.

Lord Lockhart nodded. "The objects are affecting one another without touching, wouldn't you say? Something is there between them. Something we cannot see. But it is powerful enough to draw the magnets together and push them apart. The force we cannot see is called a magnetic field."

Gaffer came to inspect the demonstration, sitting beside Lord Lockhart and watching the proceedings closely, his tail twitching from side to side.

Lord Lockhart motioned for Betsy to pass the magnets around for the other girls to inspect. While they each took a turn holding the magnets near enough to feel the pull, he ran a hand along the cat's back, and Gaffer soon made himself comfortable in Lord Lockhart's lap.

Elizabeth and Mrs. Boyle stared at one another, the secretary's open mouth and arched brows displaying the same astonishment Elizabeth felt. His Lordship appeared to have forgotten he was in a crowded hall. His focus was entirely on the students and the lesson.

Once all of the girls had the opportunity to try out the magnets, Lord Lockhart lifted a compass. "If the magnets affect one another without touching, the question is can they also affect a different object that is placed within their magnetic field?" His voice had not grown louder; instead, the room had quieted, listening.

The girls watched with rapt attention as the compass arrow followed the magnets.

Lord Lockhart scooted the cat from his lap and rose, returning to the table on the stage.

Vivian stood aside, making room for him to join her.

The two of them worked together, arranging the magnets and metal rods, demonstrating how the magnets charged the wire and in turn powered the battery. Lord Lockhart's voice was calm, his confidence growing as he explained the scientific concepts simply, keeping the attention of not only the students but the entire room.

To say that Elizabeth was surprised was an understatement.

The demonstration continued, Lord Lockhart and Vivian donning eye-protecting spectacles as devices buzzed and whirred on the table before them.

Professor Wallis looked like a proud father, standing to the side, hands clasped behind his back.

Elizabeth turned her attention to the crowd, judging their responses. Most sat quietly, their attention held by the sparks and movement of machinery on the table.

Lord Hastings and Lord Tynsdale, unsurprisingly, looked less than pleased.

Lord Chatsworth, however . . . When her eyes met his, his look of delight took Elizabeth's breath away. He nodded, his gaze darting to the demonstration and then back to her. *"Your plan worked."* She could hear his words just as clearly as if he'd said them aloud.

She raised and lowered her brows, giving a small smirk of acknowledgment. It had all gone so much better than she could have believed.

His Lordship continued to hold her gaze, his own relaxing into a gentle expression that made her breath stop completely. His lips quirked as if the two of them were sharing a secret.

Elizabeth could feel the heat in her cheeks. She felt a pull toward him, something strong, and—A crack and a flash of white light snatched her attention back to the table, where an arc of fire stretched between two rods, one held by Lord Lockhart and one by Vivian. The heat hit Elizabeth immediately, as did the smell of burning carbon.

The audience gasped.

Lord Benedict stood, holding the fire extinguisher hose at the ready.

The arc of fire was hypnotizing, its brightness unlike anything Elizabeth had seen before. It was as if they had harnessed lightning and commanded it to perform.

When Vivian disconnected the battery, the image of the bright arc still burned in Elizabeth's sight.

The audience burst into applause, the students cheered, and newsagents wrote frantically in their notebooks.

"I told you we couldn't follow that act," Dr. Jackson said to Elizabeth as they stood with the others to give a standing ovation.

The crowd started to filter out of the hall, chairs scraping and voices chattering excitedly.

Elizabeth stepped down from the stage, joining the girls as they recounted the "lightning" that had been produced with magnets.

Lord Lockhart picked up Gaffer, who was threading himself between his legs, and held the cat against his chest, scratching between his ears as Lockhart, Vivian, and Professor Wallis spoke together about some scientific hypothesis or another.

Elizabeth left the students and made her way through the crowd, but when she saw Lord Chatsworth, he was again escorting Lady Priscilla, their arms entwined. Alice was nowhere to be seen.

Elizabeth veered away, letting the throng block the couple from sight. She made a circuit of the emptying room, ending up back at the stage.

Lord Lockhart stepped in front of her. He still held the cat.

The two of them looked at one another, a tension filling the air between them. Elizabeth's chest was tight, both with fear of what he might say and what she must.

"I believe this is yours," he said at last, handing her the cat.

"Thank you." She accepted Gaffer, holding him awkwardly until he fought his way from her arms and jumped to the ground. "Your Lordship, I cannot thank you enough for what you did today. You were . . . brilliant with the students."

He cleared his throat, but he did not look away. There was hurt in his expression. And anger. "I am not a monster, Miss Miller, no matter what you may believe. I do care about people."

"Yes." Shame covered her like a wave of hot water. "I realize that now. I do." She forced herself not to look away. "I should not have made that sign. It was cruel and unjustified. I apologize."

Lord Lockhart nodded. He grimaced. "I've a need to apologize to you as well, miss." He glanced toward where he'd been seated earlier with his companions, clearing his throat. "I have not been entirely above board in my dealings with you. The factory employment policies, the increased taxation . . . that was my doing." He looked away, as if he could no longer meet her eyes. "I was . . . it was inexcusable."

"I know," Elizabeth said.

He faced her. "You know?"

She nodded.

He swallowed. "And do you intend to press charges? It is entirely within your right to do so."

"I do not, Your Lordship," she said, feeling a swell of pity for the man. Lord Chatsworth had been right about him all along. "But I do hope you will make it right."

"I will," he said firmly, glancing again toward where Lord Tynsdale and Lord Hastings had sat earlier.

"And I have an idea that may at least partially make amends for the embarrassment I caused you as well," she said.

"Oh?" he asked.

Gaffer had returned, and Lord Lockhart absent-mindedly bent down and picked him up.

"Come along with me," Elizabeth said. She glanced toward the high windows, hoping they still had sufficient daylight. "And bring the cat."

CHAPTER 18

CHARLES SAT BACK IN HIS armchair, tossing the *Times* onto the stack of broadsheets. He chuckled at the image: Elizabeth and Lord Lockhart standing in front of the Spitalfields school surrounded by children, he holding a cat and she a painted sign that read, "Lord Soft-Heart Is a Champion of the Poor." The other newspapers carried the same photograph on their front pages as well, with different versions of a similar headline: "Suffragette and Peer of the Realm Reconcile, Ending Their Feud." Miss Miller definitely knew how to garner attention.

Charles enjoyed the silence of his library. The hour before dinner was one of his favorite times. His daily work was finished, and the family was busy with their own doings. He took a drink of wine, letting his thoughts travel back to the event two days earlier. Miss Miller had been magnificent, her speech powerful, moving, and the event a success. And the woman herself . . . His stomach flopped over deliciously as he thought of her descending the stairs in her blue gown. A pity he'd not had an opportunity to tell her himself how exquisite she looked. At least Alice had had the courage to say something.

He took another drink. Apparently the residents of London's East End had been too frightening for Lady Priscilla and Miss Grey, and Charles had reluctantly accompanied them home, though he'd much rather have stayed and spoken with Miss Miller.

The event had been so unconventional, her plan to win over Lord Lockhart so unique. And from what he'd heard, the arrangements with the factories had been renegotiated, the school fully funded, and the tax rate adjusted, not to mention the *ton* were discussing next year's Spitalfields School event. Truly, the woman was a wonder. He took another sip and rested his head back, closing his eyes.

The library door burst open with such force that Charles jumped, spilling wine on his shirt and waistcoat.

Grandmother rushed inside.

Seeing the distress on her face, he jumped to his feet, a weight pressing on his chest as he tried to imagine what could be behind her upset. "What has happened?"

"Alice." Her voice choked on the word. "She is missing."

Missing? "Impossible." Charles led his grandmother to a sofa, helping her sit and offering her his handkerchief, which she took. "Mrs. Snowden does not allow the girl from her sight. She is here somewhere." He called for Nigel. "Perhaps she is hiding. You know how children are."

Nigel arrived, followed by a sobbing Mrs. Snowden, who cried, "I looked after her, Your Lordship, truly I did. But she must have sneaked away when my back was turned."

"Sit down, Mrs. Snowden." Charles's tone held significantly less compassion for the nanny than it had for his grandmother. Fear tickled the edge of his thoughts. He sent Nigel and the footmen to search the house. "Calm yourself, madam, and tell me what has happened."

"Miss Alice felt ill after breakfast," Mrs. Snowden said. She still sniffled but was making an effort to keep her voice steady. "She asked if she could return to bed, and I saw no harm in it." She looked between Grandmother and Charles, her eyes round, as if begging them to agree. "I checked in on her every few hours, but she was still sleeping, and I thought it best to let her be."

"When did you discover she was gone?" Grandmother asked.

"When I came to collect her for dinner. I thought she might regain her constitution if she ate something. But she wasn't there. The bedclothes were arranged to appear as if she were beneath them."

Charles had heard enough. He hastened from the room, climbing the steps two at a time. When he arrived at the nursery, it was just as Mrs. Snowden had described. Beneath the bedclothes was a wad of blankets. A clump of blonde hair spilled over the pillow. A hairpiece. Charles could see how the nanny had been deceived. With the curtains drawn, the room was dim. It would have appeared as if Alice were asleep in the bed.

He strode back into the corridor, calling for Nigel as he went and feeling as if he needed to continue moving in order to keep his panic at bay.

The butler met him at the top of the staircase, handing him a towel. "The search continues, my lord."

"Check everywhere," Charles said. He dabbed at the wine stains. "Each cupboard, behind every curtain. Any space small enough for her to hide. Make no exception." He wasn't certain what was behind Alice's disappearance, but from the way her bedding was arranged, there was more afoot than a simple misunderstanding.

Footsteps sounded overhead as the servants' rooms and attics were searched. Charles returned to the library, where the nanny still wept in her chair.

Grandmother paced in front of the window. "Alice has seemed so distracted lately. Melancholy," she said. "I assumed it was simply a case of the doldrums and it would pass." She dabbed beneath her eyes with his handkerchief. "What could have happened?"

"I don't know." Charles tossed aside the towel and stood in front of the hearth, his thoughts awhirl with questions. He rubbed his mustache, trying not to let his emotions overtake his thoughts. He had to consider the situation logically.

Had Alice been taken? Had she run away? The thought of the girl alone in London filled him with a dread that made it difficult to breathe. Alice knew nobody in the city aside from the family, their servants, and her tutors. *Miss Miller.* He went still. Alice adored the woman. Might she have gone to find her?

"If she is not located in the next few moments, send for the police," Charles said, starting for the doorway. "Ask for Inspector Jonathan Graham, specifically. Lady Mather will know how to reach him."

As usual, Nigel had anticipated Charles and had his gloves and hat waiting as Charles hurried through the entry hall and through the front doors. The evening was already dark and cool. Charles pushed away the image of Alice shivering in the cold and continued on. The Lancasters' home on Eaton Place was only a few blocks away from Ivy House, and he reached it within a few moments.

At his knock, an elderly butler opened the door, the slight tick of his brow the only indication of surprise at seeing a wine-stained earl alone on the doorstep at this hour.

"I am looking for Miss Miller, if you please," Charles said, stepping into the house and removing his hat. "Is she at home?"

The butler's brow ticked again, but he maintained the neutral expression on which men of his occupation prided themselves and held out his hand for the hat. "Miss Miller is in the sitting room. If Your Lordship pleases, I will announce you."

"There is no time," Charles said. He'd visited the Lancasters' house often enough with Ruben to know where the sitting room was. He started down the corridor with the butler at his heels. At the door, the man slipped past him, entering ahead. "Lord Chatsworth." He spoke in a breathless voice as Charles burst in.

Miss Miller sat on the sofa, leaning back against the armrest, her feet up on the cushion as she read from a book. Her cousin was seated in a similar position opposite her. Upon seeing him, the two ladies spun around, their feet hitting the floor at the same instant.

"Lord Chatsworth." Miss Lancaster rose to her feet first.

Miss Miller had a bit more trouble adjusting her skirts. When she stood, she regarded him with a quizzical expression, her gaze dropping to the stains on his chest. "Your Lordship?"

Charles had no time for formalities. "Have you seen Alice?"

The book dropped to the ground, and Miss Miller crossed the room to him. "Not since the event on Saturday. What has happened? Is she missing?"

He hadn't realized how much he'd wanted to be with Miss Miller, how much comfort her presence brought him, but now that he was here, the emotions he had fought forced their way to the surface. His throat tightened and he swallowed hard.

Miss Miller's hand was in his, the warmth of her touch seeping through his glove. "Come, sit down." Her voice was tender.

"Jameson, please bring Lord Chatsworth some tea," Miss Lancaster said.

Charles shook his head and remained standing where he was. The hope of finding Alice here was what he'd been holding to. "I thought she may have come here." He squeezed Miss Miller's hand, feeling strength from the touch. "I should return home. By now the police will have been summoned."

He began to turn toward the doorway but stopped, realizing he still held Miss Miller's hand. The contact felt like a lifeline, the only thing keeping him steady, and he feared that if he let go, he would be completely untethered. He needed her. "Elizabeth, will you come with me?" he asked. His voice sounded pathetic, vulnerable. If she rejected him, it would be humiliating.

"Yes, of course." The tenderness was still there, and the sound gave him a measure of comfort.

The pair hastily took their leave of Miss Lancaster and returned to Belgrave Square on foot. They walked in silence, for which Charles was grateful. Elizabeth knew nearly everything he did at this point, and reiterating the details would only increase his apprehension.

When the pair went into the library, they found it filled with people. Nigel and the footmen were speaking with two constables, and Leonard and Grandmother stood together as a man in a battered tweed coat wrote in a notebook while he spoke with Mrs. Snowden. Under the direction of the housekeeper, maids were distributing cups and saucers.

When the man in the tweed coat saw them, he said something to Mrs. Snowden, motioning for her to sit, then closed his notebook, placed it in a coat pocket, and approached Charles. He bowed, cap in his hand. "Yer Lordship." As he spoke, a scar on his cheek tugged at his side-whiskers. "I'm Detective Lester, at your service. Inspector Graham has been summoned, but we've no time to waste waiting around for him." He glanced to Charles's side and appeared to notice Elizabeth for the first time. "A pleasure to see ye again, Miss Miller."

"Detective Lester," she said, inclining her head. "I'm very glad you've come." Her voice was unsteady. She leaned closer to Charles, and he let go of her hand to touch the small of her back.

"What have you discovered, Detective? What is being done?" Charles asked.

"We've only just arrived, mind you," Detective Lester said. He retrieved the notebook from his pocket, flipping it open and taking the stub of a pencil from behind his ear. "I've spoken with the nanny there." He jerked his thumb backward, indicating Mrs. Snowden. "Thought I'd have a look at the girl's bedchamber, with your permission."

Charles and Elizabeth accompanied the detective up the stairs. He studied the bundle of blankets and the false curls in the bed, then moved to the window, trying the latch and looking closely at the windowsill. He pushed open the pane and looked down. "Doesn't appear as if anyone entered this way," he muttered, pulling back inside and closing the window.

"You think she may have been abducted?" Charles asked.

"We have to consider every possibility. When money's involved, ransom could be a motive." He looked up, as if referring to the house around them. He scratched his cheek as he looked back at the bed, then poked at the bedding, and crouched down, lifting the ruffle and peering beneath.

Elizabeth's breath hitched. When Charles looked at her, he saw that her eyes were wet. He reached into his pocket out of habit but realized he'd given the handkerchief to his grandmother.

He took her hand instead.

She was shaking.

Footsteps sounded behind them, and Inspector Graham came into the room. "Your Lordship, Miss Miller." He gave a brisk nod and stepped across the room to join the detective. "What have we got, Lester?"

"No sign of an intruder." Detective Lester pointed to the windowsill. "Linens arranged to resemble a sleeping child." He brushed his fingers over the blonde curls.

"We can safely assume her departure was planned," Inspector Graham said. He rubbed the fob of his pocket watch between his fingers as he considered. "How old did you say the child is?"

"Twelve," Charles said. "But she couldn't have left on her own. She has no money, no means of transportation. Nowhere to go."

"Was the child left alone?" Detective Lester asked.

"Alice was ill today," Charles said, "but her nanny remained close, monitoring her constantly." He glanced toward the bed. "Or, at least, she believed she was."

"Would Alice have any reason to want to leave Ivy House?" Inspector Graham asked.

"No. Certainly not. She is happy here. She . . ." For the first time, Charles felt a hint of doubt. He remembered how she'd hugged the edges of the rooms when she walked, how she'd shrunk away when his siblings spoke to her. "I believe she's happy." He spoke the last sentence quietly.

Elizabeth squeezed his hand.

"Had Alice been acting different as of late?" Inspector Graham asked. "Perhaps she made some new friends recently?"

"No, she is tutored at home," Charles said. "She has no . . . friends here." His doubt grew as he heard himself speaking the words aloud. "She has lived with us in London for only a few months." He glanced at Elizabeth.

She watched the interaction, her eyes still wet but contemplative.

"And where did she live before?" Inspector Graham spoke with the efficient tones of a person who did not allow himself to become distracted.

"Stourbridge," Charles said. "I only recently learned of her existence . . . she is the natural daughter of my father, and her mother is dead."

"Do you think she may have returned to Stourbridge?" Detective Lester asked.

The memory of the orphanage turned Charles's stomach. The institution was hardly more than a workhouse, with small dormitories overflowing with too many children and not enough beds. The children toiled in a warehouse, gluing labels and hauling crates of bottles. They were given just enough schooling to teach them to discern which label belonged with which bottle or jar. The sickly sweet odor of the glue combined with the disease and filth of unwashed children still made him ill. "No, I don't believe she would." He glanced at Elizabeth again, wondering what she was thinking.

"Even if she'd wanted to, she had no way to get there," Elizabeth said.

"In any case," Inspector Graham said, "Alice couldn't have left without assistance. This"—he motioned to the bed—"her delusion of the nanny as well as the rest of the staff required planning. And I do not believe a twelve-year-old child in an unfamiliar city could have managed it alone."

Elizabeth drew in a breath as she looked at the bed.

A wave of cold spread over Charles, and his head began to ache.

"Can you tell us," Inspector Graham continued, "when the last time you saw Alice was?"

"At breakfast," Charles said. "She . . . she was quiet. I was not surprised when Mrs. Snowden told me she felt ill."

"And did you speak to her at breakfast? Did she say anything unusual?" Detective Lester asked.

Charles thought back to the morning meal. "We spoke, just pleasantries. I asked about a book she'd been reading. She did not seem inclined to talk." The notion that Alice may have been planning an escape even as he'd made small talk caused his heart to hurt. "The conversation was rather dominated by my other sister. I . . . when I left, they were still eating."

Inspector Graham gave a curt nod, telling Charles the interview was finished. "We'll need to speak to the rest of the household, Your Lordship." He motioned to Detective Lester, who opened his notebook and held his pencil ready. "Are there any servants you suspect might be involved?"

"Certainly not." Charles was adamant on this point. "Each member of the staff has come highly recommended. Many have been with my family for decades. I trust each of them implicitly."

"Nevertheless," Inspector Graham said. "We will speak to them." He turned to his associate. "Lester, procure a list of the staff. Anyone who came in or out of the house today as well."

"Your Lordship." Elizabeth tugged at Charles's hand. She pulled him a short distance away from the police officers. "I wonder . . ." She grimaced. "I think . . . perhaps you should speak to Lady Kathryn."

"Kathryn?" He pulled away his hand, not liking the hesitance in her voice. "What has she to do with this?"

She blew out a breath, looking toward the doorway. "I just think you should speak with her."

"Lady Kathryn is . . . ?" Inspector Graham asked. He did not even pretend not to be listening.

"My sister," Charles said. He studied Elizabeth, trying to understand what she was not saying. Did she believe Kathryn was involved? Sweat dripped down his spine, and the comfort he'd felt moments before had fled, replaced by agitation. "But she has nothing to do with this."

"Send for her," Inspector Graham said.

Charles blinked. He was unused to being issued orders. This was his house and his family, and he felt his control slipping. He took a step back, lifting his chin and avoiding eye contact with any of them. "I will talk to Kathryn alone," he said and abruptly left the room.

After inquiring with Nigel regarding her whereabouts, Charles knocked on Kathryn's bedchamber door.

The lady's maid admitted him, and he entered. He hadn't stepped into his sister's room for years, and he took a moment to look around, reacquainting himself with her personal space. The dressing table was filled with bottles and ribbons, and hats and bonnets were arranged on racks. It was no longer the bedchamber of a child, he realized with surprise. His sister was a grown woman.

Kathryn turned from her seat at the dressing table. She was twisting a curl, shaping it around her finger. "Oh, Charles, do come in." She motioned to a small divan. "Oh! Your waistcoat. Is that wine?"

He sat. "You've heard that Alice is missing?"

"Yes, isn't it dreadful?" She turned back to the mirror, inspecting the curl. The lady's maid pushed an ivory comb into the arrangement.

"Have you any idea where . . . did she confide in you?" he asked.

"Of course not." Kathryn turned her head from side to side, studying the effect. She jumped up and crossed the room, pulling a rose-colored gown from her wardrobe. "I've chosen my debut dress," she said. "I debated between this and the peach one, but Madame Dubois, the dressmaker, says this color is much more flattering to my skin tone." She held the dress up before her. "What do you think?"

"Kathryn." Charles kept his voice calm. "The situation is critical. A child is missing. She could fall prey to any number of dangers on the London streets. We must find her as soon as possible."

"Don't worry about her, Charles." Kathryn flicked her fingers, as if banishing his worries. "She'll be perfectly well now that she's returned to her friends."

His gut sank. "What do you mean by that?"

Kathryn shrugged, pressing down the gown's ruffles and looking into the mirror. "I mean she must have returned to Dudley."

"Why would she do that?"

Kathryn tossed the gown onto the bed, sending the lady's maid scrambling to catch it before it slid to the floor. "Alice has no friends here. Nobody likes her. Even at the Spitalfields school the children didn't want to be with her, not with her satin dress and curled hair. She doesn't belong in London."

"Kathryn," he said slowly, trying to control the emotion in his voice. "How do you know about the Spitalfields school?"

She came to the divan, sitting beside him and taking his hands. "Charles, don't you see? It's for the best. Alice never should have come here."

He looked away, schooling his expression, and his gaze landed on the blonde hairpieces curled into various styles that hung beside Kathryn's dressing-table mirror. He closed his eyes, feeling them burn. "Kathryn, what have you done?"

"I helped." Kathryn spoke in the tone of a person entirely convinced that she'd done the right thing. "Alice wanted to go home, so I sent her there."

He was so angry that his muscles were quivering. "How could you do this? You engaged in a deception, purposely lying to me."

Kathryn sprang to her feet. She faced him, hands clenched, face red. Tears rushed from her eyes and flowed down her cheeks. "*I* am your sister, not *she*!" She stomped her foot in an action he remembered from her childhood. "Why do you worry so for an intruder?"

Charles opened his mouth to reply but closed it. He didn't know what to say.

"You used to carry me on your shoulders. We played jumping rope and blindman's buff. But now you have time for only *Alice*." Kathryn wiped furiously at her face. "You have not discussed my Season once. When I bring up the topic, it is swept away without a second thought. You wouldn't go shopping with me in Brighton. You have no time for me." She sank back onto the divan, her words punctuated by sobs. "Even Grandmother prefers to have tea parties and read picture books with Alice." She dropped her face into her hands. "As soon as she arrived, everyone forgot about me." She sobbed in earnest now, her shoulders rising and falling.

Charles was entirely dumbfounded. He thought back over the past months, his efforts to welcome Alice, to help her assimilate, to find tutors and clothes. He'd worried over her, read with her in the evenings, taken her to search for birds in Sussex . . . When he looked at his behavior through Kathryn's eyes, he saw how single-minded he'd been. He'd been so focused on one sister that he'd entirely overlooked the other.

"You're right," Charles said, very nearly sobbing himself. He pulled Kathryn into an embrace, holding her as she wept on his chest. "I have neglected you."

She sniffled, and Charles resolved to carry multiple handkerchiefs in the future.

He laid his cheek on her curls, tightening his arms around her. "I am so very sorry, Kathryn. Can you ever forgive me?"

She nodded, and her weeping slowed.

The lady's maid offered Charles a handkerchief, and he gave it to his sister, bringing her back to sit beside him on the divan.

The lady's maid pressed back into a corner of the room, doing her best to be invisible.

Kathryn wiped her cheeks, sniffling. "I know it wasn't the right thing to do," she said at last, looking down at her lap. "But I wanted my family back."

Charles put his arm around her, and Kathryn rested her head on his shoulder. "Taking on the responsibilities as the head of the family these past years hasn't been easy for me," he said. "And I can see I'm not the only one who suffers from the effects of my inadequacies." He sighed, feeling exhausted. "I have failed both of my sisters."

Kathryn remained quiet for a long moment. She twisted the handkerchief around her fingers. "Charles," she said at last. "Do not worry about Alice. I made certain she was taken safely the entire way to the children's home."

His earlier panic returned, as did his anger. "It is not a children's home, Kathryn. That place . . . the conditions are completely appalling. No child should have to endure such treatment, let alone our own sister."

Kathryn sat up, shaking her head. "Alice is with her friends there. She is happy; I know it. It can't be as bad as you think."

She looked convinced that what she spoke was the truth, but Charles could not overlook the utter selfishness of her action. "You can decide for yourself," he said, rising and crossing to the door, "when you accompany me there tomorrow."

"To Stourbridge?" Kathryn looked appalled at the idea. "Of course I can't go there."

Charles rested his hand on the door handle. "I am striving to learn from my mistakes, and as your guardian, I would be negligent if I didn't hold you to the same standard." He turned the handle, opening the door. "Actions have consequences, Kathryn. And they rarely affect only ourselves." He stopped before leaving the room, coming back inside and laying a hand on his sister's shoulder. "And once this business is finished, I am very interested in seeing all the gowns you've chosen for your Season."

Kathryn's defiant expression softened nearly into a smile.

CHAPTER 19

Elizabeth joined Lady Chatsworth in the library, watching the detectives and constables as they interviewed the household servants.

When a maid approached with the tea tray, she and Lady Chatsworth both held out their cups to be refilled. Elizabeth thought they needed the sustenance.

Lady Chatsworth dropped a cube of sugar into her tea and stirred it. "That poor, dear girl." She shook her head sadly. "What do you think has happened to her, Miss Miller?"

"Elizabeth, please." Lord Chatsworth had called her by her Christian name; it seemed only reasonable that his grandmother should as well. "Inspector Graham is the finest police officer in the city," she said, not knowing what other words of comfort she could offer. "He will not rest until Alice is found."

"But do you think he is proceeding sensibly?" she asked. "Why does he waste time interviewing the household when the person who took Alice is clearly not here?"

Elizabeth didn't know how to answer. She glanced to the doorway, wondering about the conversation between Lord Chatsworth and his sister. Elizabeth's intuition told her Lady Kathryn was somehow involved. She remembered the woman's face when Lord Chatsworth had turned down her request for a shopping trip. And surely the blonde hairpiece discovered in Alice's bed must have come from Lady Kathryn. Who else would know how to bypass the servants and arrange transportation? Lady Kathryn had more reason than anyone else to wish Alice gone.

The butler escorted in a group of kitchen staff, and the constables and Detective Lester set to work questioning them.

Elizabeth leaned forward, setting her teacup and saucer on the nearest table. She wondered if she should be finding an excuse to leave. She was adding nothing to the investigation. Why was she here in the first place?

Lady Chatsworth made polite conversation, but her thoughts were obviously elsewhere.

Nearly an hour had passed by the time Lord Chatsworth returned to the library. He spoke to Inspector Graham, who listened, nodding his head.

The inspector excused the staff and bid the women and Lord Chatsworth good evening, gathered the constables and his detective, and left.

Charles sat in a chair across from the women. He looked exhausted, his eyes red, face pale, and clothing stained. Even the wave of his blond hair that always fell carelessly over his forehead looked flat. "Alice is in Stourbridge," he said in a dull voice. "Kathryn helped her evade her nanny and Nigel and purchased a train ticket."

Lady Chatsworth sat up straight. "Of all the impertinent girls! If you'll excuse me, Elizabeth, I'll be having a word with my granddaughter now."

Lord Chatsworth held out a hand. "Please do not be angry with her, Grandmother."

She looked surprised. "And whyever not?"

He sighed, leaning forward and resting his forearms on his knees. "It was my fault," he said. "I've not cared for my family the way I should have." He hung his head forward, pushing his fingers through his hair. Elizabeth had never seen him looking upset or disheveled in any way until tonight. Pity swelled inside her. The man bore a heavy load.

"Charles," Lady Chatsworth began. She looked at Elizabeth as if she might hold the answer.

Elizabeth certainly did not. "Excuse me," she whispered, rising to leave. She had intruded long enough in the family's personal matters.

"Please stay." Lord Chatsworth looked up at her, but he did not rise.

Seeing the despair in his eyes, she couldn't refuse. She returned to her seat.

Lady Chatsworth left to speak with Kathryn.

"Your Lordship," Elizabeth said. "I am so sorry. But Alice is safe, is she not? And you know where she is. We can find solace in that, surely."

He rubbed his eyes. "I thought I was saving Alice. That by taking her away from the orphanage, providing an education, giving her security, I was improving her life. But my failing was the belief that what I could provide would bring her happiness. That this lifestyle is preferred, when in actuality, I took her from the life she knew and put her in a prison, forcing on her what I believed she needed, rather than what she wanted."

"You provided her the opportunity for a better future," Elizabeth said. "You gave her a family and a home."

"But she is unhappy," he said.

Elizabeth sighed. "Change is difficult for everyone. And finding where one belongs is not as easy as altering one's residence."

"She is my sister," he said. "I cannot just leave her there. I . . . I want Alice here, in my life. But if she doesn't want to stay . . ." He pushed his fingers through his hair again. "What should I do?"

"Perhaps the decision should be up to Alice," Elizabeth said gently.

Charles nodded. He came around the table, sitting on the sofa beside her, and slid his hand beneath hers, bringing it to his lips. "How is it that you are so wise, Miss Elizabeth Miller?"

The touch of his lips made her shiver. "I'm a teacher, Your Lordship."

A smile spread over his face, and although it didn't have its typical carefree ease, it was still enough to send a surge of heat over Elizabeth's skin.

"I could use a teacher," he said. "Might you be available to accompany me to Stourbridge tomorrow morning?"

"If thee thin' arm aboot to let ye goo tae Staahbridge alone, thee am saft as a biled taernip." Elizabeth put every bit of country accent into her words.

Lord Chatsworth laughed.

The sound set Elizabeth at ease, telling her she'd been more worried than she'd realized when she'd seen him so despondent. She laughed as well.

Lord Chatsworth's eyes twinkled. He slipped his hand behind her neck, bringing her face to his, their lips a breath apart.

The image of Lady Priscilla hanging on to his arm at the school came into her thoughts, and Elizabeth pulled away.

Hurt filled his eyes, but Elizabeth didn't change her course. She excused herself and hurried away.

She and Lord Chatsworth had developed a friendship, but beyond that . . . she knew all too well what men in his position thought of flirting and kisses with women in hers. It was just a game to them. And she'd not allow herself to be played.

Not when her heart wanted it all to be real.

❧❧

The following morning Clem brought Elizabeth to Victoria Station. The sky was heavy with gray clouds that gave an air of gloom. "A pity yer not off for another holiday," he said, looking at her small handbag.

"I agree," she said, putting some coins in his hand. "But it is just a quick trip."

He looked as if he'd reply but pulled off his hat instead, bowing. "Good morning, Yer Lordship, my lady."

Elizabeth turned, finding that Lord Chatsworth and his grandmother had come up to her.

"Clem." Lord Chatsworth's smile was not quite to its full strength. "Delighted to see you, my good man."

Lady Chatsworth extended her hand, greeting the cab driver warmly. "I've not seen you since you delivered all of those boxes of confectionaries at Spitalfields School," she said. "How helpful you were. It's nice to encounter you here."

Elizabeth noticed Her Ladyship's smile was strained as well.

Clem gave another bow and wished them a pleasant journey before climbing back into his cab.

"How do you do, my lady? Lord Chatsworth?" Elizabeth curtsied.

"Oh, Elizabeth, I'm so glad you're with us." Lady Chatsworth took her arm, any pretense of a smile falling away. Her face was drawn. The poor woman must not have slept. "Let us go find our dear girl."

Lord Chatsworth's expression was grim. He held out a hand, inviting the women to precede him.

Having no luggage to manage, the trio walked directly to the platform. The Chatsworths' train carriage was exactly as it had been the last time Elizabeth had seen it; however, this time, they boarded from the other side since the journey would be northward.

When Elizabeth entered the carriage, she was surprised to see Lady Kathryn sitting in a chair beside the window. Her arms were folded and she looked sullen, staring through the glass and purposely not meeting any of their gazes. She had obviously not joined the party willingly.

They were greeted by a porter and the smell of fresh scones. But none of the travelers had an appetite. Lady Chatsworth sat in the armchair, and Lord Chatsworth and Elizabeth took seats across from one another on the benches near the window on the other side of the carriage. They all knew to give Lady Kathryn a wide berth.

The train started off with a whistle and a lurch. The journey was quiet, a sharp contrast from the jolly excursion a few weeks earlier.

Lady Chatsworth opened a book, but she didn't turn the pages. She wiped her eyes occasionally, and within a few moments of departure, she had fallen asleep.

Lady Kathryn continued her silence, and eventually she got up and went into the sleeping berth, letting the curtain fall closed behind her.

Lord Chatsworth stared through the rain-soaked window. His worry over what would happen when they arrived in Stourbridge was palpable.

"How did you learn of Alice, if you don't mind my asking?" Elizabeth said, desperate to break the dismal silence. "You told Inspector Graham you'd not known about her until recently."

He brushed the side of his finger over his mustache. A habit she'd come to recognize as one he did when he was considering his words.

"It was Mr. Whitesides, my secretary, who discovered an anomaly in my father's private accounts. Father's man of business had remained in the position until his retirement, and Mr. Whitesides had only recently taken his place. He noticed a monthly payment to an account in Cradley Heath. I recognized neither the name nor the place and asked him to investigate."

Elizabeth knew of Cradley Heath. The village was small, hardly more than a few houses and shops.

"Mr. Whitesides located a man named Mr. Buford, a solicitor in Stourbridge who had arranged the account with my father for a Miss Jessop and her daughter."

"Alice," Elizabeth guessed.

He nodded.

"When Mr. Whitesides and Mr. Buford sought out Miss Jessop for further inquiry, they learned the account hadn't been touched in three years. You can guess the rest."

"Miss Jessop had died," Elizabeth said.

"And Alice had been taken to the orphanage in Stourbridge," Lord Chatsworth said. "When I learned my father had another child, I went to Stourbridge immediately." He looked back to the window. "When I saw her . . . I knew I couldn't leave her there. She . . ." He swallowed. "She was meant to be with me—with my family."

Elizabeth wanted to touch him, to hold his hand, wrap him in an embrace, anything to lessen the pain in his eyes.

"You cannot imagine the condition of that place," he continued. "It is foul. There is a smell of illness, a sense of despair. For her to prefer that over . . ." He rubbed his eyes. "She must have been truly unhappy at Ivy House. And I was too blind to see it."

"I don't believe she was unhappy," Elizabeth said. "She may have had moments of sorrow, but overall, she seemed to enjoy your home. She loves you and your grandmother. That I am certain of."

"Then, why would she leave?"

"She is a child, and children are susceptible to suggestion." She glanced toward the velvet curtain, glad the noise of the train kept their voices from carrying. "If Lady Kathryn spoke to her when she was particularly upset, she could have been more easily convinced that Ivy House was the source of her unhappiness."

Lord Chatsworth looked toward the sleeping berth and grew quiet.

Elizabeth let the conversation fall away. The remainder of the journey was silent, aside from the porter's offer of tea.

Eventually, the rain stopped, but the sky did not brighten. It remained a dull gray, the horizon lightening with bursts of flame from the furnace towers. The train passed by tall piles of slag, pit mounds, and enormous tanks of steaming wastewater.

When they at last arrived at the station, the porter assisted the women in stepping down onto the uneven wooden boards of the platform. Sounds of forges echoed in the distance. The air smelled burnt.

Nostalgia warred with memories best left forgotten, moving through Elizabeth in a rush of conflicting emotion. She breathed in, the air stinging her nostrils. For better or for worse, she had returned to the Black Country.

CHAPTER 20

A CARRIAGE WAS WAITING AT the small Stourbridge station. Charles assisted his grandmother and sister as they climbed inside, then held out his hand for Elizabeth.

She took it, glancing at the sky as she climbed onto the step.

Elizabeth's eyes were red, and he wondered if it was a reaction to the smoky air or if some emotion had affected her. There was definitely enough of that to go around. Poor Grandmother had wept through the night, and Charles himself had indulged in a bout of melancholy he'd not felt since his mother's death all those years earlier. There was something to be said for keeping one's sentiments hidden behind a wall of triviality and amusements. It was much less painful.

He settled in and rapped on the carriage roof, directing the driver to set off.

The tension in the carriage was thick, and Charles looked through the window, trying to distract his mind from what was ahead. What would he do if Alice didn't want to return to London? How could he say goodbye to her?

Grandmother's hand pressed on his knee, and Charles realized his leg was bouncing. He leaned forward, taking her hand and squeezing it. The same turmoil he felt was reflected in her face, and the heaviness of his familial responsibilities pulled at him, straining his already thin nerves.

Grandmother gave a small cough. "Goodness, this air . . . I feel as though I've swallowed a spoonful of ash."

"It is dreadful," Kathryn agreed, holding a handkerchief over her face.

Charles appreciated Grandmother's attempt at light conversation but could not bring himself to engage. He nodded an acknowledgment of hers and Kathryn's comments and glanced at Elizabeth. She looked through the carriage window, and he would have given a pretty penny to know her thoughts. The night before she'd departed in a rush, drawing away at his attempt to kiss her. Her action had left him confused. He'd thought their connection was growing, that she felt the same affection that increased in him with every encounter. He'd thought she may even love him. Perhaps he deluded himself in that as well.

They arrived at the Stourbridge Asylum for Orphans. A high wrought-iron fence surrounded the property, and inside was a brick-and-stone building with small windows and a tall clock tower. There was no trace of plant life in the garden, no sound of children's laughter. The edifice had the appearance of an institution, rather than a home for children.

The four stood for a moment at the gate, waiting for a gatekeeper. A flock of wood pigeons pecked the ground inside the fence.

Grandmother looked pale as she gazed around.

"Where are all the children?" Kathryn asked.

"Working." Elizabeth's mouth was set in a determined line.

The gatekeeper arrived at last, hurrying across the lawn and scattering the birds. He looked the group up and down, his curiosity obvious. Charles requested an audience with the director, Mr. Hamblin, and the gatekeeper escorted them inside, indicating benches and a few straight-backed chairs inside the front doors, where they could wait. The space was large with stone floors and high ceilings held up with wooden rafters. It was also extremely cold, the only light filtering in through windows far above the front doors.

The four of them sat together on a bench. Grandmother was between Charles and Kathryn. Elizabeth sat on Charles's other side.

The gatekeeper spoke before hurrying away down a corridor, but Charles hadn't understood anything he'd said.

"I should have asked you to manage the communication," he said to Elizabeth. "I confess I do not know if he has gone to find the director, or if he's just told us to jump into the sea."

"I will, if you'd like," Elizabeth said. "If you trust me to do so." She gave a small smirk and a wink.

She was attempting to set him at ease, but he didn't engage in repartee. The truth was he did trust her. More than anyone he knew. "That is why I wished for you to come," he said. "Not because of your understanding of the dialect but because I trust you fully."

Elizabeth studied him, likely ensuring that he was speaking sincerely, then turned away. "Thank you, Your Lordship." She spoke the words quietly.

"At this point, I think it entirely appropriate for you to use my name," he said. "I would prefer you to call me Charles."

Elizabeth darted a glance toward his grandmother and sister, her face reddening. "Very well," she said.

Grandmother was rubbing her forehead. Kathryn was watching the door where the gatekeeper had gone. Whether they didn't hear their conversation or just chose to ignore it, Charles couldn't be certain.

A hand pressed on his knee, which he realized was bouncing again. This time it was Elizabeth's. "Everything will be all right, Charles." She pulled her hand away quickly, but its heat remained, spreading until it covered him like a warm blanket.

Mr. Hamblin came into the waiting area. He was tall and slender with yellowed teeth, thick brows, and deep lines around his mouth. His lip was permanently fixed in a sneer. Charles had met the man once before, when he'd come for Alice, but they had hardly spoken. Mr. Whitesides and Mr. Buford had handled the interactions and legalities. Charles's concern had been for only Alice. The gatekeeper followed the director, coming into the waiting area and crossing the room to stand beside the door.

The visitors stood.

Elizabeth strode forward, meeting the director halfway across the room. "Good day, sir. You are the asylum director?"

Mr. Hamblin appeared disconcerted, not just by a woman taking charge of the meeting but very likely also because of the confident way in which she did it. She spoke crisply without a trace of the country accent Charles had assumed she'd employ in the circumstance.

"Yes. Mr. Hamblin." The director gave her a dismissive glance, looking past her at Charles, as if expecting him to take the lead.

Charles watched Elizabeth.

She stepped to the side, standing in the director's line of sight. "How do you do, sir? I am Miss Miller, the Chatsworth family's representative. You see behind me Lord Chatsworth, the Dowager Lady Chatsworth, and Lady Kathryn."

Mr. Hamblin bowed, but the motion held no deference. He studied them with a shrewd gaze that made Charles's skin crawl. The thought that this man was anywhere near his little sister was nearly enough to send him rushing past him and searching the school until he found her and carried her far away from here.

"We've come to speak with Miss Alice Jessop, if you'd be so kind as to send for her," Elizabeth said.

"Thought ye moight be retuhnin' 'ere," Mr. Hamblin said, looking at Charles. He ran the tip of his tongue around the inside of his lips and sucked his teeth.

"Is Alice here?" Elizabeth asked.

"Ay, 'er's 'ere," Mr. Hamblin said, still watching Charles.

"Oh, thank goodness." Grandmother pressed her hand to her chest. Charles and Kathryn helped her sit back on the bench.

"Please send for her," Elizabeth said.

Mr. Hamblin's sneer grew sinister. He said something in a thick accent to the gatekeeper, who responded in turn.

Charles understood none of their words.

"Oy ain' sid Miss Jessop in a whoyle, nah." Mr. Hamblin put his hands in his pockets. "Moit prove difficult tae locoit 'er."

"What did he say?" Kathryn asked, leaning across Grandmother to whisper at Charles.

He could only shrug.

The gatekeeper spoke again, and Mr. Hamblin continued to smirk, his eyes cold. He started to say something, but Elizabeth stopped him.

"Nah." Her voice was sharp, echoing through the stone room. "Thee bay usin' this gel." The men stared at her. "You will not use the girl to line your pockets," Elizabeth said, speaking once again in a formal accent. Her voice was stern. "Or I'm certain Lord Chatsworth will have no difficulty using his position to relieve you of yours."

Mr. Hamblin glanced at Charles again.

"Send for Alice immediately," Elizabeth said once more. She stood tall, facing down a man who physically dominated the space but somehow seemed to shrink under her gaze.

Mr. Hamblin nodded to the gatekeeper, who rushed away. The director excused himself, leaving the room in quick strides.

Elizabeth turned, coming back to join him as they both retook their seats. She blew out a breath, looking extremely pleased.

"That will teach him." Kathryn scowled toward the door and then looked at Elizabeth, obviously impressed.

"You were magnificent, Elizabeth," Grandmother said.

"Magnificent indeed," Charles said. He looked toward the corridor where the director had disappeared. "He retreated with his tail between his legs."

Elizabeth smirked, an expression Charles was coming to anticipate. She employed it quite regularly, and the sight was reassuring. "I must say that was most satisfying."

The door creaked open, letting in a slice of dim light.

Alice slipped through. She stood just inside the doorway, her face cast downward and her arms folded, looking as if she were attempting to make herself even smaller.

Good manners urged Charles to rise, but his instincts told him to remain seated lest he frighten her away.

"Oh, my darling," Grandmother said. She held out her hand.

Alice hesitated, taking a step closer. She wore the linen dress and pinafore of the orphanage uniform. Her boots were much too large. She looked up, revealing the shine of tears on her cheeks.

Kathryn gasped.

"Are you very angry with me?" Alice asked in a voice that was hardly more than a whisper.

"Of course not," Grandmother said. She dropped her hand. "Alice, my dear, we were so worried about you."

"I'm sorry." The way she stood reminded Charles of those first weeks after he'd met her, when the girl always looked tensed, as though she were ready to flee at any moment.

The sight discouraged him, especially after all the efforts he'd made to earn her trust.

"Have you come to take me back?" she asked, glancing quickly at Kathryn.

"Only if that's what you choose," Charles said. "We've just come to talk."

Alice looked surprised. She was not used to being allowed to choose anything.

Charles stood then and brought a chair closer, setting it in front of them and motioning for her to be seated before he returned to the bench between Grandmother and Elizabeth.

Alice sat, her legs swinging, as her feet didn't reach the floor.

Charles stroked his mustache as he considered how to begin. If he said the wrong thing, they could lose Alice forever.

Elizabeth's leg pressed against his, giving him a boost of encouragement.

"Alice, will you tell us why you left?" he asked.

She sat quietly, looking down at the floor.

Now that he was closer, Charles could see bruises on her legs, sending hot spikes of anger through him, but he kept his voice gentle. "Please, my dear. The truth won't offend us. We simply want to understand."

"I don't belong in London," Alice whispered.

Grandmother began to reply, but Charles placed his hand on hers, stopping her. Alice needed the chance to explain herself.

"Why do you believe that?" he asked.

Alice squeezed her eyes shut as more tears came out. "I don't speak correctly. My manners are all wrong. I don't even know how to eat properly."

Kathryn shifted uncomfortably and folded her arms.

Now that Alice had started, the words fell out in a rush. "The Spitalfields girls consider me above their station. The Society ladies consider me below their notice. Even here—" She looked toward the doorway, hunching her shoulders and rubbing a hand over her arm. "Everywhere I go, I'm out of place." She swiped her palms over her cheeks, smearing dirt and tears and barely managing to get the words out. "I belong nowhere."

Charles's heart was heavy. He gave her one of the three handkerchiefs from his pocket and scooted forward so their knees were close. "Alice, I was wrong in how I treated you."

She looked up, sniffling.

"I tried to change you, to mold you into what I thought you should be. How you should dress, how you should speak, what you should be taught." He swallowed, too aware of his failings. "But perhaps what I believed you lacked wasn't what you actually required. You are not me, and I am not you, and that is something I have learned."

"I like reading," Alice said. "Especially about animals. I enjoy reading Sir Cornelius Poppleford's illustrated handbooks. And I enjoy searching for birds."

The heaviness in Charles's chest lightened just a bit. "I enjoy those things too."

Alice sighed, lowering her face. "But . . ."

Charles sighed as well. Having similar interests wasn't enough. Alice's concerns were complicated, and they wouldn't be solved tidily.

Elizabeth leaned forward. "I understand how you are feeling, Alice," she said. "It can be an advantage to have a foot in two worlds, such as when one wishes to appeal to both wealthy donors and to factory workers." Now it was her turn to sigh. "But most of the time, it means you fully belong in neither. And it can be very lonely."

Alice sat very still as Elizabeth spoke, realizing that Elizabeth's situation was very similar to her own. "How did you find your place?" she asked, a cautious hope in her eyes.

"I found people who loved me, who helped me and understood me. My cousin, my aunt and uncle, and my friends." She looked at Grandmother and Charles as she said the last word.

"No matter your choice," Charles said to Alice, "you will not face it alone. We will always be your family. If you decide to stay in Stourbridge, I will ensure that you have access to books, to school."

"And if I return to London?" she asked.

Charles did not allow his hopes to overtake his reason. She had not given an answer. "I cannot promise it will be perfect," he said. "I am still learning. And as much as I wish to, I cannot fully understand your experience. But I promise I will try. I will be honest with you if you will be honest with me."

"Will you come home, dear?" Grandmother asked.

"Please, Alice." Kathryn spoke with a choke in her voice. "I haven't treated you as a sister, and I would very much like another chance to do it properly."

Alice scooted forward, hesitating at the edge of her seat, and then all at once she propelled herself forward and into her grandmother's waiting embrace.

Charles put his hand on her back, and Alice twisted, extending her arm to draw him in to the embrace as well, and then she reached for Kathryn.

Charles pulled Elizabeth's arm, bringing her against him and putting his arm around her. The position was awkward, but he didn't release her. She belonged in this embrace every bit as much as any of them. She belonged in his family. That thought brought him up short. It was not as if it was a surprise. He'd known for a long time that he loved her. But convincing her of it would take effort. He'd won back Alice's trust. Now to work out how do the same for Elizabeth, because Charles could not envision a future without her.

CHAPTER 21

ELIZABETH STOOD IN THE REAR of the school's assembly hall, applauding with the girls as Charles and Alice completed their presentation about the birds of London. They had brought enlarged photographs of the various birds, he and Alice taking turns describing each species and telling interesting facts.

At the end they had played a game, holding up a photograph for the students to identify. With each picture the girls called out the name excitedly, cries of "Tree sparrow," "Starling," and "Coal Tit" echoing through the hall. Elizabeth was surprised by how quickly the girls memorized the various species.

Since Alice had returned to London a month earlier, she and Charles had come three times to the school, bringing stuffed specimens, pictures, and a mountain of knowledge about the feathered inhabitants of the planet. Elizabeth had enjoyed watching Charles interact with the children. His natural cheer and quick smile made him a favorite among the girls.

Alice's speech lessons had tapered off, and Elizabeth visited her only a few times a week. She'd missed their interactions, but the girl had little need of speech training any longer. Elizabeth had seen Charles only a very few times since traveling to Stourbridge. He'd sat in on a few lessons, but he had apparently been very busy helping Kathryn plan her coming-out ball. Alice had been delighted to be included in the selection of a ballgown for her sister and had told Elizabeth repeatedly about the visit she and Kathryn had made to the seamstress together. It appeared the discord in the Chatsworth home was being mended.

Elizabeth made her way to the stage, stepping up and helping him return the pictures to a box. "That was very well received," she said. "Thank you."

"I should apologize to the feathered residents of the city," he said, chuckling. "They are going to find it difficult to be anonymous around Spitalfields."

He glanced to where Alice was talking with a group of girls. Through their visits to the school, the students had warmed to Alice, little by little. Elizabeth could see it was an enormous relief to her brother.

He stacked the final pictures into the box. "I wondered if you might spare a moment for an audience," he said. "There is a matter I should like to speak with you about."

"Yes, of course." Elizabeth studied him, trying to discern his intention. "Is something wrong?"

He motioned with a sweep of his arm. "In your office?"

He did not appear upset. Perhaps he simply had a question about Alice. She glanced toward the girls.

"Mrs. Boyle has things well in hand," he said. His arm was still outstretched.

He held her arm as she stepped down off the stage, and the pair walked through the entry hall and up the stairs. When they arrived at her office, Charles held open the door.

Elizabeth entered, stopping when she saw a painting propped up in her chair. She stepped closer, studying it. The image was of two white geese tending a clutch of eggs on a rocky shore.

Gaffer rolled over on the desk, looking at the painting and rolling back, unimpressed.

"What is this?" Elizabeth asked.

"Snow geese," Charles said. He stepped up behind her. "They are native to the Americas. Aren't they glorious?"

"Very beautiful," she said, noticing the black tips of their wings.

"Snow geese—and most geese, in fact—are special, in that they choose one mate for life."

Something in his tone had changed. His words were spoken earnestly, as if it were important for her to understand.

He took her elbow, turning her around to face him. "I am not my father, Elizabeth. I saw the toll his disreputable conduct took on my mother, the lack of respect from his colleagues, the lives he damaged." His glance darted to the doorway, and she knew he was speaking of Alice and her mother.

"I inherited his reputation, and I played the part of the frivolous pleasure-seeker. It was easy enough because I was resigned to the fact that I would one day have to marry . . . someone, but I never intended to fall in love." He slid his hands down her arms, entwining his fingers in hers. "Until I met you."

"Charles . . ." She drew back but could not move very far without knocking over the painting. Her thoughts spun. Was Charming Chatsworth actually declaring his love? For her? Was this a jest? "But you . . . I . . ." She pulled away a hand, pressing it to her cheek. Her heart was pumping blood straight to her face, betraying her reaction.

He pulled her hand gently away from her face, holding both of hers against his chest. "I am in earnest. Lower your defenses, Elizabeth. Allow yourself to trust me."

Did she trust him? Could she trust him? He was, above all else, a man. A powerful man, exactly the type she'd fought against at every point in her life. But she thought of Uncle Eldon, of Clem, and even Lord Lockhart. Was her pride preventing her from seeing that not every man was determined to control her, to silence her?

"Did you say you are in love with me?" she whispered.

His lips pulled in a tiny smile. "I am."

She looked back at the snow geese. One mate for life. Charles was not like his father. He'd shown it again and again. When she'd told him she didn't wish to be teased, he'd stopped. When he'd learned of the Brookline Group's interference, he hadn't stepped in and put it right. He'd allowed her to decide how to proceed with the information. He'd come to her when Alice was lost, trusted her to speak to the orphanage director. Charles valued her. He believed in her. And he'd given her every reason to trust him in return. If she could only find the courage to allow herself to love, to be loved. His heart beat beneath her fingers. She kept her gaze on his lapels. "My defenses, as you call them, have protected me for so long that I'm afraid to . . ."

She mustered her courage and looked up into his eyes, seeing in them assurance and such adoration that it made her ache. He had bared his heart to her, holding nothing back and leaving himself vulnerable.

"I am in love with you too." She blinked, surprised to hear herself say the words aloud.

A slow smile spread over his mouth as he took her in his arms. Elizabeth's fingers wound in his hair as they kissed, and in that moment, her doubts fled. Charles was everything he said he was and more. And in his arms, she felt cherished.

He held her cheeks in his hands, kissing her cheek, her jaw, her chin, the whiskers of his mustache tickling her skin. "I may have left out the part where I ask you to marry me." He pulled back to watch her face. "The geese painting was supposed to imply it, but I didn't say the words implicitly."

Elizabeth glanced over her shoulder at the painting. At the birds and their nest. She could not think of anything that more appropriately represented this man she loved.

He watched her expectantly. "I will marry you," she said, feeling immensely shy as the words left her mouth. She laid her head against his chest, hiding her face until the heat calmed. "I do have one question, however."

"Oh?" His voice rumbled beneath her ear.

"As your wife, will I automatically have membership in the West Sussex Order of the Friends of Fowl and Feather?"

He laughed aloud, wrapping his arms tightly around her. "As Lady Chatsworth, you will have anything money can buy. Ask me for diamonds, ask me for a palace—it is yours. I will do anything for you, my dear." He drew her away, holding her by the shoulders. "But I am afraid that is one title you must win on your own merit." His smile grew wide, his teeth flashing, dimples showing in the glorious image that had captured the admiration of so many readers of the society columns.

Elizabeth could hardly look at him without her heart feeling as if it were overflowing.

"I have a question for you as well," he said.

"Oh?"

If you will remember, almost a year ago, in the Marquess of Molyneaux's sitting room, before you tossed the contents of my wineglass over my borrowed shirt and waistcoat, you made a vow. 'I will never dance with you as long as I live,' were, I believe, your exact words."

Elizabeth narrowed her eyes playfully. "That is not a question."

He nodded, his smile somehow managing to grow even wider. "My question is this: Kathryn's debut ball will be in less than a month, and I do hope that, as my fiancée, you will consent to standing up with me—at least once?"

Elizabeth had forgotten about that day, about that vow. It seemed so silly now. She'd not known to whom she was speaking, that it was a generous, kind, honorable man she'd tossed the wine at. She felt sorry for the version of herself who didn't know the truth, because to her, it was the most valuable knowledge she possessed. "I will dance with you," she said. "Though, I am afraid you will be disappointed at my skill."

He cupped her head in his hand, drawing her to him for another kiss. "If that were your only skill, I would be very disappointed indeed, but knowing you as I do, seeing firsthand your accomplishments and intelligence, a small thing such as dancing hardly deserves mention." He brushed a kiss over her lips. "You are exceptional, Elizabeth."

She reached for him, pulling him close, her kiss a hope and a promise.

QUOTED IN
EDUCATING ELIZABETH

Mary Kalantzis and Bill Cope, "Catherine Beecher on the Role of Women as Teachers," *Works & Days*, https://newlearningonline.com/new-learning /chapter-5/supproting-materials/catharine-beecher-on-the-role-of -women-as-teachers, from Catharine Beecher, *Suggestions Respecting Improvements in Education: Presented to the Trustees of the Hartford Female Seminary, and Published at their Request* (Hartford, CN: Packer & Butler, 1829), 7–8, 10–11, 15.

George Washington, "From George Washington to Bushrod Washington, 15 January 1783," https://founders.archives.gov/documents/Washington /99-01-02-10429.

AUTHOR'S NOTE

Before I began this project, I spent some time considering what exactly I wanted to say. What is important enough to me that I'm willing to spend an entire series exploring it? What have I learned, or what do I want people to know or to reexamine in their own perceptions?

Still looking for a direction, I read quite a few books and watched some movies, and after a while, I began to notice a trend that was so contrary to my own experience that I was surprised I'd never realized it before. It involves how women's relationships with one another are portrayed in fiction, especially in romantic stories, and it's something I'm guilty of in my own writing. Women are often represented as rivals, either to provide competition for the main character in vying for the same man's affection or simply to give the main character someone to compare herself to. Other times, they are under-developed secondary characters the heroine confides in when she wants to talk about the hero.

Neither scenario quite reflects my own experiences. From the moment I was born, my mother, sisters, grandmothers, aunts, cousins, friends, and teachers cheered for me, encouraged me, and offered advice as I grew up. And now I still find myself surrounded by strong, intelligent, supportive women in every area of my life. Women are my friends, my mentors, and my heroes. I turn to them when I'm hurting or unsure or happy, and time and again, I've been bolstered and comforted and inspired by my own Blue Orchid Society. The women I know are complex and interesting and filled with wisdom. And that is what I hope to represent in this series—the sisterhood that's often overlooked in stories but so prominent in the lives of real women.

I love the time period of this story. The industrial revolution was changing the way people worked and lived. Florence Nightingale was instructing nurses, and women were being admitted to colleges and inheriting property. Colonies were pushing back against English expansion. The suffrage movement was growing in both England and America. Women were working as detectives in the Pinkerton Agency and starting to get credit as writers and teachers.

It feels like such an exciting time, and such a turning point in history, and I wanted my characters to be smack in the middle of it, navigating these modern developments and adjusting to a changing world.

So this book is meant as a tribute to them—the women who came before—and to us, the women who follow in their footsteps. And to the sisterhood that has marched along throughout history, often silently and unnoticed, and shaped our world.

JENNIFER MOORE

SOLVING

Sophronia

A Victorian Romance

THE BLUE ORCHID SOCIETY

CHAPTER 1

DETECTIVE JONATHAN GRAHAM OF LONDON Metropolitan Police Force's Criminal Investigation Department stood in front of the bustling Paddington Railway terminal. He took a paper sack from his pocket and retrieved a peppermint, popped it into his mouth, and nodded to the constables accompanying the prisoners—the jewel thieves Alvin Marley and Boyd Wardle—as the wagon started east toward the H Division police headquarters in Whitechapel. Once they were well underway, he turned and strode to where Sergeant Gordon Lester waited, holding tightly with both hands to a leather satchel. Two blue-uniformed constables, Brunswick stars glinting on their helmets and collar numbers shining in the few rays of sunlight that pushed through the afternoon fog and smoky air, stood on either side of the sergeant.

The small amount of space the Duchess of Attenborough's jewels occupied inside the bag was at odds with their immeasurable value. One small gem was worth more money than any of these men would see in their lifetimes, and yet they'd not hesitated to risk their lives in returning the jewelry to the duchess. Jonathan felt a swell of pride as he looked at the men. Agents of law enforcement were, at best, offered grudging respect, typically disregarded or criticized, and more often than not, treated with contempt and outright hostility. Yet, there they were, walking their beats day after day, putting in long hours to return a lost child or apprehend a thief, and doing all within their power to protect the citizens of a rapidly swelling city.

As Jonathan approached, one of the constables caught his eye. Constable Ernest Merryweather looked dead on his feet. His uniform was rumpled, and his eyes were red. The man had been working since the day before, when they'd been called to the scene of the robbery. He'd proven himself to be tireless. And hadn't it been Constable Merryweather who'd discovered the broken latch on the cellar window?

The onlookers who had gathered to watch as the arrests were made had dispersed, but the street was still crowded.

Jonathan noticed Merryweather shift closer to the sergeant as a group of young lads darted past. The man's movements were subtle, his eyes alert. Good instincts, that one.

Sergeant Lester held out the bag of jewelry. "Still too early to knock off for the day." His smirk pulled at a scar that ran through the thick muttonchops on his cheek. The sergeant's voice was gravelly and low, but he spoke loudly enough to be heard over the sounds of carriages and crowds.

Jonathan waved for the sergeant to retain the satchel. "Suppose so." He glanced at his pocket watch, then raised his brows and gave a small smirk of his own. "Pity we apprehended them so early. Left ourselves time to write up the reports."

"Congratulations, sir," Sergeant Lester said, and his mouth spread into a genuine smile. "Nice bit of detective work."

The praise made Jonathan uncomfortable, but he shrugged it off, looking away across the street and rubbing the pocket watch fob between his fingers. "It was a group effort, Sergeant. All of the men contributed." He motioned with his chin in the direction the prisoner wagon had gone. "Even Mr. Wardle and Mr. Marley contributed—unintentionally, of course. Only a matter of time before a criminal makes a mistake; that, you can count on."

Sergeant Lester laughed. "You're being modest, if you don't mind me saying so, sir. Poor blokes had no way o' knowing you'd investigate them so thoroughly. And I'll not soon be forgetting the look on their faces when we stormed the passenger carriage."

"Their disguises really were terrible, weren't they?" Jonathan grinned.

Beside them, Constable Merryweather snorted.

Jonathan watched the street traffic for a moment longer, then gave a sharp nod. "Right, then." He motioned to another of the constables. "Constable Hutchings, we'll be needing two hackney cabs, if you please. Direct them to wait. You others, be on your guard." He motioned to the satchel in the sergeant's hands. "I'm not interested in hunting down this bag a second time."

Seeing the men's acknowledging nods, Jonathan crossed Praed Street to a vendor and purchased a bag of tarts. The small gesture was by no means adequate compensation for his comrades' work on this case, but he wished to express his gratitude all the same. One solved theft hardly made a dent in London's crime situation, but it was still commendable, and he wanted the men to have a moment of celebration.

An hour later Jonathan stepped through the door of the H Division station and removed his hat.

Bert Abner, the desk sergeant, glanced up. "Detective Graham, I've some mail for you." He pulled a pile of envelopes from a compartment and reached forward to hand the bundle over the tall desk.

"Thank you, Sergeant."

Sergeant Abner grinned, showing missing teeth beneath an enormous red mustache. "Been an exciting day, sir." He chuckled. "Appreciated the package ye sent."

Jonathan smiled at the reference to the jewel thieves in their ridiculous disguises. Sergeant Abner had no doubt signed them in only moments earlier. "Thought you'd enjoy that." He leaned an arm on the tall desk beside the sergeant's penny-dreadful novel.

"The wig . . ." Abner chuckled again, the sound growing into a full belly laugh that had the man holding his sides. "And the lady's gown with the"—he waved his hands in front of his chest—"the cotton padding. Wish we'd a photography camera here at the station." He wiped his eyes. "There's a photograph I'd keep framed on me mantel."

The constables in the main room of the station laughed at this.

As Jonathan glanced through the letters, he chuckled as well, but he couldn't help thinking how beneficial photographs of criminals would actually be. There were often repeat offenders, and to easily identify them . . .

Seeing Constable Merryweather walk past, Jonathan was pulled from his thoughts. "Constable, I do hope you're headed for home."

The young man clasped his hands behind his back. "I'm on duty in an hour, sir."

"Nonsense," Jonathan said. "You haven't had a wink of sleep in a day and a half."

Merryweather shrugged. "If I might be so bold, sir, you've not slept either."

"That is entirely different," Jonathan said. "I don't have to walk a four-mile beat for the next—"

The station door opened, and a boy ran inside. "Come quick! There's been a murder!"

"What's all this?" Sergeant Abner scowled and leaned over the tall counter, pointing. "You, there. Boy! I will tolerate no yelling in the station house."

The boy breathed heavily, and his cheeks were flushed. He'd no doubt been running. "But sir—"

Jonathan set the letters back on the reception desk and approached the boy. "Now then, calm yourself. What's your name, lad?"

"Freddy Payne, sir. Constable Hutchings sent me. Said to fetch Detective Graham right away."

"I'm Detective Graham." He clasped his hands behind his back. "What's this about a murder?"

"A woman, sir, in a blue dress. She's dead in an alley off Wentworth. Behind the Porky Pie."

Spitalfields, of course. Jonathan glanced through the station's window; the summer evening was still light—at least for the next hour. Extreme poverty, disease, overcrowding, and crime made Spitalfields one of the most dangerous slums in the city. An ideal place for criminals to disappear, Spitalfields was a complicated warren of dark alleys and crumbling buildings. Pubs, bawdy houses, and opium dens were the primary businesses of the rookery, and in the interest of safety, police walked the street in pairs. Not that any of these concerns gave him a moment's hesitation. He was an officer of the law, after all. "Well, then." Jonathan put on his hat. "Off we go."

He motioned with a flick of his head for Sergeant Lester to follow.

"If I might accompany you as well, Detective"—Merryweather hurried toward them, bucket hat underneath his arm—"the Porky Pie is on my beat."

Jonathan nodded. He glanced up again when the group stepped outside. The fog was thickening into dark clouds. They would need to hurry before rain washed away evidence or the night became too dark to investigate properly. Poorly maintained streets and late-afternoon traffic would make the journey much quicker on foot.

"Lead the way, Freddy."

The boy planted his feet, fists on his hips. He scowled, lifting his chin defiantly. "I was sent to find one copper. Escortin' the three of ye'll raise the price."

Sergeant Lester opened his mouth to argue, but Jonathan tossed the boy a penny. "You'll get another when we reach the Porky Pie."

"Yes, sir!" Freddy grinned and tucked the coin into a pocket, then set off at a quick pace.

The men followed.

Jonathan smirked at the boy. Creative, he'd give him that. And cheeky. The Porky Pie was easy enough to find, with or without Freddy's help, but Jonathan would not begrudge the lad. Based on where the boy'd come from and the way his clothes hung loosely on his small frame, he knew a penny meant one less day with an empty stomach. Jonathan had felt childhood hunger pains firsthand.

As they all walked, Merryweather caught up to the boy, his long strides keeping time with Freddy's short ones. "You look familiar, Freddy. Payne, did you say?"

"Yes, sir."

"I've come across a Martha Payne a time or two on my beat. Works as a laundress. You know her?"

Freddy's small shoulders stiffened. "My mum never committed any crime."

"No, I apologize. That's not what I meant. Try to learn the names of all the people on my beat, I do. You've a good mum."

Jonathan wondered what it was about the woman that made Merryweather remember her. He hoped the circumstance was as innocent as the man had said, but he feared the odds of that were low. Hunger drove the most honest of people to breaking the law, and the woman had a child to feed.

A crowd had gathered outside the alley beside the Porky Pie, with constables holding the curious gawkers back from the crime scene.

As promised, Jonathan gave Freddy another penny.

Constable Hutchings met them at the edge of the gathering, falling into step beside Jonathan. "A young woman, sir. No blood. Best guest is she was strangled."

"We won't know for certain until Dr. Peabody inspects the remains," Jonathan said. "You've preserved the scene?"

"She's not been touched since we arrived, other than to check for a pulse," Hutchings said. "But there's no telling who might have been here before we were called."

"Keep an eye on the people, Merryweather," Jonathan said. "Watch for anyone acting unusual."

"Yes, sir." The constable broke off from the others and began making his way among the gathered citizens.

Jonathan and Sergeant Lester followed Hutchings to the mouth of the alley, the other constables making a path through the crowd. Jonathan glanced around for Freddy, wanting to ask the lad a few questions, but as soon as he'd gotten the coin in his hand, the boy had made himself scarce. Jonathan didn't blame him. It wouldn't improve Freddy's reputation to be the one bringing the police into his neighborhood.

Nightfall was approaching quickly, and the narrow alley was already cast in shadow. The nearest gas lamp was half a block away. Jonathan blinked, waiting for his eyesight to adjust. Even if it hadn't been evening, this area of the city was always dim beneath a layer of smoke. "Fetch some lanterns, Hutchings."

"Yes, sir."

Jonathan took another peppermint from his pocket and sucked on it as he surveyed the scene. Placing his feet carefully, he studied the ground as he stepped toward the body in the blue dress. The paving stones were uneven, and quite a few were broken or missing. Searching for footprints would be pointless.

The victim lay on her front, head turned to the side. One arm was beneath her body, and the other was outstretched above her head. Her hair had come partially unfastened and spread on the ground in a mess of blonde curls.

Jonathan tugged up on the pleats of his trousers and crouched down to examine the body closer. "What do you see, Sergeant?"

"Appears to be in her twenties, sir." Sergeant Lester moved the woman's collar. Even in the dim light, bruising was visible on her neck. "I'd say Hutchings is right. Looks like she was throttled."

Whether or not that was the cause of death was still to be seen. When the lanterns arrived, he could possibly discern more clues from the body. Jonathan stood and took note of the alleyway—one entrance from the street and, at the other end, a brick wall too high to climb. When he kicked aside a broken bottle, a cat dodged past, no doubt in pursuit of vermin of some kind. Pieces of crates and other rubbish littered the space, giving the air a foul odor and contributing to the rodent problem. A door on his left led into the Porky Pie, and above, on either side, were windows of upper stories from which lines of drying clothes were strung over the alley. He wondered vaguely if their owners would pull them inside before the rain started.

He tried the door handle. Locked.

Circles of light spread through the alley as Hutchings returned with two lanterns.

Sergeant Lester took one, and Jonathan the other. "Ask around inside the pub, Constable," Jonathan said to Hutchings. "Learn who has a key to this door and whether anyone noted anything suspicious."

"Yes, sir." The constable started away.

"Do you think the killer escaped through the pub?" Sergeant Lester asked. He tried the door handle as well, with the same result.

"If so, he either had a key or was assisted by someone inside."

Raised voices came from the crowd, Merryweather's among them. Jonathan shared a look with the sergeant, and they strode to the mouth of the alley to investigate.

"Let me through, sir." A young woman was attempting to push past the constable. "I insist you move aside directly."

Jonathan brought the lantern light closer. The woman was short with light-brown hair pulled up beneath a flower-embellished hat. Her skirt was striped, and she wore a matching fitted jacket over a blouse with a lace collar. A brooch with some sort of blue flower was pinned to her lapel. But the most conspicuous characteristic was the woman's cleanliness. Her clothing was laundered and her shoes unblemished. It was obvious the garments were costly, even to a person with no knowledge of fashion. Her appearance stood out like a beacon in the grimy street.

"I'll handle this, Constable," Jonathan said. He turned to the woman and tugged on his hat brim. "Detective Jonathan Graham, at your service, miss."

"Sophie Bremerton." She inclined her head.

"How might I be of assistance, Miss Bremerton?"

"Thank you, Detective." She darted a sharp look at the constable. "This man refuses to let me past."

Jonathan glanced at Merryweather, then back at her. "With good reason, miss. This is an active crime scene."

"Yes, I realize that, Detective. It is the very reason I'm here."

In just that moment Jonathan took her measure. She was confident and well-spoken, with an aristocratic accent. The woman was no doubt slumming—a favorite pastime of the privileged and bored. Curious wealthy tourists visited impoverished neighborhoods for amusement. The idea of these people seeking a thrill from witnessing the hardships of their fellow man made Jonathan's blood boil.

Very well, he'd teach this Sophie Bremerton a lesson. Show her the people he protected were not simply here for her entertainment.

"Stand aside, Merryweather." He took Miss Bremerton's elbow and pulled her into the alley with long strides, holding up the lantern so the body on the ground was completely illuminated.

Miss Bremerton cringed back. "Oh my. Do you know her name?"

"No."

"She's so young."

"Was young," Jonathan said, satisfied that the interloper had gotten more than she'd asked for. "So tell me, Miss Bremerton, is this what you hoped to see? Is it tragic enough for . . ." His words trailed off when he realized she was not listening but had stepped away and begun to speak with Sergeant Lester. Jonathan scowled and followed her.

"A pleasure to meet you, Sergeant," she was saying. "What do you suppose happened to this poor woman?"

Sergeant Lester knelt, set down his lantern, and pulled back the dead woman's collar.

Miss Bremerton knelt on the other side of the body, arranging her skirts around her and then leaning close to study the woman's neck. "She was strangled," she said.

"That's our guess, miss," Sergeant Lester said. "The doctor will know for certain."

"How terrible." Miss Bremerton's voice was much softer. It seemed she finally understood this was not simply a carnival show but a life cut short in a violent manner.

"Yes," Jonathan said, coming to stand behind her, glad the exercise had had its intended effect. "It is, as I told you, a crime scene—a murder scene. Of course it is not pleasant. Now, if you're quite done . . ." He reached out a hand to assist her to rise.

Sophie Bremerton apparently suffered from convenient hearing loss. She didn't even glance up as Jonathan spoke, but tipped her head to the side, looking at the body. "She didn't intend to go out of doors, I think. She wears no hat nor gloves."

"They may have been stolen," Sergeant Lester said.

"But not her ring?" Miss Bremerton pointed to the silver band on the woman's finger. "I do not think it is very valuable, but it is surely more so than a pair of gloves."

"Perhaps the thief did not see it in the dim light," Jonathan said. "At this point, we can't rule out any possibilities. Now, if you please . . ." He held out his hand again, but as before, she ignored him.

"The gown is very distinctive," she said. "Custom-made raw silk with Brussels lace." She sat back on her heels. "But it was not sewn for this woman."

"How do you know that?" Jonathan asked, curious in spite of his irritation.

"The sleeves are too short." Miss Bremerton pointed to the woman's wrists. "And of course the tournure is all wrong for this skirt."

Sergeant Lester looked up at the detective with a confused expression that Jonathan was certain matched his own.

"Tournure, miss?" the sergeant asked.

"The bustle," Miss Bremerton said.

Sergeant Lester furrowed his brows. "You mean the contraption that makes a hump on a lady's bum?"

Miss Bremerton nodded. "I suppose that's as good a description as any." Her voice trembled the slightest bit, and Jonathan thought she might be holding back a laugh.

"And how can you tell she was wearing the wrong bustle?" Jonathan asked, wanting to return the conversation to the business of solving the murder.

"You see, here." She pointed to the bottom ruffle of the woman's dress. "The rear of her skirts have been dragging. The proper tournure would have lifted the hem off the ground."

"So we can assume the woman purchased the gown secondhand, without the proper underclothing," Jonathan said. "While it is interesting, it is not unusual."

"I agree, Detective," Miss Bremerton said. "But a dress such as this . . . its value is very dear. I believe it was made for last year's Season. The collar design and color were the very height of fashion, and the basque-style overskirt had not yet been replaced by a polonaise."

The men shared another bewildered look.

Miss Bremerton continued. "If we can discern where the dress is from or how she came to be wearing it, perhaps it would lead to her identity."

Jonathan didn't like the woman's use of the word *we* or the way she was taking charge of the investigation. "Obviously, that is—what are you doing now?"

Miss Bremerton had pulled a notebook from her bag and started sketching. "It will be dark soon, Detective. And it looks like rain. I intend to document as much of the scene as possible. Would you move your lantern closer?"

Jonathan plunked down his lantern beside Sergeant Lester's in front of the lady. His irritation was evolving into something much more like anger. He'd had quite enough of this woman's presumptions and uninvited observations and intended to tell her. But before he had the chance, Sergeant Lester called to him. "Sir, have a look at this." He motioned him toward the victim's feet. "The backs of her heels are scraped."

"She was dragged here," Jonathan said. He noticed the young woman's boots were old and worn. They were nowhere near the quality of the gown she wore. Perhaps Miss Bremerton's observations about the woman's clothing would be useful after all. But the idea that she'd offered helpful insight grated at him.

Dr. Peabody entered the alley, his cane making a clicking sound where it hit the paving stones. He nodded to the men and knelt next to Miss Bremerton, showing no surprise at her presence, as was his way. Dr. Peabody was rarely rattled. "How do you do, miss? Dr. Phinneas Peabody. I don't believe I've had the pleasure."

"Sophie Bremerton. And the pleasure is mine, Doctor."

"Delighted." The older bowed awkwardly from his kneeling position, then looked down at the dead woman. "Now, what have we here?"

"We believe the victim was strangled." Miss Bremerton spoke before Jonathan could respond.

Sergeant Lester returned to kneel across from the others. He held his lantern closer. "Bruises on her neck, Doctor."

"Skin's cold," Dr. Peabody said, touching the woman's cheek with the back of his fingers. He lifted her arm and bent the elbow, checking for rigor mortis. "Hasn't been dead long." He pulled down her collar.

Jonathan crouched beside the sergeant, leaning forward for a better view, though so many people gathered around the body made it difficult.

"Definitely could indicate asphyxia," Dr. Peabody said. "Have you finished your initial examination of the scene, Detective? Might we turn her over?"

"Yes." Jonathan and Sergeant Lester turned the woman onto her back.

"Hold a lantern, if you please, Miss Bremerton." The doctor examined the deceased woman's neck, then pulled up her eyelids. "Ah, look here."

The three leaned closer, the flowers of Miss Bremerton's hat effectively blocking Jonathan's view.

"Petechial hemorrhaging," Dr. Peabody said. "Another sign of asphyxia." He lifted the victim's outstretched hand, studied it, laid it beside her, and then reached across the body to lift the other. "No defensive wounds."

"You think she did not resist her attacker?" Miss Bremerton asked.

"Impossible to say," Dr. Peabody replied. "I'll know more once I can examine her in the morgue." He looked closer at the hand he held, turning it over to study the nails. "Soft hands. A gentlewoman, perhaps?"

Jonathan spoke quickly before Miss Bremerton had the chance. "I'd considered it, but her clothing and jewelry would indicate otherwise."

"Well, that is your area of expertise, not mine, Detective." The doctor set the hand back.

"How long has she been dead?" Jonathan asked.

"Two hours, perhaps three." He moved to stand.

Miss Bremerton jumped up and helped the doctor to his feet, retrieving his cane.

"Thank you, my dear."

Jonathan and Sergeant Lester stood as well.

"I'll let you know my findings," Dr. Peabody said.

"Thank you, Doctor." Jonathan and Miss Bremerton spoke at the same moment.

The lady took the doctor's offered arm and accompanied him to the mouth of the alleyway, where he directed the waiting students from the medical college to retrieve the body and deliver it to the morgue.

Sergeant Lester picked up his lantern and Miss Bremerton's notebook and bag and followed.

Jonathan clasped his hands behind his back and took one last look at the scene, wishing for daylight or a photographer. He had very few clues as to the dead woman's identity and knew finding witnesses willing to talk would be difficult, if not impossible. As he walked to the mouth of the alley, he ground his teeth, frustrated that this would very likely be another unidentified woman in an unsolved case file.

"What is the next course of action, Sergeant Lester?" Miss Bremerton asked.

"We'll interview potential witnesses, look into the lady's identity, and hope the doctor is able to find anything on the body to give us direction."

She nodded, writing something in her notebook. "Very good. As far as the gown—"

"That's enough." Jonathan had reached the end of his patience. "Listen, Miss Bremerton. I've had quite enough of your thrill seeking. This is a police matter. It is not your place to advise my sergeant on police procedure, nor for that matter, should you travel in this part of the city alone."

"But I am not alone, sir. My carriage driver waits just—"

"Go home, Miss Bremerton." He took her arm and led her from the alley. "Make yourself a nice cup of tea. You've had sufficient adventure in the rookery to earn the envy of your friends."

"Detective Graham, I resent your implication. I—"

"Constable, see that Miss Bremerton gets home safely." Jonathan motioned to Merryweather, who took the lantern from the lady and moved to assist her. He felt no guilt ignoring her protests. He turned and strode away without even waiting for an acknowledgment. He could hear Miss Bremerton arguing behind him, but he was not worried. Merryweather would see his assignment completed. The woman would be sent away whether she wished to be or not.

Jonathan stopped in the light of a gas lamp outside the Porky Pie and checked the time, unconsciously rubbing the uneven edges of the fob hanging from his pocket watch chain as he considered the case. He had no real leads aside from an expensive dress and ill-fitting bustle. He doubted Hutchings would gather much from interviews. People tended to their own business in this part of the city. Perhaps the doctor would discover more, or perhaps the ring might reveal something upon closer examination.

When Sergeant Lester joined him, the two started back toward H Division.

With so many factors unknown, two things he was certain of: a young lady belonged nowhere near a murder investigation, and Miss Sophie Bremerton belonged nowhere near him.

CHAPTER 2

Sᴏᴘʜɪᴇ ᴛʜᴀɴᴋᴇᴅ ʜᴇʀ ᴅʀɪᴠᴇʀ, Jᴀsᴘᴇʀ, as he helped her from the carriage on Park Lane. When she stepped inside the house, a maid took her gloves and hat. A wave of fatigue moved over her as she climbed the stairs, but instead of continuing on to her bedchamber for a nap, she followed the upstairs passageway toward the first-floor sitting room, where Mimi, her grandmother, would be at her writing table.

After returning from Spitalfields the night before, Sophie had stayed up into the early hours of the morning, sketching images of the murder scene and making notes when she should have been finishing the illustration she'd promised to deliver to the newspaper editor by tomorrow morning. Then, after only a few hours of sleep, she'd left early for Bond Street to call on various dressmakers in hopes of discovering who had made—and purchased—the gown the dead woman had worn. But lack of sleep was not the full cause of her exhaustion. Sophie couldn't avoid her mother forever, and anticipating the inevitable confrontation left her weary.

Last night Sophie had missed the Hamptons' ball—her third conspicuous absence from an event this week as she'd gone in search of a story. Her mother, Lady Mather, took personal offense to unconventionality of any kind. As it was, a daughter working for the newspaper was nearly more than the countess could endure.

But, in truth, pleasing her mother was not something Sophie imagined she'd ever be capable of. Not when she'd been presented four Seasons earlier and still remained unmarried—a failure of the highest degree in her mother's eyes, and one Lady Mather did not neglect to remind her daughter of on a daily basis.

When Sophie entered the drawing room, the dowager countess set aside her fountain pen, stood from her desk, and smiled. "Good morning, dearest."

From the floor beside the window, Dorrit, Mimi's beloved pug, jumped up and barked.

Warmth relaxed the tension inside Sophie as she took her grandmother's outstretched hands and allowed her to kiss both cheeks. "Good morning, Mimi."

In spite of her age, Sophie's grandmother was extremely active, both socially and physically. She was a member of various societies, a champion of causes, and a chairwoman of fundraisers. She also served on school and hospital boards and participated in a ladies' badminton league.

Her grandmother picked up the dog's leash from the desk. "Dorrit and I are just headed to the dining room, my dear. Have you eaten?"

"I had some toast earlier."

"Well, that is hardly enough to sustain you. The hour is nearly noon." Mimi shook her head, making her gray curls bounce around her face. "Come along."

"I'd love to."

"Time to eat, Dorrit." Mimi spoke in a cooing voice, then gave a whistle.

The dog ran to her mistress and allowed the leash to be attached to her collar.

Sophie linked arms with her grandmother as they walked down the stairs. "How was your ride?" Sophie could hardly hold back her grin at Mimi's most recent infatuation. She and a group of her friends had all purchased penny-farthing bicycles and met regularly to ride through Hyde Park in the mornings before the paths became too crowded. Six elderly women pedaling along the paths on the high-wheeled contraptions was certainly a sight to behold.

"It was lovely." Mimi waved her hand as she spoke. "The morning hours are spectacular. The air is crisp, birds sing, and a feeling of hopefulness prevails as the city wakes."

"I'm glad you enjoyed it," Sophie said. "And no falls today?"

"Oh, there are always a few." Mimi shrugged "But we don't let that stop us. Physical activity and fresh air are good for the body and soul, though the hard ground is not always good for my elbows and knees."

Sophie chuckled. She loved her grandmother's eccentricities. And while the rest of her family simply tolerated the foibles with a roll of their eyes, she felt jealous of them. At what age did it become socially acceptable to . . . not act socially acceptable?

They reached the dining room, and a footman took the leash from Mimi and led the dog away to eat in the kitchen.

Sophie took her place beside her grandmother at the dining table. The meal was served, and she poured the tea.

Mimi took a bite of fish. "You returned very late last night. Did you find your story?"

"Yes." The excitement of the investigation returned, making Sophie's stomach flutter. She dabbed pastry crumbs from her lips and leaned toward her grandmother. "I stumbled upon a murder in Spitalfields."

Her grandmother stopped with her teacup partway to her mouth. She opened her eyes wide. "Gracious, my dear. Jumped right in with both feet, didn't you?"

Mimi's reaction was exactly what Sophie had expected. Her grandmother never fussed or lectured but gave constant encouragement. Though she didn't know for sure, Sophie was almost certain Mimi had been the one who'd convinced her parents to allow her to take the position with the newspaper in the first place.

Sophie scooped fruit onto her plate. "The circumstance was extremely lucky." Seeing her grandmother's raised brows over her teacup, she shook her head. "No, not lucky for the victim, of course, but for me to have arrived right as the police did. I was able to assist with the examination of the scene. Watching the investigators at work, seeing what they noticed and what they were able to deduce—it was all fascinating."

"Do you know the victim's identity?" Mimi asked.

"No," Sophie said. "She was a young woman, and her dress . . ." She pulled her bag from beneath the table and slipped out the drawings she'd made the night before, leafing through until she found the one she wanted—a picture of the victim's clothing. "I hope the dress will lead to her identity." She set the paper between their plates.

Mimi looked through a quizzing glass, studying the drawing. "Not a gown one would expect to see in Spitalfields, is it?"

"Exactly what I thought," Sophie said. "Madame Delacourt, the modiste, recognized the pattern but was not certain whom this particular dress was made for, as the specific embellishments and alterations were done by various seamstresses in her shop, some no longer in her employ. Her records did indicate three gowns in this periwinkle-blue color were sold last year, and she gave me the names of the women: Julia Westerfield, Charlotte Grey, and Abigail Scott. I am acquainted with all of them, to some degree."

"But you did not recognize the victim. She was not one of the young ladies to whom the dresses were sold?"

"No. Someone wearing one of their dresses, I believe." Sophie explained to her grandmother about the gown's too-short sleeves and the tournure.

"How very intriguing." Mimi dabbed her lips with a napkin. "You truly have a gift for observation and deduction, Sophronia."

Sophie's chest warmed at the praise. She bit into another pastry, set it down, and then wiped the crumbs from her fingers before returning the drawing to her bag. She debated showing the others to her grandmother but decided pictures of a murder scene were hardly appropriate at the breakfast table.

"Do you believe the gown was stolen?" Mimi asked.

"I do not know. The doctor pointed out that the woman's hands were very soft, so she must have enjoyed some level of comfort."

Mimi nodded. "But if so, why was her dress not altered to fit properly?"

"Why indeed," Sophie said. "I intend to pay a visit to Misses Westerfield, Grey, and Scott this afternoon." She winced, glancing at the clock. The young women were very likely not taking visitors this early, and if she was to attend Mrs. Jeffries's garden party this evening, she needed the entirety of the afternoon to prepare her article and drawing that were due tomorrow morning. She blew out a frustrated breath. "Or perhaps tomorrow."

"Since when are you friends with any of those young ladies?" Priscilla's voice came from the doorway.

Sophie and Mimi turned in their chairs.

"Good morning, dear," Mimi said.

"It would be a good morning if I hadn't awoken so early." Prissy flounced into the dining room and sat in a chair on the other side of the table. She reached for the basket of pastries.

"And what are you doing today, Prissy?" Sophie turned the subject away from her investigation and onto her sister's favorite topic—herself.

"Paying visits with mother this morning." Prissy rolled her eyes, but then she tipped her head, giving a superior smile. "Everleigh has invited me to a picnic at Kensington Gardens tomorrow." She sighed, clasping her hands. "He is so handsome, and he quite prefers me, you know."

"And why wouldn't he, Priscilla?" Mimi said. "A gentleman would be foolish not to take notice of my lovely granddaughter."

Prissy smiled. "Thank you, Mimi." She blinked as if an idea had just occurred to her. "You should come as well, Sophie. Really, you must. All the Casanovas and Darling Debs will be there."

Sophie was surprised her sister would make such a suggestion. Prissy had certainly never sought her company socially—let alone acknowledged in public at all the fact that they were related.

"Thank you for the invitation, but I'm afraid I have plans tomorrow."

Prissy pouted, setting down her teacup with a clatter and folding her arms. "But Everleigh's dull railroad friend *Hans*, from Germany, is invited." She spoke the name with a groan and rolled her eyes. "If you came, you could keep him occupied, discussing . . . whatever it is tedious people discuss."

Ah, this explanation makes sense. Sophie did not take offense. Her sister seldom thought before speaking, nor realized how her words would be received.

"That does sound very tempting, but I'm afraid I will be busy," Sophie said.

"What could you possibly need to do that is more important than picnicking with the most prominent members of high Society?" Prissy wrinkled her nose. "Drawing pictures, no doubt?"

"Illustrations for the newspaper are hardly more frivolous than—" Sophie bit off her witty rebuke when Lady Mather entered the dining room, and at the sight of her mother, the muscles in Sophie's neck tightened.

Lady Mather sat beside Prissy and nodded in acknowledgment as the others bid her good morning. She slid her teacup closer and stirred its contents. "I heard the carriage earlier." She glanced at Sophie. "You've been out already?"

"Yes." Sophie pushed the bag with her drawings farther beneath her skirts. "To the dressmakers'."

"I take it your waist has expanded beyond your corset's capacity to contain it." Her mother sighed. She shook her head, glancing at Sophie's plate. "You are not taking your reducing diet seriously, Sophronia. How many times have I told you to limit your pastries? And now your gowns must be altered . . ."

Mimi snorted. "Honestly, Maxine. Sophronia's waist is perfectly suitable for its purpose of housing her vital organs, and the idea that she must conform to Society's ideal of—"

Mimi's words stopped as Sophie clasped her hand beneath the table, giving it a squeeze. She knew Mimi would understand that as grateful as she was for her grandmother's defense, the argument was unnecessary, as her mother's mind would not be changed by a lecture on the abstract criterion of feminine beauty.

"The dressmakers'!" Prissy obviously took the pause in the conversation as an invitation to speak—or, more accurately, to complain. "I have need of new gowns as well. I've seen two other young ladies in the very color I'd intended to wear to the opera tomorrow. Could you imagine my humiliation if we were all attired similarly?"

Prissy continued speaking, but years of living with the young woman had given Sophie the ability to ignore her sister's prattle. She caught her grandmother's eye, giving a grateful smile. What would Sophie ever do without her staunch support? She thought how Elizabeth Miller adored Mimi and imagined her grandmother must have been very much like her new friend when she was young.

". . . I am being courted by Lord Everleigh, and I cannot afford to look anything less than spectacular," Prissy continued to her mother. "The gown I wore last night was so ordinary—Everleigh hardly noticed me at all. He spent most of the evening in private conversation with that dull German. I've half a mind to give the dress to my lady's maid and be done with it."

Sophie stared at her sister, and her mind spun with what the younger woman said. She'd not considered that the dead woman's gown might have been a gift from her mistress. Could its method of coming into her possession be so simple? A lady's maid was often the recipient of the gowns the woman she served no longer wanted, and that would explain perfectly why it did not fit her.

She considered what she knew of the three women whose names the modiste had given her. Which of them might be inclined to give away a costly gown after wearing it for only one Season? The answer was immediately clear. Charlotte Grey was one of the Darling Debs, and if Sophie had to choose a young lady who was nearly identical in temperament and behavior to Prissy, Miss Grey would be at the very top of the list.

"Sophronia." Lady Mather's voice was sharp, cutting into her thoughts. "You will do me the courtesy of listening when I speak to you."

Sophie shook herself from her thoughts. "I apologize, Mother. My mind was wandering."

Her mother sighed, and her jaw tightened. "I was reminding you about Mrs. Jeffries's garden reception this evening."

Sophie forced her shoulders to remain down instead of hunching. "I plan to attend, but I have quite a few obligations this afternoon that might interfere."

Her mother's right brow ticked upward, and though it was a miniscule movement, Sophie winced. Lady Mather's anger was never displayed in fits of yelling but with carefully worded attacks. And her sharpest weapon was guilt.

"We made apologies for your absences last night and the night previous," Lady Mather said.

"Not to mention Mrs. Rothschild's luncheon," Prissy added helpfully.

"The position this puts me in"—Lady Mather's voice grew softer, which was far more frightening than if she'd screamed—"coming up with excuses day after . . ." She sighed. "Finding a husband for you has been difficult enough with your"—she motioned with a wave of her hand—"ordinariness. And after *four* Seasons—"

"I have not asked you to apologize for me." Sophie could sense Mimi preparing to interject. She knew better than to interrupt her mother, but she didn't wish for the argument to grow or for her grandmother to have to defend her again. Sophie shifted, feeling heat rise to her cheeks. "I will do my best to attend, but I am very busy today."

"She'll probably arrive with Dahlia Lancaster and her bluestocking cousin." Prissy spoke her former friend's name with a contemptible curl of the lip.

Anger flashed through Sophie.

"Priscilla." Mimi's voice held a reprimand. "That is unkind. You used to be dear friends with Dahlia."

"Well, of course, that was before Lord Ruben rejected her," Priscilla said. Her expression did not show one bit of remorse. "It makes one wonder what is wrong with her if he'd not have her."

"Quite so," Lady Mather agreed. "And it appears he was wise to escape when he did. I hear Miss Lancaster has since taken to the company of suffragettes and misfits."

"Such an embarrassment. He is very lucky to be rid of her." Prissy shook her head.

Sophie could typically ignore her family's insults, but today she was tired, and the affronts to herself and her friends were more than she could overlook. She set her napkin on the table and stood. "I'm afraid I am in complete disagreement with both of you." She lifted her bag over her shoulder. "If anyone is to be congratulated, it is Dahlia Lancaster for escaping not only an unfaithful man but spiteful friends as well."

"Well, I never," Prissy sputtered. "Mother, did you hear?"

"Sophronia, that was quite uncalled for," Lady Mather began.

Sophie ignored the outburst from the other side of the table. "Have a lovely day, Mimi." She kissed her grandmother's cheek, received a private wink and a smile in return, then left the room without a backward glance.

ABOUT THE AUTHOR

JENNIFER MOORE LIVES WITH ONE husband and four sons, who produce heaps of laundry and laughter. She earned a BA from the University of Utah in linguistics, which she uses mostly for answering Jeopardy questions. A reader of history and romance, she loves traveling, tall ships, scented candles, and watching cake-decorating videos. When she's not driving carpool, writing, or helping with homework, she'll usually be found playing tennis. Learn more at authorjmoore.com and on Jennifer's social media.

    Facebook: Author Jennifer Moore

    Instagram: jennythebrave